Praise for
SHATTERED HEARTS

"From the onset, *Shattered Hearts* grabbed my attention and held it until the end. Rich Schiesser's characters are intelligent, charming and relatable. The MacDonald's story is intensely sad, delivering a powerful message of love, understanding, family togetherness, and the ability to overcome. I cannot wait to see what he writes next."

—Ronald Belfort, author of *Brooklyn Girl*

"*Shattered Hearts*, where three very different families' lives collide in a tale of violence and sadness, mixed with a good dose of hope."

—Heather Weidner, author of *Secret Lives and Private Eyes* and part of the Virginia is for Mysteries anthology series

"Still madly in love and celebrating their 20th anniversary in Paris, Julie and Greg have the perfect life. But perfection is fragile, and a family can be broken into pieces as easily as a crystal ornament. Rich Schiesser's novel soars as high as the Eiffel Tower and then plummets through Atlanta's gangs to a parent's worst nightmare. Absolutely un-put-downable."

—Mary Arno, award-winning author of *Thanksgiving*

"Rich Schiesser is a talented writer and a polished storyteller. I believe he is off and running with *Shattered Hearts*."

—Glen Alan Burke, author of *Jesse*, Chanticleer Book Award, First in Category, winner in Paranormal

Three families. Three separate conflicts. One collision. With twists that will keep you engrossed until the end.

—Betsy Ashton, author of the *Mad Max Mystery Series*

"If you have raised or are raising a challenging teen whose unique gifts and personality make these years fraught with conflict, anxious parental nights, and deep concern for the outcome, Rich Schiesser's *Shattered Hearts* will ring true. This story portrays a decent middle-class family who love one another yet encounter teen drug use in their home. The author captures the confusion and pain the parents face as they strive to understand and help their struggling son.

Simultaneously, this seventeen-year-old on the cusp of manhood is shown from many viewpoints with all his flaws and his strengths. The reader sympathizes with all involved as they interact with a teen whose lack of judgment and quick temper spur his decisions. Doug, the challenging but good-hearted rebel, is well fleshed out and was my favorite character.

In a realistic and nonjudgmental way, the author portrays how family conflict spirals out of control on both sides, bringing law enforcement and the Tough Love program into the picture. Remorse, confusion, and angst on the parental side clashes with bravado, deception and finally faltering growth on the teen side. Law enforcement and a wonderfully balanced and kind grandmother play strong supportive roles.

High praise goes to Schiesser for his sympathetic look at troubled teens and their anxious family members. Adult and YA readers will root for all involved as they face more than one event that produces urgent concern and hope that this family will work it all out in time to prevent disaster."

—**Melinda Inman**, award-winning author of *Refuge*

"Schiesser's emotionally complex yet realistic drama about three families' struggles with their own form of tragedy catches you by surprise all the way through, and leaves one to ponder the truth of whether we are, indeed, all the same despite it all."

—**Christopher Leibig**, Next Generation Indie Award winner for *Almost Mortal* (Best Religious Fiction, 2016)

Shattered Hearts
by Rich Schiesser

© Copyright 2016 Rich Schiesser

ISBN 978-1-63393-232-6

All rights reserved. No part of this publication may be reproduced, stored in a retrieval system, or transmitted in any form or by any means – electronic, mechanical, photocopy, recording, or any other – except for brief quotations in printed reviews, without the prior written permission of the author.

This is a work of fiction. The characters are both actual and fictitious. With the exception of verified historical events and persons, all incidents, descriptions, dialogue and opinions expressed are the products of the author's imagination and are not to be construed as real.

Published by

◤köehlerbooks™

210 60th Street
Virginia Beach, VA 23451
212-574-7939
www.koehlerbooks.com

SHATTERED HEARTS

A NOVEL

RICH SCHIESSER

All the best!

Rick Schiesser

VIRGINIA BEACH
CAPE CHARLES

the best!

With admiration,

For my loving wife, Ann,

who helps me turn dreams into reality,

and reminds me that all things are possible.

CHAPTER 1

DOMINIC WILLIAMS PRESSED the barrel of his loaded handgun against the right temple of the homeless man and threatened to pull the trigger. The anguished beggar pleaded with Dominic to let him go. But the gunman in the black leather jacket was not about to let the booze-reeking wino off so easy. Dominic put his finger on the trigger and tilted the handle of the gun slightly forward.

The eyes of the homeless man bulged.

"Come on, man," the man pleaded. "Didn't mean no harm. Can't you hook a brother up? Been starving for days."

"Shudup, bitch," Dominic hissed. "Tired of your nightly begging. Say goodbye."

Dominic started squeezing the trigger. The man gasped and nearly fainted. But Dominic knew the gun would not discharge. He intentionally left on the safety. Shaking his head in disgust, Dominic shoved the man back and snarled, "You're pathetic."

The homeless man's chest heaved as he tried to catch his breath. Dominic reached inside his jeans pocket and threw some money at the man, who quickly crawled on his hands to gather up the five dollar bills. "God bless," he blurted out.

"Beat it, scum," Dominic ordered. "I ever see your punk bitch ass here again, you won't be walking away."

Dominic's bodyguard stood expressionless watching his boss harass the beggar. Tall and muscular, he was known only as Raven because of the long jet-black hair that was slicked back behind his ears. Reaching inside his jacket, he pulled out his Glock and pointed it at the man now hunched over and trembling, clutching the fistful of bills.

"Want me to finish him, boss?" Raven asked very matter-of-factly.

"Nah," Dominic replied. "Your bullet's worth more than that little piss ant."

Dominic and Raven put their guns back inside their jackets and watched the homeless man scamper into the darkness.

The two men walked away from the scene and departed the sprawling expanse of land known as Stephenson Park. It was Atlanta's largest public area.

During the day most portions of the park were welcomed recreation spots for families to enjoy numerous activities with their children, but late at night the southeast section harbored a different type of cliental—sketchy low-lifes dealing in drugs, illegal gambling, weapons, and prostitution.

Dominic frequented Stephenson Park to conduct some of his own business. He was leader of the notorious Atlanta motorcycle gang, the Raptors. Raven had accompanied him to finalize some arrangements with a key supplier of high-grade marijuana. The dealer was a middle-aged Colombian who chain-smoked Marlboros.

Dominic learned early on to accommodate the idiosyncrasies of his drug-dealing partners, no matter how peculiar they might appear. He and the dealer talked business for a while until the Colombian was satisfied with the terms. He shook Dominic's hand and then the three men left the park.

Dominic and Raven approached a giant arch known as the South Portal as they exited the park. The gray concrete structure stood over fifty feet tall and was considered one of several Atlanta landmarks. On its surfaces were sculptures and engravings of numerous significant events depicting the history of Atlanta. Dominic gazed up at some of the images as they walked underneath.

It was a few minutes before eleven o'clock and a chilly light breeze caused Dominic to rub his hands together. He was pleased at the deal he had just sealed, but his mind was on a much larger venture. This was the night that Dominic planned to expand his empire significantly.

"That Colombian's gonna make me rich," Dominic declared. Raven nodded in agreement. Dominic had confided to Raven earlier his plans to expand his fledgling drug business into Atlanta's junior high schools.

While Atlanta had its share of drug users, a number of the schools were relatively drug-free. Dominic saw this as a hugely untapped market, especially the southeastern side. This was a poor neighborhood with many single mothers struggling to feed their kids. There were dozens of junior high schools in this area. Most of the boys here spent much of their time on the streets. They often admired gang members and aspired to become one of them.

Dominic essentially owned the streets on which many of these junior and senior high schools were located. He saw those attending the schools as potential users or dealers. This was his marketplace. Dominic had worked hard to establish a network of contacts at dozens of junior and high schools. He had almost a sixth sense at detecting the telltale signs of juveniles who were likely to succumb to the temptation of addictive drugs. The Colombian drug deal was the last piece that allowed his plans to fall into place

Dominic was only twenty-six and considered young by some of his rivals. What he lacked in age he more than made up for in experience and sheer brutality. More than one person had met his death challenging Dominic's authority and leadership.

The police had never been able to charge Dominic. They knew the gang leader was behind several murders, but they had no proof. He learned to cover his tracks well. The killings were usually by gunshots or stabbings. The weapons used were never found and there never seemed to be eyewitnesses.

Dominic demanded ultimate loyalty and respect from those in his organization. It had served him well. His gang had more than forty members. He rewarded their respect and loyalty with booze, drugs, sex, money, and turf. Perhaps the most valuable benefit was the respect that came from being a member of one of the most feared gangs in Atlanta, if not the entire Southeast.

///

Dominic and Raven walked two blocks to the rear of a small but clean donut shop called the Kozy Korner. Attached behind it was an abandoned warehouse that Dominic had acquired and converted into his gang's headquarters. The outside was remarkably nondescript, making it the perfect cover. Dominic had contractors transform the interior into a comfortable place for bikers to hang out. There was a well-stocked bar, poker and pool tables, a stripper pole and an office for Dominic.

A dozen Raptor motorcycles were parked outside.

Dominic and Raven spent some time inside their clubhouse and then walked outside to their motorcycles. Another homeless man with a stout build approached them. He was new to the area but already had made himself a pest at the local donut shop. He had been bothering Dominic for several days now. Dominic first tried to ignore him, but Sammy was more persistent than ever.

"You ain't so tough. When I was your age I never needed guns or knives. Bare hands is what I used and I could use them a hell of lot better than you, Willy-boy."

"Told you never call me that," Dominic shouted as he slugged Sammy across his face. Sammy collapsed next to a dumpster overloaded with garbage. He picked up an empty Budweiser tall neck beer bottle and smashed the bottom of it against the curb. The heavy base of the bottle shattered into several pieces. Sammy waved the makeshift weapon as he struggled to stand. *So much for his claim of bare hands conflict*, Dominic thought to himself.

"Come on, man; you's got to have some money on you. Just a few bucks, dude, just a few bucks." Sammy looked a disheveled mess. He had long, graying, scraggly hair and was wearing a tattered brown overcoat covering a dirty, light-blue sweatshirt. Dominic pushed him away and ignored him. Dominic had far more important matters on his mind that night.

Sammy started ranting and raving while waving the broken bottle. "Come on, dude, show me what's you got. You don't own these streets the way you's think you do. You ain't near as tough as you think you are. Now give me some money, you gangbangin wannabe."

Dominic glanced over to Raven with a look of frustration. Raven reacted instinctively. He calmly pulled out his Glock, pointed it at Sammy and fired two successive shots into the man's chest. Sammy fell to the ground in one crashing heap. Raven looked up at Dominic.

"Done."

"Damn, bro, you are one heartless bastard. Just the kind I like. Good work," Dominic responded. Sammy was lying facedown with blood seeping out from his chest. The pool of liquid was thick, dark and slowly expanding. The body was not moving, but just to be sure Raven bent down and felt for a pulse.

"He's dead," Raven said with no emotion. Minutes later police sirens blared in the background. The clerk from Kozy's had heard the gunshots and had called 911.

"Come on, we better get out of here," Dominic said.

As they started walking away, Raven said, "That takes care of two issues tonight." Dominic asked, "What do you mean, two issues?"

Raven answered, "Whether Tartikov's gonna partner with you, and what to do about Sammy."

"I guess you're right. Come on, let's get out of here." The two of them headed over to their Harley-Davidson motorcycles and quickly rode off.

CHAPTER 2

AS THE HAPLESS homeless man died in Stephenson Park, three thousand miles away in Paris the amorous life of a middle-aged married couple was being rekindled. Greg and Julie MacDonald had planned for years to celebrate their twentieth wedding anniversary in the city of lights. They were doing just that.

It was Friday morning and the couple had already spent six magical days and nights in this most romantic of cities. This day, their anniversary, would be the most special. The stylish alarm clock in their luxury suite sounded with a soft purring hum at precisely eight. Greg had set it the night before to go off with a very light tone to avoid startling his light-sleeping wife. What he had not planned on was that both of them would awaken some two hours earlier, engaging in passion that lasted almost an hour. It was mutually spontaneous, which made it all the more satisfying. She had fallen back to sleep and he stared at her lovingly.

Greg leaned over and kissed Julie lightly on the cheek, hoping the alarm had not fully awakened her. Then he whispered into her ear, "Happy anniversary, Sweetheart. I love you."

Julie whispered back to her husband, "Happy anniversary, my love."

Greg thought about the satisfying session with his wife and asked, "Do you have any idea how amazing you have been?"

"Do tell, my husband," Julie responded with a phrase she used often.

"Not much to tell, my love. Just asking if you are aware of how truly amazing you have been."

"Well, do you mean during the last twenty years, or during just the last twenty minutes?"

Greg laughed. "Both." He lightly kissed her again and whispered, "I'm getting up."

"And I'm not," Julie said. "Will you be going down to the workout room or out for a run?"

"Out for a run. Likely clear around the park. I haven't been doing much lately and I feel like getting the old heart pumping. I'll probably be gone for an hour. What about you? What are your plans for the morning?"

His wife blinked a few times, obviously not interested in engaging in any lengthy conversation. "I'm going back to sleep and then will take a nice, long, warm bath. Don't expect to see me for several hours."

Greg climbed out of bed and sauntered into the richly appointed master bath. Julie watched her husband out of the corner of her eye as he strolled out of the room. Greg was tall and fit with a muscular build and a full head of thick, brown unruly hair. His handsome looks belied his forty-eight years. Both he and the blonde Julie were avid runners and appeared athletic, even in their sweats. But Julie, three years younger than Greg, also knew how to dress to the nines and could flaunt her teasing sexuality when business or social settings called for it.

She stretched out a bit and enjoyed the feeling of the plush, expensive linens. She thought back for a minute to the exquisite sensation of passion she had just experienced with her husband, and then dozed off, content and smiling.

Greg slipped on his running clothes and glanced back at his wife. He saw she was fast asleep and whispered, "Goodbye, my love. See you soon." Then he quietly left their room and within a minute boarded the elevator.

The lobby of the hotel was quiet, with only a half dozen people milling about and three others in line for checkout. Greg strode by them and out past the neatly dressed doorman.

"*Bonjour, monsieur,*" the doorman pleasantly greeted Greg as he walked past him.

"*Bonjour*, you too," Greg replied, realizing he once again had mixed his French and English translations. This was a trait he exhibited several times while in Paris. Whenever he did, Julie teased him about it.

The doorman responded "*Avoir une belle course.*" Greg was not sure what that phrase meant but presumed he was saying something about having a nice run. Greg kept walking and waved his hand back toward him without turning.

A block from the hotel was an expansive city park with a hiking trail that Greg had been jogging on for about ten minutes. Eventually he veered left out of the park and walked briskly for another three blocks. He crossed the street and jogged down the sidewalk.

In the distance he spotted the majestic spire of the stately Notre Dame cathedral that Julie and he had visited the day before. Though they were only periodic churchgoers, they both appreciated the centuries-old architecture and artistry of the structure. Moments later Greg slowed to a walk as he approached an upscale boutique specializing in fine jewelry and crystal sculptures.

As he entered the store a well-dressed middle-aged gentleman smiled, walked up to him and extended his arm for a handshake.

"Good morning, Mr. MacDonald," the man said as he shook Greg's hand firmly. "Nice to see you here so bright and early."

"Good to see you as well, Gabriel. Please, call me Greg."

"All right, Mr. Greg."

"Is my special gift ready?"

Gabriel's eyes brightened. "Indeed it is. I think you'll enjoy it. Please, let me bring it out for you to be the judge."

Greg waited while Gabriel retreated to a back room. When he returned Greg's eyes widened.

"So what do you think?" Gabriel asked, smiling proudly as he set the object on the counter.

Greg almost gasped as he looked at it closely. "It is beautiful. More magnificent than I imagined."

"So you approve?"

"Absolutely. My wife will be thrilled."

"Very good. Is there anything else you'd like?"

"No, that should do it."

"Very well. Then I will have it sent over to your hotel within an hour if that is good for you?"

"That would be perfect, Gabriel. Thank you so much."

Greg exited the store and started jogging back to his room. But he could not contain the broad smile.

When Greg returned to his room Julie was just getting ready to take a long, relaxing bath.

Greg used the time to catch up on some leisure reading. After a few hours the couple enjoyed a tasty brunch at one of the many charming sidewalk cafes. Then they walked hand-in-hand along flower-bordered pathways. Late in the afternoon they prepared for a romantic evening of drinks during sunset, an intimate dinner and then back to their room for Champagne and passionate lovemaking.

Julie walked out in a snug fitting black dress that nearly took Greg's breath away.

"Oh my, sweetheart. You look absolutely gorgeous."

She was wearing the pearl necklace, pearl earrings and other jewelry Greg had given her on previous anniversaries. Her three-inch stiletto heels and silver clutch purse completed her ensemble.

"Thanks, honey. You look pretty good yourself," Julie replied taking in Greg's well-fitting dark pinstripe suit.

"Come here, you," Greg said, walking toward her with open arms and giving her a huge warm hug. "Mmm. You smell so good"

Julie purred back at him. "This feels nice."

Greg's hands slowly moved down Julie's back causing her to murmur softly. As his hands continued moving lower and rubbing across the thin material of her dress, he flashed a devilish smile.

"Feels like someone's been to Victoria's Secret," Greg mused as his fingers traced the outline of what felt like a garter belt.

"Not exactly," she breathed back into his ear, which led to a lingering kiss.

"No?" Greg said with a bit of surprise in his voice. He was sure that whatever she was wearing underneath her flirty dress, it was not something she would have picked up at Target.

He did not want to kill the erotic buzz, but couldn't resist teasing. "So what then? Did the Home Shopping Network have an adult special for the ladies?"

Julie breathed into his ear, "Funny . . . not."

"They're actually from Agent Provocateur," she said, referring to the line of erotic lingerie.

"Really? Well, now you're talking." Greg's hands started roaming all over both of her shoulders, leading down her back to her backside. "Why don't we skip dinner and go straight to dessert?"

Julie smiled, knowing she was teasing him, but desiring a romantic dinner in Paris.

"Be patient, my love. You know what they say about good things coming to those who wait. Besides, I really want to experience the Eiffel Tower at sunset. So let's go have dinner. I promise I will give you a dessert like you've never had before."

Greg's eyebrows rose. "Seriously? Like never before? You do realize we've been married for twenty years?"

"Trust me. We will have a night to remember, my handsome husband."

"I can hardly wait, my sexy wife."

///

Less than an hour later they were seated at a window table in a rotating restaurant atop one of the tallest buildings in Paris. They watched a beautiful sunset slowly sinking into the horizon just as their plush booth turned to face it. The timing was perfect. Off in the background was their beloved Eiffel Tower.

They welcomed the chance to catch their breath from a hectic and busy life of working, parenting and coping with life's many unexpected surprises. This was a time to rest, relax and reflect on the good life they had. And reflect they did. They talked for hours over drinks and dinner about the many memorable and amusing instances they had experienced together over the past twenty years.

"Speaking of memorable events, do you recall our tenth anniversary back in Las Vegas?" Greg asked.

Julie started laughing. "Oh, my God, talk about memorable. That is one event I will never forget."

"I so wanted us to spend the entire weekend at Paris-Paris Hotel Casino. I should have made the reservations earlier," Greg confessed.

"You had no way of knowing so much was going on in Vegas that weekend and that all the rooms at our special hotel would be sold out. At least you were able to get us a room."

"Yes, indeed. I had no idea what a Luxor even was," Greg said.

"Who suggested the Luxor in the first place?" Julie asked.

"The reservation clerk at the Paris-Paris Hotel did. She suggested it when I told her I wanted a really nice room for us to celebrate our tenth anniversary. She felt bad that she could not accommodate me, especially after I told her this was where I had proposed."

The Luxor was another major hotel casino resort on the famed Las Vegas Strip. It was Egyptian-themed and in the shape of a huge black pyramid. All of the rooms had floor to ceiling windows that were slanted inward to accommodate the pyramid's shape. The windows were tinted black on the outside but completely see-through from the inside. On the night of their anniversary, Greg and Julie decided to darken their upper floor suite to take in the incredible spectacle of neon seemingly everywhere below.

With thousands of lights to gaze upon, they soon pressed up against the window in a passionate embrace. Julie moaned when Greg pulled her tightly toward him. Her body trembled as the exquisite sensations washed over her and ended in pleasurable release.

Suddenly Greg exclaimed, "Sweetheart, don't move."

"What? Why?"

Greg slowly and carefully pulled her back away from the glass and then pointed to the bottom of the window. Etched into the glass was the following warning:

Do not press up against the glass. Windows are designed to pop out during an emergency.

"That was quite the night, alright," Julie said, still laughing at the memory.

They discussed other memorable events in their twenty-year marriage. Eventually they talked about their two sons and the many trials, tribulations and triumphs they had encountered. Finally, after a decadent chocolate dessert they headed back to their room.

Julie suggested that before they devote the rest of their evening totally to themselves, they first give their two sons back in Atlanta a quick call.

"Couldn't we wait until the morning?"

"No, sweetheart."

Greg nestled up to his wife and gave her a small hug. "Are you sure? They might be in the middle of something."

"Darling," Julie replied somewhat firmly, "It will be in the very early morning for them if we call them tomorrow before lunch. There's a six hour time difference."

"What if we call them tomorrow after lunch?"

"We will be busy packing and heading to the airport tomorrow afternoon. This will only take a minute. Then I promise you I am all yours."

"All right." He dialed the long sequence of international digits. In less time than he expected the phone started ringing.

Michael picked up."

"Hey, Michael, this is Dad calling from Paris."

"Oh, hi, Dad. Wow! You sound like you are right next door."

"Modern technology, I guess. So how are you and Doug doing?"

"We're fine. Grandma is coming over in a little while. I'm going to spend the night at her house and Doug is going out with Lisa."

Greg spoke for a short time with both his sons before handing the phone to Julie. She chatted with the two boys long enough to be assured they were surviving each other, and without their parents, just fine. She told them she loved them and then ended the call.

With both of them assured everything was calm on the home front, Greg asked Julie, "Honey, close your eyes. I have something for you."

"What is it?" she replied.

"I can't tell you or it would ruin the surprise," he said.

Then he went back, quickly assembled the crystal Eiffel Tower and brought it out to her.

"Now open your eyes," he instructed.

When Julie opened her eyes she nearly gasped, "Oh, sweetheart, it's beautiful. It's breathtaking. It is the most exquisite piece of crystal I have ever seen."

It was a magnificent crystal replica of the Eiffel Tower. Julie went on for another five minutes just talking about and admiring the piece of art. Greg asked her to stand back a few feet away from the sculpture. He then dimmed the room lights and turned the switch that illuminated the crystal.

"Oh, my, sweetheart, that is incredible. It is magical." She hugged her husband and gave him a long lingering kiss.

The replica was constructed out of the most expensive Waterford crystal. It was securely mounted on a rich dark mahogany wood base just over a foot square and about four inches thick. The tower itself was just over three feet tall, exactly one meter.

Greg pointed out the intricacies in the structure.

"It's positively amazing," Julie said. "The details of the beams and girders are incredible."

"Look at the engraving," Greg said. He directed Julie's attention to a small golden plaque on the front of the wood base. Engraved on it were their names, the date of their wedding and the inscription *Lovers Forever* and then the current date.

Greg motioned for Julie to look at the tiny inscriptions that Gabriel had engraved in each of the lower four corners of the tower. On the front left in stylish calligraphy was Julie's first name. Greg's name was similarly etched in the lower front right corner.

"Your name is to your left to signify I am your right-hand man."

Julie gave her husband another warm kiss.

Next he directed her attention to the two corners in the back of the crystal. At the right rear junction Doug's name was beautifully inscribed, and to the left of it was Michael's.

Julie kept admiring. "It's breathtaking, but how will we get it home?"

Greg smiled knowingly. As he switched off the sculpture's

light he said, "Watch." He unfastened four hidden latches on the inside of the latticework, just above the second level of the tower. The structure came apart and he turned the top half upside down and placed it neatly inside the lower half and then secured the two pieces together again using the same latches. It was an ingenious design intended to facilitate packaging for transport.

He quickly re-assembled and illuminated it again as Julie looked on.

"It represents our entire marriage: intricate, beautiful, fulfilling and lasting," Greg whispered in her ear. "Do you really like it?"

"Let's go to bed, and I'll show you how much I appreciate it."

"You don't have to ask twice."

Greg drew her close and then cupped her face in his hands. Slowly he leaned in. He lifted her hair and took in the still evident aroma of her scented shampoo. He lightly kissed her ear and her neck and enjoyed the fragrance of her lavender body lotion. Her sighs and his movements felt intoxicating to them both. They quickly undressed each other and climbed into bed.

The expensive sheets on their king-sized bed in their luxury suite felt sensual. They snuggled for several minutes before slowing exploring each other. They spent the next hour enraptured.

The following day they wrapped up their memorable vacation. They had had an incredible time, but now looked forward to the peaceful setting of warm, stable home life and family. As they rode to the airport Julie noticed swarming black clouds. They contrasted sharply to the white puffy clouds and the spectacular setting of lights from the day before.

CHAPTER 3

IN A MIDDLE-CLASS Atlanta community called Crescent Estates, Doug MacDonald had just awakened from a restless afternoon nap. He and his brother, Michael, had spoken an hour earlier with their parents, who were in Paris. The sunlight was peaking in through his partially closed blinds. He wiped his eyes and took a deep yawn as if to throw away the last remaining elements of sleep.

Before Doug climbed out of bed, he picked up his iPad and surfed local news websites. Several had short articles about the killing of the homeless man known only as Sammy. Doug read carefully the sparse details provided. Nothing he read deterred him from his plans for the evening at Stephenson Park.

He dragged himself out of bed and pulled on a T-shirt and jeans. His stomach was churning. Doug stood six feet three and weighed just over two hundred pounds, and his seventeen-year-old body needed to be fed. So he bounded down the stairs and turned left toward the kitchen.

His paternal grandmother, Francine MacDonald, would be by in half an hour to pick up thirteen-year-old Michael, who would be spending the rest of the day at her house seven miles away. The boys had enjoyed free rein of the house this past week with their parents in Paris.

Doug had been diagnosed with several physical, mental and psychological ailments. Among these were high anxiety stress syndrome that could lead to debilitating panic attacks. It had taken Greg and Julie years to understand the complexity of Doug's disorders, but only during the next few weeks would they fully appreciate the depths of Doug's conditions.

Doug felt very insecure in unfamiliar and crowded places. In spite of this, or perhaps because of it, Doug had found some comfort and peace in the section of Stephenson Park where rebellious misfits like him hung out.

Doug was a complex combination of contrasting aptitudes and attitudes. He had both street smarts and computer savvy. He took great delight in learning about and mastering computers. It had all started with video games. When Doug was four his father had given him his first home video game. Doug became mesmerized by the bright colors, amazing graphics and clever logic challenges that the games presented.

By the time Doug was eight he had begun mastering sophisticated versions of several video games. He had even started writing manufacturers with questions, comments and suggestions for improvements. When some of the companies started writing back to him with questions of their own as to his uses and preferences, he would frame their responses. Although Doug was starting to struggle with schoolwork, his curiosity about video games continued to progress and evolved naturally into a keen interest in computers. His fascination with computers was less for academic reasons and more for the enjoyment of video games and for communicating electronically with others who had similar interests and abilities.

Doug strode into the kitchen. He grasped the freezer door of the refrigerator with his strong left hand and roughly pulled it open. Little of what Doug did was ever performed gently or with much finesse. This was a trait that his female companions often found both frustrating and exciting.

He scanned the freezer to determine which frozen delicacy he would select for his early evening dinner. Ham pocket sandwiches and macaroni and cheese seemed to be the perfect choice. He popped them into the microwave and finished them in ten minutes. A short time later the doorbell rang and Doug opened the door for his grandmother.

"Well, hello, Douglas, how are you?" Francine asked cheerfully. Doug responded to her in a friendly voice, "I'm fine, Grandma. How are you? Come on in."

Francine laughed. "Oh, I'm doing okay for a lady my age. Is Michael ready to go?"

Doug yelled for his brother.

Francine mused to herself, *Well, I guess that's better than texting him*. Francine often teased her two grandsons about their obsession with technology.

Michael showed up from around the corner of the foyer. Francine saw him first and said, "Ah, there you are. That's a nice shirt. Did you pick that out yourself?

"Yeah. It was on sale at Tilly's."

Michael appreciated his grandmother's eye for fashion, even as it pertained to currently popular style of clothes for teenagers. Michael had an uncanny sense of fashion, something he likely inherited from his mom whose artistic knowledge included not only fashion and jewelry but also furniture, floral arrangements, sculptures and paintings.

"Thanks for watching him today, Douglas. Have you had your dinner yet?"

Doug and Michael answered at the same time, "Yes." "No." Each stared at the other as if to say, "She was talking to me." Francine rolled her eyes.

"Douglas, do you mean you made dinner for yourself and made nothing for your brother?" Francine inquired.

Doug replied nonchalantly, "Well, yeah. Michael knows how to operate the microwave just as well as me."

Francine rolled her eyes again and looked at Michael. "Don't worry. I'll fix you a nice meal at my place." Michael's eyes widened, "Thanks, Grandma. That sounds good."

Doug murmured to himself, "Whatever."

As Michael and Francine started walking out of the house she turned to Doug and said, "Tell you father and mother tomorrow that I said hello. It will be nice to have them back home."

"Will do," Doug replied, though the thought of his father caused him to frown. They did not get along. Some might blame it on hormonal changes in adolescent boys, but it went deeper than simple puberty.

One of the effects of Doug's psychological problems was an intense distrust of anyone in authority. This included parents, teachers and especially any form of law enforcement. The fact that Doug's father had a police detective as a best friend was a constant source of tension. His rapport with his mother was only slightly better, but mostly because Julie avoided confrontations with her son. Doug's relations with young women generally fared better.

Doug was good looking with a mysterious and rebellious nature. Most girls his age found his conflicting traits to be very appealing. To a few he was even intoxicating. He could be scary but exciting; gentle but quick-tempered; intelligent but unpolished. Doug saw himself more as a lover than a fighter, but given the choice of fight or flight he would usually opt for the fight.

Doug later checked his texts and emails, and then sent a suggestive message to his girlfriend, Lisa Gilbert. She texted right back, saying she would be ready in two hours. Doug had met Lisa at the Continuing Education Charter High School of Greater Atlanta, a school for at-risk teenagers who were struggling to fit in with a normal school environment. Doug qualified in part because of his various psychological problems. Lisa qualified because she was dyslectic.

Despite her dyslexia Lisa was a very intelligent and communicative. Her long blonde hair cradled her beautiful face. She was tall and curvy and could easily have her pick of boyfriends, but she found something appealing about Doug and discovered they had quite a bit in common. Both shared a rebellious streak, enjoyed video games and savored smoking marijuana. Their parents would be surprised if they knew about their pot smoking, especially Lisa's mom, Katherine, who still thought of her daughter as her little girl.

Lisa's mom had worked at a local Coca Cola bottling plant ever since her husband was killed in Iraq eight years prior. Katherine liked Doug but thought he might be a bad influence on her daughter. Katherine did not always like his manner of dress and the fact that he smoked cigarettes. She was not aware that Lisa may have been influencing Doug in ways that her mother might not approve, particularly in showing Doug new ways to satisfy a woman.

After Doug sent Lisa a racy text, he brought up the World of Warcraft video game on his iPad. He had been playing WoW for five years and was very proficient. His skills enabled him to acquire highly desired but difficult-to-obtain weapons, territories and personnel. He could then sell these items to fanatical but less skilled players from around the world for respectable amounts. Even more revenue was possible when auctioned off on eBay. Doug also discovered another source of income by sharing some of his know-how as a WoW consultant.

It brought Doug a special satisfaction to know that his understanding and mastery of computers and video games had resulted in him generating revenue. Doug did not ever see himself locked into a boring nine-to-five job such as those of his mother and father. Doug was very much anti-establishment and a non-conformist.

///

Doug realized he had been engrossed in his game for almost an hour. During that time he had interacted with players in China, Brazil, India and Des Moines, Iowa, and accumulated over ten thousand points, worth about twenty dollars. Content with his performance, Doug signed off the game and powered down his computer.

Doug felt a rush of anticipation as he thought about the events that would later unfold. He had been planning this transaction for some time. He would go out that night to purchase an item he had long desired, the final functional article that would complete his persona. He would meet with Tommy Bertello, a sketchy arms dealer who he met through a WoW connection. The get-together would take place just beyond the Southeast Portal of Stephenson Park.

Doug slipped on his black leather jacket. His clothing looked tough and street rugged but there were no gang affiliations on it. A gleaming silver steel chain hung a good eight inches over his loose-fitting Levis, and was attached to the right-side belt loop of his jeans with a spring-loaded eye-hook. The other end of the chain was permanently attached to his wallet.

Doug walked through the laundry room and hit the button that activated the garage door. He checked out all of the surfaces of his blood red Chevy Silverado. His father had agreed to let Doug have a vehicle provided that his attendance and grades at school remained satisfactory. Another part of the agreement was that Doug had to find summer work.

During the first few months of spring, this strategy seemed to work as Doug's attendance at school and his grades improved. He also landed a summer job at a distribution warehouse. But during the last several weeks Doug's grades and school attendance started to slip. Greg and Julie were not yet aware of how much Doug's behaviors had changed for the worse, but they would soon find out.

Doug completed his quick inspection of his truck from the outside and then walked over to open the driver door and climbed into the cab. The truck was functional but lacked fancy options. Doug was not into prestige or status but he did insist on a high-quality, over-the-top stereo system.

Before backing up he set his iPod. As he turned on to the street he pressed his remote to close the garage door and then drove off.

Doug pulled up to Lisa's house and walked up the steps and gently tapped on the outside screen door. A minute later Lisa opened the door.

"Hi, Babe, come on in." He stepped inside and they gave each other a warm hug. Lisa closed hers eyes and sighed momentarily as Doug wrapped her up in a close embrace. She felt safe and secure in Doug's strong arms and enjoyed that he never hurried to break out of his clasp. She wanted to stay in the comfort of his arms but knew that her mother would be waiting on them. So she kissed him lightly on his lips and reluctantly pulled back out of his embrace.

"Hey, is that T-shirt new?" he said.

"Yes. I was wondering if you would notice. Do you like it?"

The T-shirt was a tight-fitting, low-cut V-neck. It was dark blue with black lace embroidery around the top, bottom and sleeves. It was casual yet classy and matched well with the light blue jeans she was wearing.

"Yeah, it's okay."

"It's just okay?"

"Well, yeah, I mean it's really okay."

"Good enough for me." Lisa knew by now that fashion opinions from Doug were few and far between, and a complimentary one was even rarer. So she relished the fact that he had given her outfit tacit approval.

"Did you have to park very far away?" she asked.

Doug responded to her question, "Not really. About half a block up the street on this side."

"Good job," Lisa acknowledged as they walked toward the living room.

Doug looked over at Lisa's mom. "Hi, Mrs. Gilbert. How are you doing tonight?"

Katherine looked directly at Doug and responded, "I am doing quite well, Douglas, quite well. Thank you for asking."

Katherine usually addressed Doug by the more formal version of his name. He was not certain if this was expressing more a form of respect or more a form of scolding. But he did not let it bother him and cheerfully responded, "Oh, you bet."

"So where are you two off to tonight?" Katherine asked.

Lisa looked over at Doug and studied his expression. She was certain he would not reveal the details of his plans. He knew her mom would not approve of him taking her daughter to join him in meeting with a weapons dealer. Lisa also knew that Doug did not want to deceive her mom, and was curious as to what he would say to her.

"Oh, we're just going out to cruise for a little bit and then meet up with some friends. Maybe grab a bite to eat afterward." Lisa smiled slightly at Doug's maneuver. Tell part of the truth but not all of it. Just enough to keep the parents at bay.

Katherine stood. "Well, just be careful out there. I'll expect you to have Lisa back by midnight."

Doug concurred. "Yes, ma'am. I'll have her back by eleven."

"Good night, mom. Please don't wait up. I'll be home on time."

As they approached his vehicle he walked around the back of his truck to open Lisa's door. Lisa learned months earlier not to open the door herself. She noticed how close Doug was able to position the truck right next to the curb without scraping the sides of his tires. She looked over at Doug, smiled and complimented him on his excellent parking skills.

"You sure know how to maneuver this vehicle," she said, obviously impressed once again by his ability to parallel park a car. This was one technique Lisa had not mastered and was always amazed at how easily Doug could negotiate a tight spot next to a curb.

Doug got a mischievous glint in his eye and glanced over at Lisa. "That's because I have all the right moves."

"Yes, you do."

She climbed into the cab and slid over to the center of the bench seat to sit as close to Doug as possible. She was deeply in love with this man and was not shy about showing it. Doug was more perceptive than most seventeen-year-olds about such things and sensed the longing Lisa had for him at that moment. He closed her door and walked around the rear of the truck.

As he got inside his truck he looked over at her and had never felt such an attraction for a woman. He leaned over, wrapped his muscular arms around her and pulled her close. He cupped her face with his hands and very slowly positioned his lips on hers. Their long, lingering kiss would be one of many memories that would be created over the next few weeks that Lisa would cherish forever.

CHAPTER 4

MICHAEL STEPPED QUICKLY ahead of his grandmother and opened the driver's side door for her.

"Why thank you, Michael," she said. "You're always such a gentleman."

Michael was considerate of others and a straight-A student and a good athlete, too. He rarely sought accolades, but the approval of his grandmother was very special to him, and something he did not take for granted. Francine's tone and demeanor were so warm and sincere that it gave her compliments much more meaning.

Michael was only thirteen and still young enough to be influenced by the warmth and tenderness of a loving grandmother. Often times, Michael felt closer to her than to anyone else in his family. She was someone he could always count on. She never judged him harshly and often was the voice of reason during the inevitable family disputes. He trusted her, and felt totally comfortable in her presence.

"Dad always says you won't earn a woman's respect if you don't first treat her with respect."

Francine smiled. "That's very true, Michael. Very true."

As he fastened himself in his seat he turned to Francine. "Hey, Grandma, did you know your tags are about to expire?"

"Why yes, Michael, I did know that. Good of you to notice and to remind me. I've just had a few things on my mind lately, and have been putting it off."

"That doesn't sound like you, Grandma. So what kinds of things are on your mind?" His insecurity showed. "Anything involving me?"

"No, Michael, nothing involving you. At least, nothing about you that concerns me. Of course, I think about you all the time. I think about how smart you are with you always getting straight A's; I think about how athletic you are in all the sports you play; and I think about what a handsome young man you are growing up to be."

"Thanks, Grandma. Mom always says Doug and I inherited our dad's good looks."

"That you did. But don't count your mother out on this matter. She is a very attractive woman as well."

"Oh, I know, Grandma."

"And just how do you know that?" Francine teased.

"Because I hear dad telling mom how beautiful she is, especially on the weekends."

Now it was Francine's time to smile as she thought about her son commenting on his wife's appearance perhaps less as a sincere compliment and more for personal pleasure. Still, she knew that Greg truly loved Julie and had seen him demonstrate his affection for her many times.

"So, Grandma, if it's not me on your mind, what is it you are concerned about these days?"

"Just the normal worries a grandmother at my age has."

"Like what?" Michael asked.

"Well, like making sure your mom and dad had a good time in Europe, and that they get back home safely," Francine replied.

Her answer seemed to satisfy him. He knew his grandmother had a very real fear of flying, even though Greg and others had tried to reassure her. When Francine was in her early twenties a close friend of hers was killed on a flight between Atlanta and Chicago. Though it was ruled as a freak weather-related accident, the jolt of losing her friend so tragically never left Francine. She knew that flying was so much safer now, and even acknowledges that it may be the safest means of travel today, but she still worried whenever Greg or Julie flew. This was especially true when the flights were out of the country.

"Oh, they seem to be having fun. We talked to them just before you showed up," Michael explained.

"You did? Well, that's good," Francine replied. "So they are having a good time?"

Michael enjoyed his role as momentary family news reporter. "Oh, sure. They sounded like they were having a great time. Mostly they asked how Doug and I were doing."

"And what did you two say to that question?" Francine asked.

"We told them we were doing fine. Doug told them how he modified his truck stereo to get more decibels out of it. That's a measure of sound volume."

"I know, Michael," Francine chagrinned. "I am very familiar with what a decibel is. Hard as it may be for you to believe at times, I was not born yesterday."

"Oh, I know, Grandma. You definitely were not born yesterday."

"So what are you saying, Michael? That I'm really old?"

"Oh no, Grandma. I just meant that you have been around for a lot longer than me. Heck, you've been around longer than Mom and Dad. But that doesn't mean you're old."

Francine was amused at Michael's attempt to smooth things over. *There may be a politician in this boy,* she thought to herself. She steered the conversation back to the phone call from Greg and Julie as they stopped for a red light.

"What else did you and Douglas tell your parents?

"I told them how I had aced my algebra test."

"Very good, Michael."

He tried to avoid smiling at his grandmother's remark of approval, but could not hide his satisfaction at having pleased someone with whom he felt so close. Michael was at that awkward stage of trying to break away from behaviors that he perceived to be too childish for someone his age, while still relishing adult praise.

Michael did get along well with his parents, but he found his grandmother to be a very calming influence over him. This could be particularly helpful as he navigated the often-troubling waters of adolescence.

"Well, it sounds like they're having a great time," Francine said cheerfully. "But it will be great to have them back."

"Yeah, I guess so," Michael replied.

Francine could sense something was amiss. "Is everything okay between you and your parents?"

"Oh, yeah, we're fine," Michael responded with slightly more energy.

"Michael, you know you should always try to go to your parents, either together or separately, to discuss whatever is on your mind. You are reaching an age when life will start becoming a bit more complicated. You will start having questions and conflicts that they can help sort out. You should never feel like you have no one to talk to about things."

Michael simply nodded and said in a low voice, "I know, Grandma."

Francine was not sure Michael was sold on the idea. As tenderly as she could she made a suggestion to her grandson.

"Michael, I want you to know that if ever you feel the need to talk to someone about anything troubling you, I would always be happy to talk with you about things. Even if it's just for me to listen."

"Thanks, Grandma, but what kinds of things do you mean?"

"Oh, most anything. Your grades, teachers, new hobbies." She paused and then said slowly, "Girls."

"Girls? Grandma, what do you know about girls? I mean, I don't want to sound unkind, but it's been a while since you were in junior high school."

The light turned green and as Francine stepped on the accelerator she smiled. "Trust me, Michael, it may have been a while since I was your age, but some things about young men and young women do not change much."

"I guess I'll take your word for it, Grandma."

"Well, I think you should. You may find it serves you well." They both laughed as the vehicle approached the last few miles to her house.

Once inside the house the two of them went separate ways, Michael to the guest room and Francine to the kitchen where she heated up some leftover casserole. Over dinner Michael discussed his art project, and Francine talked about a mystery novel she was reading. After they finished eating Michael retired to the guest room to work on his project.

An hour later Michael wandered into the living room and sat down next to his grandmother. Francine looked up and greeted him warmly. She could tell something was on his mind. "Well, hello there. I thought you might be heading off to bed."

"I will be shortly. But I was thinking about what you said earlier in the car."

Francine was not sure to what Michael was referring, "Well, we talked about a lot of things. What specifically?"

Michael's voice was low and soft. "You said that if I ever felt the need to talk to someone about something that you would always be happy to listen."

Francine laid the book down on her end table and looked at Michael with attentive eyes. "Why yes, of course." Then she placed her hand on his knee and said, "I can see that something is troubling you, Michael. What is it?"

"It's everything, Grandma, just everything."

His grandmother drew in a breath and tried to be supportive without sounding condescending. "I know that junior high can be a very difficult time for a young man. So many changes, so many questions and so few clear answers. But why don't you start with what is bothering you the most?"

"It's Doug. He's always chirping me."

"Excuse me, Michael. What do you mean by chirping?"

"I mean like he's always criticizing me. Trashing me for the things I do and am interested in. Calling me a geek. Calling me a jock. Now he's even started mocking me by calling me an artist."

Francine seemed puzzled by his last remark. "An artist? Why would that be so insulting? Your mother is a bit of an artist. Wouldn't that be more of a compliment?"

"He says all male artists are gay. Can you believe that?"

Francine had to stifle a small smile. "What do you think about gay people?"

"I have no problem with them. A classmate of mine is pretty sure he's gay, and because we get along so well he wonders if I might be gay."

"What do you think?"

"I'm pretty sure I'm not. There's a girl I like, but I get the feeling she only likes me because I'm Doug's brother."

"Why do you say that?"

"Because she keeps asking me about video games and stuff that she thinks Doug would know." What Michael did not say is that the girl really wanted Michael to score her some pot from Doug.

"Michael, I know those comments from Doug are not easy for you to take, but I'm sure your brother doesn't mean to hurt your feelings."

"Oh, I think he does. It's just seems so unfair."

Francine wanted to get more to the root of the matter so she asked, "What seems so unfair about it?"

Michael sighed. "I work so hard trying to get good grades, trying to do well at student government, trying to win at sports. But I get no recognition for all that. Mom and Dad hardly notice because they're spending all of their time with Doug and his so-called problems."

Francine knew exactly what Michael was talking about. Doug had been diagnosed with a host of emotional ailments since he was seven years old. In the last year he was suspended twice from the special needs school he was attending due to physical altercations and temper tantrums. His parents suspected he was smoking marijuana, and possibly doing even harder drugs. He had kept his parents busy for sure. By comparison, Michael was almost a model child. As such, he received nowhere near the attention that his older brother did. And that seemed to be what bothered Michael the most.

Francine tenderly put her arm around her grandson. "Michael, have you mentioned this to either of your parents?"

"Grandma, I have tried talking to both of them. They say the same thing, that as long as I keep getting good grades and stay out of trouble that I will be fine. It's almost like they take me for granted."

Francine used both of her arms to turn Michael's shoulders so that he was facing her. She spoke quietly but firmly.

"Michael, I want you to listen to me. I know for a fact that both of your parents love you very much. They are so proud of all that you have accomplished. It may seem to you at times like they are taking you for granted, but they most definitely are not. They are very busy with their own careers and with the extra issues that Douglas brings them. But they still find as much time for you as they can."

Francine paused for a second. "Think about all of your sports activities for a minute. Doesn't your dad make a special effort to attend all of your games, and even several of your practices whenever he can?"

Michael thought about this and had to agree. "Well, yeah, I guess so."

"Well, see, maybe they don't really take you for granted as much as you think they do."

Michael retuned to the matter with his brother. "Maybe, but it still seems like Doug gets a lot of favoritism over me. Dad and him are always talking computer stuff that I don't understand. It's like Dad and Doug have much more in common than Dad and I do. Even their names sound similar. My name doesn't sound like anyone's around here."

Sibling rivalry, Francine thought.

"Having a unique name can be a good thing, Michael. It sets you apart from others. Having a distinguishable name can benefit you, don't you know?"

"I suppose."

Francine could sense there was something else upsetting Michael. "What is really bothering you about Douglas? Has he been violent toward you?

"Gosh no, Grandma. It's nothing like that."

"Then what is it?"

"I know this is going to sound crazy, what with Doug's temper problems and poor grades and all." His voice trailed off.

"Michael, are you feeling a little bit jealous of your brother?"

He hesitated. "Yes, grandma, I guess I am. Maybe just a little bit."

"Now why on earth would you be jealous of Douglas? You play sports better than him, get better grades and certainly draw better pictures."

Michael took a deep breath. "Because, grandma, everyone thinks he's cool."

"I don't believe that everyone thinks he's so cool. I'm sure your parents don't always think he's cool. And when he loses his temper or gets in trouble at school, I don't think he's cool."

But Michael was hearing none of the rebuttal, and was only getting started. "He's big and strong, he always sounds confident, his friends all look up to him, and he has no problem getting girlfriends. Did you see the girl he was dating last year? She was gorgeous. And his current girlfriend, Lisa, is even more beautiful. I think they may even be having sex."

"Michael! That's a terrible thing to say."

Michael sounded perplexed. "What? You think sex is terrible?"

"No, I don't think sex is terrible. But it's not appropriate between couples that young." Michael grinned slightly.

"I think you may be teasing me right now, so I'm going to get off this subject and get back to you and Douglas. You have nothing to be jealous about. You have just as many friends as your brother and they all look up to you. But there's something about your brother you're not considering."

"What's that?"

"That he actually may be a little bit jealous of you."

"Of me? No way! There's nothing about me he likes or appreciates."

Francine knew the opposite was true. Doug had confided recently to Francine how he wished he had some of the mental ability and athletic coordination that his younger brother displayed. She had tried to encourage him to do what he does best, which was programming computers and solving video games. But she would not betray his confidence in her by commenting on the conversation between Doug and her.

"Michael, do you trust me?"

"Of course, Grandma; why would you even ask that?"

"Because I want you to trust me when I say that I know how much Doug admires you. He may not always show it, but deep down he thinks the world of you. There is much about you that he wishes he were more like. Your ability at math, at sports, even art. Sometimes when a person criticizes another it may be because they miss not having the ability the other person has. Does this make sense?"

Michael thought for a minute. "I guess so. But if Doug feels that way why doesn't he just say so?"

"Because he would be admitting that part of him may be inferior to you, and that a part of you may be superior to him."

"So what should I do, Grandma?"

"First, don't let what Douglas says bother you. In fact, you should never let anyone's criticisms of you effect you. That just makes them win and you lose. Only you have total control over how you react to someone's negative comments. Don't let them control you; only you have the final control over your feelings. Now if it is constructive criticism, meaning it's truthful and not mean-spirited, then you should listen and try to improve yourself accordingly.

"Second, the next time the opportunity comes up, try paying Douglas a compliment."

Michael seemed puzzled, "A compliment? On what? I don't think there's anything to compliment him on."

Francine lowered her head and raised her eyes. "I agree with you when you say you don't think. You're just not thinking hard enough. What about his computer skills? Didn't you say you sometimes ask him for help on computer assignments?"

"Well, yeah."

"And isn't he very accomplished at some of his video games?"

"Yes."

"And isn't he pretty knowledgeable about cars and trucks and the stereo systems that go in them?"

Michael lifted his arms as if in surrender. "Okay, Grandma, okay. I get it. There are some things I could compliment him on."

"You might find the good deed will come back to you when you expect it the least, and when you may need it the most."

"Sort of like pay it forward, Grandma?"

"Precisely, Michael. It is exactly like pay it forward. And there's one other thing to consider about your relationship with Douglas."

"What's that, Grandma?"

"You and your brother will always be four years apart, but the difference in years will diminish as you both grow older."

"I'm not sure I understand what you are saying. Doug will always be fours older than me, won't he?"

"Yes, of course, he will. But that's called your chronological age, measured only in the years that you have lived. What I'm talking about is your emotional age, or your age of maturity. When you were eight and he was twelve, didn't he seem much older to you then than what he seems now?"

"Yes, I guess so."

"And when you are sixteen and he is twenty, the difference will seem even less. By the time you are both in your twenties you will likely seem almost the same age as your brother. Do you see what I am saying?"

"I do. But it still doesn't make my life any easier right now."

"I know, Michael. But believe me when I say, as you get older you will likely find you have more in common with Douglas than you realized."

Michael sat motionless. Finally he said, "Thanks, Grandma."

"For what?"

"Just for being you. And you were right about talking things out. I do feel better."

"You're very welcome. Anytime you want to talk I'll always be here for you. But don't forget to give your parents the first chance to hear you out."

"I know. I think I'm going to turn in now. Getting a little sleepy." With that he stood up and gave his grandmother a nice hug. "Good night, Grandma."

"Good night, Michael. Sleep well."

Michael walked back to the spare bedroom. As Francine resumed reading, she thought for a few minutes about her talk with Michael. She was keenly aware that before too long Michael and Douglas would indeed start having more things in common than not.

CHAPTER 5

DOUG CONFIDENTLY WOUND his Silverado around the curving streets of the residential neighborhood. He gripped the steering wheel firmly with his left hand as his right fingers tapped out the rhythm of the heavy-metal music blaring on his stereo. As the vehicle turned sharply the shoulder strap tightened over Doug's muscular torso and held him comfortably in place. The snugness of the lap and shoulder belts made him feel secure inside his truck, just as the purchase he was about to make would make him feel secure outside his truck. He thought how good it felt to be finally completing what he had started so many weeks before. He was sure he was doing the right thing both for him and for Lisa by making this purchase.

Lisa also was having her own feelings about security, but not the kind that had occupied Doug's thoughts. She was replaying the slow, soft kiss that she had experienced with Doug just moments before. She felt safe and protected in his arms. She had no illusions about Doug's shortcomings. Lisa knew he would never be a scholar or an athlete. But those drawbacks were of little concern when weighed against his sense of loyalty. Doug's intrinsic insecurities and distrust of authority resulted in him choosing his friends very carefully. Once a person had earned Doug's trust, his loyalty became unconditional.

Lisa felt an overwhelming desire to touch him. She stretched her left arm out behind Doug's head and started stroking the slightly curled thick brown hair on the back of his neck. She kept staring forward but looked slowly out the corner of her eye to gauge his reaction. Just as she hoped a wry grin formed across his lips. This brought a slight soft smile to her face.

"I love you," she whispered.

"I love you too," he responded. "What brought that on?"

"Oh, nothing in particular." She was hoping he would inquire a bit more, but Doug just kept on driving. Finally he echoed her comment. "Nothing in particular?"

"No, nothing in particular. Just life."

"Life?"

"Yes, life." Then she smiled again and stroked his hair one final time before returning her arm back to rest in her lap. She was content in the moment.

Doug was just about to turn right when Lisa suddenly spoke up. "Turn left."

Doug slowed his truck and instantly asked, "What? Why?"

"I'd like to enjoy the view from the lane for a minute."

"Uh, okay," Doug replied. He pulled off to the left down a narrow road that ended in an open parking area. Commonly referred to as Lover's Lane, the vantage point afforded an unobstructed and spectacular view of downtown Atlanta and the surrounding countryside. The sight was breathtaking, even for Lisa and Doug, who had seen it numerous times before. Doug turned left and picked a spot to park far away from any distractions. He turned off the engine and set the parking brake.

Lisa gazed out at the incredible vista and unbuckled her seat belt. She then snuggled over to Doug, who wrapped his arm around her and drew her close. Her fingertips tapped on the back of his hand as he gently stroked her arm. He leaned over and slowly brought her face up to his. It was a long, enduring kiss of young, passionate love.

When they finally broke away she whispered in his ear, "I love you, Douglas MacDonald."

"I love you too."

"You need to be going. Your public waits."

He loosened his grip on her slightly as she began to pull away. Suddenly he tightened his hold on her and pulled her back close to him. He cupped her face with his hands and kissed her forcibly on the lips. She was taken aback momentarily then quickly responded to the unexpected display of affection. After a few seconds Doug used his hands to move her face ever so slowly away from his.

"Wow, what brought that on?"

"Sudden impulse." He paused just long enough to smile and add, "And maybe the view had something to do with it."

"Really. And here I thought it was my ravishing beauty."

"That too."

"Too late. Not buying it."

"No, really. When I said the view had something to do with it I meant my view of you."

"Right." They both smiled widely at each other's remarks. Lisa leaned up and gave Doug a light kiss on his cheek. "You're so cute. Nice safe recovery."

Lisa paused for a minute. "Speaking of a safe recovery, did you ever get that safe you were talking about?"

Doug's expression noticeably brightened as he answered, "Yes. Two days ago."

"Well, I know you had talked about getting it. Is it everything you expected?"

"Everything and more. The locksmith put a personalized combination on it as I requested. And he oiled all of the gears and chambers and hinges. It was quiet as a mouse when I opened and closed it." Doug bought the floor safe at an auction for twenty dollars. It was a relic from the Prohibition era and had a two-foot square enclosure.

Lisa looked pleased. "Well, I'm glad that all worked out for you. But we need to go."

"You're right about that." Doug fastened his seat belt and looked over at Lisa as if to urge her to fasten hers, which she promptly did. "Let's come back here later. I have some primo grass. We can mellow out on it."

"Sounds like a plan to me."

Soon they were back on Parkway Drive that led into the southeast entrance of Stephenson Park. A mile in he turned left down a sparsely traveled gravel road which led into a small parking lot. Doug drove down to the far left side of the lot and parked in one of several spaces. Then he walked around the truck to open the door for Lisa.

A few minutes later a red pickup pulled up and parked. Behind the wheel was a young, large male who sluggishly climbed out of his vehicle. The man seemed almost as wide as tall. He was just under six feet and weighed nearly three hundred pounds. His name was Robert Henderson, but all his friends called him Tiny. The nickname was intended to be endearing, which was how Tiny took it.

He had been born with a malformed brain. Doctors could not identify any direct link for the malady and attributed it to a rare freak of nature. Tiny's paternal grandparents suspected that his mother had been doing hard drugs well into her pregnancy. Whatever the cause, it left Tiny with slow, simple mental capabilities and a severe case of stuttering.

Doug first met Tiny when both were attending freshman orientation at the continuation school. Afterwards Tiny needed a restroom, but he could not get the words out very quickly. Doug patiently endured Tiny's stammering request and then directed him to the men's room. Tiny was forever grateful.

Rather than feeling pity for Tiny, Doug saw loyalty and persistence. Tiny told Doug he would be willing to do anything Doug asked as payment. Doug didn't think much about it at the time, but every few months Tiny would remind Doug of the offer. Though he never took Tiny up on the proposal, Doug was touched at Tiny's childlike faithfulness.

Along with loyalty, Doug was also impressed by Tiny's dogged persistence to accomplish a few personal pursuits. Tiny had shared with Doug his desire to one day legally drive his recently deceased father's old Ford pickup truck. It would be an uphill battle.

In order for Tiny to accomplish his goal, he would have to read and thoroughly comprehend Georgia's basic driver's manual to score high enough on a written exam. Then he would have to overcome tremendous stress by passing a driving performance test. Finally, he would have to master learning the intricacies of driving a manual shift vehicle. Although it took him two years and several attempts at the written and driving tests, Tiny finally earned his driver's license.

Doug was a big help. No one was prouder than Doug when Tiny eventually showed his rehabilitated mother how well he could drive, backup and even parallel park his late father's truck. The bond between Doug and Tiny was forever sealed.

"Heeeyyyy," Tiny stuttered cheerfully to Doug.

"Hey yourself," Doug replied smiling.

The three teens chatted briefly and then walked to a secluded area and waited next to a rusting picnic table. Ten minutes later a black Ford Fusion drove up and a tall, thin man in his early thirties climbed out. Doug recognized him as Tommy Bertello and introduced everyone. Tommy was well-dressed in black slacks over fashionable loafers and a grey mock turtle neck sweater under an expensive leather bomber jacket. He carried a black leather bag that he set on the table, unfastened its clasp and reached inside.

"I believe you may be interested in this." Tommy pulled out a long leather sheath and handed it to Doug who stood motionless for a second. "Open it up and tell me what you think."

Doug held the black cloth case in his left hand and pulled open the tiny zipper at the top of the sheath. He pulled out a long gleaming steel encasement. For a second he just stopped to take in the full experience. He wanted to seal it in his memory. The metal felt colder to his touch than he expected, but not uncomfortably so. It was slightly heavier than he had anticipated but the grip seemed to mesh perfectly in his palm. There was no doubt from the expression on his face that he was pleased. The others slowly drew near.

Doug stroked his right hand fingers along the shaft of highly polished stainless steel. He turned it over and noticed the subtle ridges that had been machined into the two handle portions. He also found the tiny release latch that was countersunk ever so slightly so as to not accidently release open the several movable parts of the weapon. For several seconds no one said a word as if giving Doug the time he needed to take it all in.

The weapon was a specialty type of switchblade called a

butterfly knife. It had first caught Doug's attention while he was playing an advanced version of WoW in which the knife was described as a highly coveted weapon. Doug felt it would be the perfect final addition to his repertoire of rebellious accessories. Now he was holding it in his hands. He stood silent and felt both excited and nervous.

"Do you like it?"

"Yes, I do. It's awesome. Everything I expected and more." He looked up at the others who had all gathered around more closely to get a better view.

To Doug the weapon was both dangerous and beautiful, and captured those rare combinations of being deadly and artistic, sleek but sturdy, friendly but potentially lethal, concealable yet unmistakably attention grabbing.

"And you haven't even opened it yet."

The group first acknowledged this fact thoughtfully and then chuckled at the humor of it.

"Do you think you can figure out how it opens?" Tommy inquired.

"I think so."

Doug held the knife in his right hand and squeezed the latch pin. He immediately sensed one of the two handles releasing from its locked position. He then used his left hand to rotate one of handles around a pivot pin to end up one hundred eighty degrees opposite from the other handle. He heard the blade snap into a locked position. Next he released a tang pin to rotate the first handle back toward the first and exposing the knife's cutting blade. Once the first handle came back to the second one he secured the two handles together with the latch pin.

Doug starred at the gleaming steel weapon held firmly in his right hand. He turned it over with his fingers and inspected its entire length from every angle.

"How long is it?"

"The blade is six inches and the casing is seven," Tommy said. "The blade is made of the highest-grade titanium combined with high carbon, tungsten and alloyed stainless steel. It's what gives the blade its incredible strength and razor edge sharpness." He paused momentarily for effect. "It's also one of the things that make this knife illegal in most states." Suddenly the group became a bit more solemn as they realized this was far from an ordinary pocketknife.

Tommy looked at Doug. "Since you seem to like it, it's time to pay up."

Doug reached into his pocket, pulled out five one hundred dollar bills and handed them to Tommy who promptly stashed them into the inside pocket of his bomber jacket. Lisa saw the exchange and whispered to Doug, "Whew, that's a lot of cash for one knife."

Tommy overheard Lisa's remark and whispered back to both of them. "Let me tell you something about this knife. I had it shipped directly from the Philippines where it was manufactured to the highest standards possible. My direct shipping line connections give me a handsome discount that I passed on to my good client Doug here. That knife could easily bring in over a grand on the open market. Your friend is getting a real bargain here."

Lisa looked at Doug with a surprised expression and Doug simply shrugged as if to say he knew that all along. Tommy raised his eyes, surveyed the entire group. "Are there any other questions I can answer about this most rare and unique of weapons?"

"Why is it called a bu-bu-butterfly knife?" Tiny asked, trying to mask his stuttering.

Tommy quickly closed up the knife and held it up as if he was a magician preparing to perform an act. He squeezed the latch pin to release the two handles then slowly pulled back the outer one that covered the other to reveal the knife blade.

"The blade inside this handle is sort of like a butterfly ready to emerge from a cocoon. Inside a cocoon a butterfly is safe, protected and almost benign. Once it breaks out from its enclosure it is free to experience a world it has never known, but because the world can be a very violent and evil place, it needs a way to defend itself so it transforms into this."

Tommy stood back a bit and quickly flicked his wrist. This caused the encasement to flip back and revealed the nearly five inches of the gleaming stainless steel knife blade. As his hand continued on in one fluid motion, the encasement latched back to become part of the handle. Then he quickly reversed the direction of his motion to cause the razor-sharp blade to lock into place. The onlookers were enthralled. Although the entire action took less than a few seconds, it was like a weapons ballet. Tommy had performed the transformation so seamlessly and flawlessly it was if with just a few rapid motions of his hand he had waved a magic wand and changed an innocent appearing cylinder into a deadly looking instrument.

No one was more impressed than Doug, who leaned over to Tommy. "You've got to teach me that, dude."

"Sure thing," Tommy replied.

They shook hands. "It's been good doing business with you, dude. I'll be looking forward to that first lesson on WoW."

"You got it," Doug replied.

He and Lisa started heading back up the trail with Tiny close behind. As Tiny caught up to them, Doug noticed two tough-looking young men walking toward them. They were dressed in gang-affiliation colors. The person in front walked very purposefully and seemed to be the leader. Doug looked directly at him and nodded slightly as they passed. It would not be the only time their paths would cross.

"Do you know who those guys were? They looked mean." Lisa said.

Doug lowered his voice, "They're part of the Raptors gang. The first dude was Dominic Williams, the gang's leader."

"What about the other guy. The one with the slicked black hair. He looks scarier than the first. Did you see the slash on his left cheek?"

"Don't know much about him. Maybe he's new to the gang."

Minutes later Doug and Tiny drove their vehicles out of the lot. Soon Doug pulled his truck into the lover's lane and parked away from all others. He cracked his windows slightly, turned on some soft rock music, lit up a joint for the two of them to share and then partook in some serious lovemaking. It wasn't sophisticated, it wasn't experienced but it was wonderful for the two of them. Raw, primitive and totally physical.

///

The next morning Doug slept in and decided to skip school for that day. He spent most of the afternoon practicing with his new knife. When Michael arrived from school in the late afternoon Doug was still perfecting his techniques at opening and closing the knife. Michael walked by Doug's room and saw him maneuvering his wrist as if playing with a toy.

Michael stopped by Doug's open door.

"What's that? What are you doing with it?"

"Get out of here. It's none of your business."

Michael was taken aback a bit by Doug's reaction. "What's the big deal? It's just a simple pocketknife. I had one like that in Boy Scouts."

"You never had one like this in Boy Scouts." Doug quickly opened the knife, locked it into its final position and pointed it at his brother. Michael stepped back.

"Big deal. So you got a gangster knife. It's not as if you'd ever do anything with it."

"You'd be surprised."

"Speaking of surprises, can I ask you a favor?"

"What?" Doug snapped.

"A friend of mine wants some pot."

Doug shoved his brother against the wall. "Don't you ever ask me that, you hear? Never."

"Okay. Okay."

"Get the hell out of here. You have no idea what you're talking about."

Michael made a heavy sigh and simply said, "Whatever. I've got homework to do. Go play with your new GI Joe toy thing."

"Just get out of here," Doug yelled as Michael was walking away. "And don't you dare tell Mom or Dad about this, understand?"

"Yeah, yeah," Michael replied. He was perplexed, confused and frustrated. He tried to apply what Francine had told him the night before, but it just wasn't working. So he simply started thinking ahead to his next day's homework assignment.

CHAPTER 6

GREG AND JULIE returned home to Atlanta safe and sound on the following Saturday. Greg spent most of the weekend going through stacks of mail. He felt good to be home, back on familiar territory and reunited with his children. He loved to travel and the twentieth anniversary trip to Paris was magical. But by Monday it was time to think about getting back to work.

Greg thoroughly enjoyed his job in the city of Atlanta's Information Technology Department. He had worked hard and was steadily rewarded with several promotions. His leadership skills and excellent performance reviews had earned him the position of IT manager eight years ago. Four years later he advanced to senior IT manager with a staff of nearly forty professional analysts and engineers.

He really thought he had reached the pinnacle of his career and felt he could never be professionally happier. That was before the idea of an Atlanta's joint IT/Police task force took hold. When he was offered the position to co-chair the task force with a key representative from the police department, Greg jumped at the chance. He had been notified of this new assignment on

Friday afternoon just before leaving on his weeklong anniversary vacation. The other co-chair from the police department, Detective Jim Barnett, would be named the following Monday.

Jim had been enrolled at Georgia Tech studying for a degree in criminal justice at the same time Greg was pursuing his degree in computer science. During the end of his junior year Jim applied for and was accepted into the Atlanta Police Department's intern program. At the same time Greg made a similar application for the IT internship at the city's IT department.

Their friendship had endured from the start of their internships, a span of over twenty-five years. During that time both attended each other's weddings, and the christening of each of their children. Jim and his wife, Sharon, had their first child, Ken, five years before Greg had his first child, Doug. Jim and Sharon had their daughter, Cheryl, the year before Doug was born. Doug and Cheryl both played youth soccer and Greg and Jim were coaches for their children's soccer teams. Greg and Jim would frequently attend soccer workshops and coaching clinics together, making their relationship even closer.

It was not uncommon for them to cross paths on the job, but it had been years since they had worked closely together. Jim had been promoted to lead detective five years earlier and had successfully investigated and closed several high-profile cases.

Greg was not surprised to learn that he was picked to be the primary IT representative on the joint IT-Atlanta Police Department task force. He had much experience working with many of the IT services that the APD used, and Greg knew many of the key stakeholders within the APD who used these services. But he was curious as to who would be selected as the primary APD representative. So when he returned to his work that Monday morning, one of the first things he sought out was the name of his co-chair on the joint IT-APD task force. He was delighted to learn it was none other than his good friend Jim Barnett. One of the first things Greg did after he found out about Jim's assignment was to call and congratulate him.

"Jim, this is Greg," he began cheerfully. "How are you doing, old buddy?"

"Greg, good to hear you're back in the U S of A. How was Paris?"

"Paris was incredible. The museums, the restaurants, the wine. And the locals were much friendlier than we expected. Overall it was a great experience."

"Plus it was your twentieth anniversary . . . and they said it'd never last."

"Who said that?" Greg teased back at his friend.

"Mostly your ex-girlfriends," Jim teased.

"So I hear you've been assigned to co-chair the joint task force."

"Yes indeed. I was really glad to hear you'd be heading up the IT side of the group," Jim said.

"I felt the same way about you being on it. Sort of takes me back to our intern days," Greg replied.

"Those were some great times. We were so young and naïve and full of ourselves," Jim recalled.

"So I guess not much has changed," Greg responded making them both snicker. "So we talked a while back about getting together for lunch today. You still available?"

"Absolutely. I want to hear more about what all you saw and did in Paris. The Eiffel Tower alone should be good for most of the lunch hour."

"Sounds good. Though I may want to squeeze in a few questions about your thoughts on the task force," Greg said.

"Sure thing. Does Dario's sound good to you?" Jim asked, referring to a popular deli located a few blocks away from their buildings, which were across the street from each other.

"Definitely," Greg replied. "Let's make it twelve-thirty. I have a staff meeting up till noon."

"Sounds like a plan, guy. See you then."

///

Dario's was a popular deli noted for their thick salami sandwiches on sourdough bread among many other tasty offerings. As Greg neared its entrance he could see the line extending outside. Jim had just arrived and Greg joined him in line just inside the doorway. The owners had both worked at the world-famous Varsity fast-food restaurant known for their super-efficient ordering in which several dozen customers could be served in a matter of minutes.

There were tables in the far back that afforded some level of privacy amidst all of the hustle and bustle of the busy eatery. Jim ordered a roast beef on wheat bread while Greg ordered Dario's signature salami on sourdough. The two men chattered about their work a bit and then their families.

"Greg, how are your boys doing?"

"They're doing fine. Michael is a standout scholar and is doing well with his sports. Doug is still fighting his emotional demons of sorts, but we think we have it under control. I think you know he is in a special continuation school now."

"Yes. Weren't you having some problems with him smoking pot?"

"Yeah, that's right. Julie and I have found some drug paraphernalia in his room and have smelled it on his breath a few times. He finally admitted he's tried it but made it sound like it was more as an experiment. I'm keeping a close eye on him, though. I do worry about him. I tried to tell him the consequences of doing it but I'm not sure he got the message. Teenagers tend to have their own way of communicating and it's not always a method parents understand."

"I hear you. Let's just hope it doesn't lead to him experimenting with harder drugs. You said that Michael is doing well?"

"Michael is doing great. He was voted class president, is a straight-A student and is helping to lead his soccer and basketball teams. He's also starting to show some artistic skills with some graphic art work." Greg paused and grinned. "Michael obviously gets his creative talents from his mother."

"No doubt," Jim smiled. "It's good to hear that Michael is doing so well."

"And how are your kids doing these days? I haven't seen them in a while."

"Well, Cheryl is doing fine. She's a freshman at the city college and is thinking of transferring to Georgia State next year."

"Good for her. And how about Kenneth?"

Jim rubbed his right hand across his left cheek as if searching for the proper words. "I don't know. I haven't talked to him in almost six months."

"Wow. Have you tried calling him?"

"Sure, but I can't reach him. Apparently he's changed his cell phone number and moved into a different apartment. He called Sharon a month or so ago and said he might be leaving the area for a while."

"What if you or Sharon need to get in touch with him about an urgent family matter? Say one of you gets into a serious auto accident?"

"Sharon asked him about that and he told her that if something came up that was really urgent she could text him at an emergency number he changes each week and gives to his sister."

"That sounds like a lot to put on Cheryl."

"Tell me about it. She's only eighteen and just started community college." Jim said.

Greg chose his next words carefully because he knew something about the origins of the disagreements between Jim and his son. "Does this all go back to you wanting Ken to go to law school?"

"Well, it sort of started there but it wasn't just about law school. It was really two other things that were at the core of our disagreements. You see, it wasn't just that Kenny did not want to attend law school as I'd hoped. He didn't even want to go to college at all."

Greg was very stunned. "Really? I'm surprised to hear that. He was always such a good student. What was the other thing that came between you two?"

"His career choice. I never wanted him to go into police work."

Jim went on to explain how during the last year he and his son had grown estranged. He wanted Ken to go to college full-time and to enjoy the full college experience. He wanted his son to see more of life and to consider other careers that would be available to his son. Jim wanted his son to experience the fun, the revelry and the parties that a college life could provide him.

Ken only wanted to go into police work, just like his dad. This greatly displeased Jim. He knew the toll police work could take on a family, on a marriage, and on raising children. It wasn't that Jim did not like his job. He certainly did, but Jim wanted his son to have that which most any other father would want for a son and that was to have a better life than he had endured.

As much as Jim tried to talk Ken out of it, Jim knew he could not stop his then 18-year-old son from pursuing the career of his choice. So Jim begrudgingly accepted the fact that his son was going to become a police officer. He watched with mixed emotions as his son graduated from the Atlanta Police Academy at the top of his class a year later.

Ken took to police work like a duck to water. He enjoyed every facet of the work including the training, the camaraderie, the equipment, the uniform, but mostly the notion of actually helping others in dangerous situations. On a few occasions he outwitted criminals and derived much satisfaction from out-maneuvering a lawbreaker with more brain than brawn.

"So when was the last time you saw or talked to Ken?"

"Saw him not quite a year ago at Christmas. He was tall and still skinny with long blonde hair like a surfer. I talked to him about six months ago, but it did not go well. We disagreed again about his career choices. I was hoping I could talk him into studying law at some point in the future. Thankfully, he realized that he needs a college degree to advance within the department, so he's been attending night school. I want him to keep going with his education. He ended the conversation saying he might just head off to California and take up surfing."

"You say he looked like a surfer. Is Ken interested in that?"

"Oh, yeah. He's always had this interest in surfing. Go figure. A kid from Atlanta wanting to become a surfer."

"Well I guess there's worse hobbies he could take up. If he is interested both in police work and surfing he very may have moved to southern California."

"It's possible that Kenny may be off in Australia surfing the beaches of Brisbane or Sydney."

"Why in the world would Ken go so far away as Australia?"

"Because Australia has some of the greatest surf in the world," Jim said. "Plus they also have some of the greatest topless beaches in the world." They both grinned. "And some of the sexiest girls in the world frequent those beaches."

Greg raised his glass and offered a toast. "To the topless beaches of Australia, and the big-breasted women who frequent them."

"And to the medium-breasted women who also frequent them," Jim said. They both laughed out loud.

Jim changed the subject. "So did you ever show Julie the two safeties of your handgun?"

"Oh, yeah," Greg responded, referring to his Colt model 1911A firearm that he kept for security. "It took her a while but she finally got it."

"Good," Jim replied. "You'd be surprised how many people forget that small but important feature."

They talked a while longer about each of their sons. Then Jim spoke.

"I need to get back. I hope you guys can keep Doug on the straight and narrow, and away from the drugs."

"And I hope you eventually get in touch with Kenny," Greg offered.

CHAPTER 7

IT HAD BEEN two weeks since Julie had returned from her magical anniversary trip to Paris. She thought often about the crystal replica of the Eiffel Tower that Greg had given her as an anniversary gift. She had placed it on an elaborately carved oak coffee table in her living room adjacent to the large brick fireplace.

The light from the flames illuminated the crystal, producing dazzling effects. The light bounced off the many angles of the structure like a mini laser light show. All four members of the family, plus Francine, were transfixed the first time they witnessed this amazing combination of glass, fire and crystal.

Every time she walked by it and gazed, she would think of that memorable evening in Paris with her husband. Then she would let her mind drift back to savor the intoxicating feelings of pleasure and contentment she had experienced.

Julie took a little longer applying her makeup because she had several important meetings to attend. She picked out a smart-looking navy blue pantsuit with a satin white blouse with lace trim underneath. She accessorized her outfit appropriately and checked out her look several times in the mirror.

Julie was an independent contractor working as a licensed interior designer for a large architectural firm headquartered in downtown Atlanta. When she realized she was running late she cut her primping short and gave herself one last look. She hurried out to the kitchen to say goodbye to Michael before he left for school. He was finishing up his breakfast.

"Hi, Mom," Michael said without looking up. His voice sounded more energized as he said, "Wow, Mom, you look good today. Something special going on?"

"Well, thank you, sweetheart. That's a nice thing to say. You mean I don't look good every day?"

"Not really."

"What?"

"Just kidding, Mom. Of course you look good all the time. But you seem to look more rad today. So what's going on?"

"I have a couple of important meetings this morning with some key clients. And then I meet with my boss for lunch. What about you? Is there anything out of the ordinary going on with you?"

"Well, my soccer coach said he may switch me from goalie to forward. And I have a history test this morning."

"So have you studied for your test?"

"Oh, yeah. I know I'm going to ace it. I always ace my history tests."

Julie frowned slightly at her son's remark, but then smiled because she knew he was likely correct. Most courses came easily to him, especially math and history, so his seeming arrogance about grades was more factual than boastful.

"Do you have your lunch money?"

"Yeah." Michael put his dishes in the washer and slung his backpack over his shoulder. He gave his mom a kiss on the cheek. "I need to go. Doug is waiting in the driveway. Good luck with your meetings."

Michael trotted out of the house and several minutes later Julie did the same. She set the GPS unit on her car dash to the address of her first appointment and headed out. Twenty minutes later she parked in front of a stately mansion.

Julie knocked on the expensive walnut front door adorned with colorful stained glass. Within a minute the wife who had hired Julie answered the door and let her in. They chatted pleasantly for a few minutes and then got right down to business. The wife wanted to transform the rather pedestrian interiors of the house into a well-integrated theme of the grand elegance of the old South. Julie knew exactly how to accomplish this.

From the color and types of draperies, to the styles and locations of hardwood, to the kinds and textures of wall coverings, Julie had the experience and know-how to bring it all together. She spent just under an hour with her first client, who was very impressed with Julie's obvious expertise and with the specific recommendations she suggested. The client was certain the goal she envisioned would be accomplished.

Then it was on to the next client. The second job involved a suite of offices in a moderately sized law firm about twenty minutes away. Julie met with two senior partners. She listened intently as they described their general requirements for their office suite. But it was obvious the two middle-aged gentlemen were unfamiliar with the notions of blended colors and complimentary furnishings. She guided them through that part of the discussion deftly, leaving them with the feeling that they were in very capable hands.

Julie had enjoyed a very productive morning resulting in two satisfied clients. But now she looked forward to a leisurely lunch with her boss and good friend, Eric Spencer, at a popular restaurant. They pulled into the lot at almost the same time and parked next to each other.

"Great timing," Eric cheerfully called out.

"Indeed it was."

The two of them entered the restaurant and were quickly seated. They spent the first half of their lunch discussing Julie's memorable anniversary vacation. It was the first time since Julie had returned from Europe that the two of them had a chance to talk about the trip at length. Eric was divorced and wanted to hear all of the romantic details. Julie was only too willing to share them.

Eric eventually asked about Julie's boys.

"So it sounds like Michael is doing well at sports. How about his schoolwork? Is he still bringing home the straight A's?"

"Pretty much. He had a history test this morning. He informed me at breakfast that he was officially going to ace it, in his words."

Eric smiled. "I guess there's something to be said for confidence."

"I guess. The thing is he can usually back it up."

"And what about Douglas? How is he doing these days?"

Julie took a breath before responding. She and Eric had confided in each other over the years and Julie felt comfortable sharing some of Doug's emotional maladies with Eric. He knew that Doug had struggled academically and for the past two years was in a special continuation school.

Julie had, in recent months, become more and more concerned with her older son's erratic behavior. She felt Doug was displaying behaviors beyond the normal transformation of a young boy growing into manhood. The vision of watching a son struggle with puberty versus admitting much more ominous behavior was often blurred by her maternal instincts.

"You've taken him to counselors, correct?"

"Yes. We have had him to school counselors, doctors, psychologists, therapists and a psychiatrist. They recommended tutors, which we tried and seemed to help but only temporarily. They have suggested counseling which only served to highlight his debating skills. He did seem to start to establish a constructive relationship with his psychiatrist until the doctor suggested the deal breaker."

"The deal breaker?"

"Medications. The psychiatrist prescribed some medications for Doug's emotional instability and mood swings. Doug was adamant that he was not going to alter his bio-chemistry, as he put it, by ingesting any artificially manufactured, mood-altering drugs."

Eric raised his eyes. "You're saying he will not take any man-made drugs?"

"None."

"And why is that?"

"He says he doesn't trust the pharmaceutical companies. He believes that because they are so profit-motivated, it is in their own best interest to produce drugs that keep people sick rather than make them healthy. Can you believe that? I don't know where he gets such ideas."

"So he won't take any medications his doctors have prescribed?" Eric asked.

"Not if it has been artificially manufactured."

"Will he take any natural medications?"

"Yes. His psychiatrist recommended some herbal-based medication that Doug tried, but it had little effect. Doug asked if there were any natural-based drugs he could try but none were available."

Eric took his final bite of cheesecake.

"Sounds like he's reasoned out his use of drugs and medications."

Julie just rolled her eyes.

"Oh, he is very good at reasoning things out. His Harvard-trained psychiatrist told me Doug had innate debating skills. He believes Doug's arguments often are well thought-out and his logic, flawless. That's what's so frustrating. He is not ignorant or dim-witted. He is actually very intelligent. Several teachers told me he has such good potential, but these other emotional inhibiters are holding him back."

"Emotional inhibiters," Eric replied. "That's a good way of putting it. I really hope he finds his way through all of this. It must be difficult on you and Greg."

"Oh, it is. Greg does his best to be patient and supportive, but it can take its toll."

They chatted for a while longer until the check came. As Eric was preparing to pay for it, Julie's cell phone rang. Eric glanced up at Julie and watched her expression change from curious to surprise to shock.

"Yes, this is Julie MacDonald." After a short pause Julie asked, "Are you sure? He left this morning at the usual time." Julie's expression changed a few times before she finally ended the call. "Yes. I understand. We will certainly look into this. Thank you for contacting me about this. Please call me any time if something like this happens again."

Julie sighed as she put away her cell phone. She looked up at Eric. "That was the assistant principal at Doug's high school. He never showed up for any of his afternoon classes today. So he has been marked truant. This is the third time this month."

"I'm sorry to hear that. Do you have any idea where he

may have gone?"

"No. Two weeks ago he said he wasn't feeling well and headed off for the park. Greg and I told him he should have told his teachers and us about his illness, and then should have come straight home. He became very upset and his short-tempered anger got the better of him. I'm concerned this may be turning into a more serious pattern."

Eric gazed at his friend and gently placed his hand on hers. Then he asked Julie, "Do his teachers have any suggestions about how to handle this? They often are closest to the situation and may be able to spot some aspects of it that he keeps from you and Greg."

"Well, the assistant principle said that Doug's counselor at his school recommended we consider the Tough Love program. But I'm not sure I want to subject Doug to that."

"What is the Tough Love program?"

"It's a program for troubled youths and juvenile delinquents jointly sponsored by the school district and the Atlanta Police Department. It's intended to get them back on the straight and narrow."

"Why don't you want to have Doug be a part of that?"

"Oh, it's not that I don't see the benefit of such a program," Julie said. "I'm sure it serves the community well, but I have heard it's pretty much populated with gangbangers or gangbanger wannabes. I just don't think Doug would get much out of that."

Eric nodded. "I understand." He felt Doug might benefit from such a program, but decided to keep his thoughts to himself. Julie needed collaboration at this point, not confrontation.

They talked for a short while longer before leaving the restaurant. Both agreed it was best for Julie to call the parents of some of Doug's friends. Eric could plainly see how distressed Julie was about the call she had just received.

Eric walked Julie to her car. "If there is anything I can do to help, please let me know. I can see how difficult this is on you."

"Thanks, Eric. You have always been so supportive of me and my family. I really appreciate that. But this is something I think Greg and I will need to work out with Doug and his counselors."

Eric gave Julie a warm, long embrace. Julie briefly wondered what it would be like to be with him. They smiled at each other and then turned away to walk toward their cars. Eric watched as Julie drove away.

///

Once home Julie tried calling Greg but it went straight to voicemail. Then she remembered Greg telling her he would be at an offsite meeting with a key vendor for the rest of the afternoon. He would likely have his cell phone off for several hours.

Julie had other friends she could have called at a time like this, but there was really only one person that she felt could offer her the advice and comfort she sought. That person was Greg's mother, Francine. Prior to getting married Julie had heard the usual nightmare stories from her married girlfriends about how demanding and unreasonable a typical mother-in-law could be. It was no wonder that Julie was pleasantly surprised that Francine had none of the stereotypical traits Julie had feared. Right from their first meeting they forged a very close and trusting relationship.

Julie had no sisters and her own mother had succumbed to cancer just a year after Julie's wedding. Francine was the perfect substitute for Julie in two separate roles. One was as the older, wiser sister who could offer support and advice as if to a younger sibling. The other was as the warm, loving mother who could dispense the wisdom that could only come from having lived such a full, enriching life.

For Julie's part, she also served in an important role for Francine whose only daughter lived nearly a thousand miles away in Albuquerque, New Mexico. Julie was more than just a daughter-in-law to Francine. At times like these Julie would often turn to Francine for her perspective on matters of child rearing, adolescent conflicts and the stresses of raising teenagers. Julie called her and she answered immediately in her always-comforting voice.

Julie tried not to sound alarmed. "Hi, Mom, it's me." Julie had long ago felt more like a daughter than a daughter-in-law to Francine. It just seemed normal to Julie to refer to Francine as her mom, and Francine certainly did not mind. She much preferred it that way. But Francine could also decipher voices and inflections better than most. She immediately knew Julie was concerned about something.

"Honey, what's wrong? I can tell something is bothering you."

"Doug's school called. He's been truant again."

"Oh dear. Sweetie, I am so sorry to hear that. What do his counselors say?"

"They suggest we put him in a Tough Love program."

"What is that?"

"It's a closely monitored program for at-risk youths. Very structured, and very disciplined."

"Is that something you're considering?"

Julie sighed, "I don't know. I'm not sure I want Doug thrown in with criminal elements like that."

"What does Greg think?"

"Well, it's run by the Atlanta Police Department where his best friend works. So he would probably be in favor of it."

"Probably? You mean you haven't talked to your husband about this?"

"Well, his best friend, Jim Barnett, is a police detective, so I suspect Greg would likely go for it."

"Julie, you have to talk to Greg about this, and soon. Whatever actions you take concerning Doug's behaviors, they have to be mutually agreed to by you and Greg. Any disagreements between you two would spell disaster."

"I know. You're right."

Even though Greg and she agreed on most decisions of child rearing, they sometimes had their differences. In this case it was imperative that they both be on the same page. Julie assured Francine that she would do just that and thanked her for the talk. Before signing off she promised to keep Francine apprised of future developments. Then she headed home with much on her mind, and much to discuss with her husband and older son.

By the time Julie pulled into her driveway it was mid-afternoon. She went inside and called out for Michael. Hearing no response, she prepared herself a cup of almond vanilla tea. She tried to enjoy its pleasing aroma. As she began sipping the hot liquid, Michael burst through the front door.

"Hi, Mom," he said as he slung his backpack down on one

of the kitchen chairs. "Are there any marshmallow crispy treats left?"

"Well, hello to you too. Yes, there are some treats on a plate under the cake saver. Grab a few and then come over here and sit. We need to talk."

Michael recognized the tone in his mother's voice. He did not hear it often but when he did it usually meant trouble. He picked up a few of the crispy treats, pulled out a chair and sat down. "Am I in trouble, Mom?"

Julie's expression softened. "No, Michael, you are not in trouble. How was your day today?"

Michael breathed a little easier. "Pretty good. Nothing out of the ordinary. My history test got pushed back a day. And the beans and franks were pretty good for lunch. Is that what you wanted to talk to me about?"

"No. It's about Doug. Did he get you to school okay this morning?"

"Ah, yeah, sure. With fifteen minutes to spare? Why?"

"Because he cut all of his afternoon classes. The school called me right after lunch." Julie paused for a second and then looked directly into Michael's eyes. "Michael, I need to know if Doug said or did anything out of the ordinary the last few days. Think carefully."

Michael started replaying in his mind the various encounters he had recently had with his older brother. He remembered the incident he had experienced several days earlier when he spotted Doug practicing with a new knife.

"Did you think of something?" Julie asked as she studied Michael's expression.

Michael recalled vividly Doug instructing him not to dare tell their parents about the knife. Michael felt conflicted. Should he come clean and reveal to his mom what he had seen? What if something bad or even tragic had happened to his brother?

Still, he had given Doug his word that he would not tell anyone. In the end his yearning to build a bond with his brother won out. He would not disclose to either parent what he knew about Doug's knife. At least for now. Michael believed Doug would eventually show up.

"Not really, mom. Just that Doug was showing off his new

stereo to me this morning. Can I go now? I have some homework to do."

Julie shrugged. "Okay. Just let me know if you think of anything."

"Okay." Michael was not sure where Doug was, or when he would return, but he was certain of one thing. Whenever Doug returned, it would not be pleasant.

CHAPTER 8

DOUG'S PHONE SOUNDED its distinctive tone. It was Lisa.

"Hi, sweetie. Are you at work?"

"Uh, no. I needed to take the afternoon off and met up with Tommy."

"Who is that?"

"You know. He was the guy who sold me my knife. I needed to talk with him about it. Then we decided to shoot some pool."

Lisa sounded mildly annoyed. "Pool? So you cut classes? Again? Aren't you supposed to be at work?"

"Well, yeah, but I wasn't feeling too well. So I called in sick."

"Too sick to work, but not too sick to play pool? I see."

"I know. I just didn't feel like putting up with all of the crap today. I just needed some time off."

"Doug, you were let go of two other jobs due to absences. Doesn't that tell you something?"

He was totally serious. "Yes, it tells me that I haven't found my ideal job yet."

"Well good luck with that search. Listen, I was calling to make sure we were on for tomorrow night. But as long as you're not at work can we meet tonight?"

"Sure. Like when?"

"How about right now?"

He agreed to pick her up as soon as he could drive over to where she was on the other side of town at a girlfriend's house. It took him nearly an hour to arrive. By the time they climbed back into his truck they were both hungry and decided to grab a bite to eat. They stopped by one of their favorite burger joints for a quick order of food and then headed over to Stephenson Park. That was their favorite place to go to talk, walk or just enjoy being together.

Doug drove to their favorite part of the park and pulled the truck into an isolated area. He pulled out a bag of high-quality weed and offered some to Lisa.

"No thanks."

"Are you sure?"

He was surprised at her answer because Lisa was not one to turn down good grass, especially when she wanted to talk something over. In the past they had covered a myriad of subjects while high on weed.

"I'm sure. Just not in the mood at the moment."

Doug decided to just let it go. Even though he was only seventeen, he well understood a woman's inclination to change her mind, and her moods, on what may have seemed a whim. Doug could not know Lisa had good reason to pass on his offer.

"Well, do you mind if I light up?"

"No. Make yourself mellow."

Just as Doug was about to roll his joint, he noticed a young lady by herself being hassled by a street thug who appeared intoxicated. Lisa saw the same woman at about the same time.

Doug unfastened his seat belt. "That chick needs help."

"All right, but be careful."

"I will."

Doug walked up to the man. "Hey, you. Leave her alone."

The man was barely coherent. "Beat it, dickhead. This don't concern you."

Doug reached into his jeans pocket and pulled out his butterfly knife. The man's eyes widened as he watched Doug perform his orchestrated maneuvers to quickly open, unlatch and then lock into place the blade of his deadly weapon. The thug immediately backed down.

"Get that thing away from me, man. Are you crazy?" The intoxicated man let go of the woman and ran off.

Doug instantly understood and appreciated the power of his recently purchased weapon. Not only would the knife complete his rebel outfit appearance, it would influence the outcome of potentially dangerous street behaviors. It turned out the woman was Tanya Peterson, the girlfriend of Dominic Williams who headed up the notorious motorcycle gang known as the Raptors. She was supposed to meet Dominic at the park but she had arrived sooner than expected. Dominic and Raven approached just as Doug was freeing her from the hoodlum.

As the man started running away, Raven rushed toward him and yelled. "Hey, punk, stop. Right now."

The man turned and hesitated. It was long enough for Raven to walk up to him, wind up his clenched right-handed fist and land a wholesale roundhouse punch into the man's jaw. He backed up and stumbled to the ground.

Raven stood over him and just glared at him. "You picked the wrong chick to mess with."

Dominic asked Tanya if she was okay and then briefly admonished her for walking in the park alone after dark instead of waiting for him in her car as they had agreed. Then he walked over to the man who had accosted his girlfriend.

Dominic raised both of his fists and said to the trembling drunk who was kneeling on the ground, "If you ever lay a finger on that woman again you'll be a dead man."

Raven glanced over at Dominic and spoke in a menacing tone. "I think we should kill him right now."

The man started pleading for his life, saying he was sorry and that the whiskey had made him do it.

Doug was standing nearby and could not believe what he was hearing.

Dominic turned to Raven. "Teach him a lesson. But don't kill him. The booze may have had something to do with it. But whatever you do, make sure he remembers it."

Raven nodded and then sneered at the man. "You lucky bastard. Don't move."

The man just cowered and kept trembling. Raven looked over the parking lot and the adjoining grassy area. He noticed that two of the low concrete barriers at the front of adjacent parking spots had rusted bent rebar jutting from their tops. About five feet past the parking stops in the grass was a steel sprinkler head.

Raven walked over to the other side of the parking lot where his motorcycle was parked. As he started pulling some chains out his right-side saddlebag Dominic approached Doug to thank him for intervening.

"Appreciate you stepping in like that. You're pretty handy with that knife."

"Thanks."

Dominic extended his hand and shook Doug's hand in appreciation.

"I'm Dominic. The other guy is Raven. I head up the Raptors."

"Good to meet you," Doug replied. "I'm Doug MacDonald and this is Lisa."

Lisa felt uncomfortable as the gang leader nodded to them. They chatted idly for a few moments about what each of them was doing in the park. Then Dominic startled Doug with a surprising offer.

"I have been looking for someone about your age who is handy with a weapon. How would you like to hang with my outfit for a while, and earn some extra money on the side?"

"Ah, what? Ah, no. I don't think so," said Doug, trying not to appear nervous.

Dominic remained persistent and started listing the various benefits of joining the gang. These included protections, camaraderie, street credibility, assuming the appearance of a true rebel, free access to booze and drugs. Dominic pulled Doug aside outside the earshot of Lisa and told Doug of another benefit of easy access to fast and loose women. Doug was intrigued by the offer. Joining the gang would be a complete repudiation of his father's conservative, establishment-oriented lifestyle. Doug thought about it for a few minutes but eventually declined the offer.

"No thanks, man. I appreciate the offer, but I'm good flying solo."

"Are you sure? What about earning some extra money with drugs? I could use someone your age."

"Naw, don't think so. But thanks anyway."

Raven returned with two chains each about three feet long. He dropped them next to each of the two rusted rebar and then dragged the legs of drunkard over to the chains.

"Hey, whadja doing man?" he asked in a shaky voice.

"It's time to teach you a lesson, scumbag." Raven wrapped one of the chains around the left ankle of the man and then fastened it tightly to one of the bent rebar. He quickly did the same with the other chain so that both ankles were fastened in a spread-eagle position to the concrete barriers.

The man struggled but he was no match for the muscular Raven.

"Hey, whadda ya going to do, man?"

Raven had noticed the man's loose fitting belt had come undone so he roughly pulled it off the leg-bound man. Pulling the man's arms over his head, Raven used the belt to tie the man's hands to the sprinkler pipe. Satisfied that his victim was securely immobile, Raven started walking toward his motorcycle.

The man started yelling after him, "Hey man, where're you going? Are you just gonna leave me here? You can't do that."

Raven ignored him. Dominic seemed mildly amused. He was not sure what Raven was up to, but whatever it was Dominic was sure it would be effective and entertaining, in a gangland sort of way. Doug and Lisa stood off to the side and watched with morbid curiosity.

///

Raven mounted the large Harley and started it. He revved the engine a few times filling the air with the distinctive low-sounding growl that only a Harley could produce. His customized exhaust pipes heighten the distinctive throaty roar of a Harley.

After he backed it up and turned it in the direction of the spread-eagled man, Raven gently engaged the clutch and started driving the heavy motorcycle toward the man.

He started screaming out, "Hey, man, what are you doing? Stop. You're crazy, dude. What are you planning to do?"

Raven gunned the bike and it took off in the direction between the man's two legs. As he approached the panicked target, the man started screaming again. As the bike neared the man, Raven let off of the accelerator and quickly applied the brakes.

The man was nearly hysterical. "Are you out of your mind? What are you trying to do?"

"Teach you a lesson. I'm gonna run over you."

The man's eyes nearly popped out of his head. He screamed back. "You can't do that. I'll be crushed. That bike must weigh over five hundred pounds."

Raven smiled. "More like double that. You should get the feel of it all right."

"Wait. Stop. You can't do this. Please! Just let me go. I promise I'll never touch her again. I'll never touch any woman like that again."

"You've got that right."

Raven backed his bike up and rode it to other side of the parking lot. This time he revved the engine to full throttle, then backed it off and popped the clutch. The bike raced toward the now-terrified man. As the loud machine approached, the man yelled out an ear-piercing scream.

Dominic watched with keen interest. Doug stared as he followed the bike on its path. Lisa was frozen, not wanting to watch but unable to turn away.

Just as the bike was about to make contact with the man's body, Raven turned the handle bar ever so slightly to the right and popped a wheelie while applying the back brake. The front of the bike lifted up about a foot off of the ground and came to rest just past the man's right thigh while the back tire slammed into the man's knee, just barley grazing it.

The man opened his eyes back up and started hyperventilating. Raven looked down at him and simply said, "Never again, understand?" The man just shook his head violently from one side to the other. Raven lowered his kickstand and dismounted the bike. In an instant he undid the three restraints that had bound his victim who quickly scampered out from under the bike. He backed away slowly and then started running. Raven yelled after him, "Never again." The man just waved his hands and kept running.

Dominic walked over to Raven and patted his back. Then they turned to leave. As they turned to leave, Dominic turned back to Doug. "Well, if you ever change your mind, you can usually find me here."

///

Doug grabbed Lisa's hand and the two of them headed back to his truck. They cracked their windows slightly and Doug put on some music. Doug again pulled out his bag of weed and offered it once more to Lisa. She immediately declined it with a shake of her head. Doug resumed his task of rolling his joint, a task he had begun some twenty minutes earlier.

He took his first hit on the joint and then slowly exhaled. He took in the full essence of its herbal aroma and then said to Lisa, "So you said you wanted to talk about something?"

Lisa took a deep breath. "Doug, I was late."

Doug looked puzzled and paused for a second. He felt the need to comfort her and tried to do so. "Babe, you weren't that late. You were ready to go almost as soon as I showed up."

Lisa shook her head and half smiled. But just as quickly her expression turned serious.

"Doug, I'm pregnant."

"What? Are you sure?"

"I'm sure. I did the test twice last week and both times it came back positive. I had an appointment with the doctor this morning and he confirmed it."

"You told me you were on the pill. Did you forget or something?"

"I am on the pill. And no, I did not forget."

Doug was becoming noticeably agitated. "Then how did this happen?"

Lisa was close to sobbing as she said, "I don't know. I'm sorry. But I don't know."

Doug's fragile personality caused him to start racing through a combination of conflicting emotions. He first felt shock, then confusion and finally disbelief. His mind started acting like it was scattering in a dozen different directions. Try as he may he could not seem to gather his thoughts coherently. Without thinking clearly, he blurted out what many men might ask in similar circumstances.

"Are you sure I'm the father?"

Lisa almost screamed at him. "What? Seriously? Yes, you're the father."

Lisa's loud voice and temperament momentarily snapped Doug back to his senses. In a soft voice he apologized.

"I'm sorry. I didn't mean that. My mind's reeling." He reached over and gave Lisa a warm, tender hug.

"I know, babe. I know." She slowly started stroking his arm. "I have to figure out what I'm going to do now."

Doug turned to her firmly. "Correction, babe. We have to figure this out. Not just you. It's we. It's both of us together. I'm just as much a party to this as you are."

"It was sort of our partying that led to this."

"I know. Does your mom know?"

"Not yet. Not until I decide on an option. One is that I could give birth and raise the child myself."

"You mean we could raise it ourselves."

"Another is that I give the baby up for adoption."

"Would you really do that?"

"Or maybe I just have an abortion."

"An abortion? Really? You'd seriously consider that?"

"I don't know."

"What about us raising the child together?"

Lisa looked at him with tender eyes and replied softly, "Sweetheart, you know I love you, but you know you're not the most stable person all the time. You struggle at school, and you struggle to get work."

"But we could make *this* work."

"I don't know that we could."

Doug raised his voice, "Well I know. I know that we could make this work."

"Stop shouting at me."

"I'm not shouting."

"Yes you are. And it's upsetting me. And it's upsetting *my* baby."

Eventually they both calmed down and agreed that the best thing to do would be to call it a night and to go home and process all that had transpired. Doug took the last drag off of his joint and held it longer than normal. He had much to think about and wanted to dwell on as many creative solutions to their complicated dilemma as he could.

He crushed out the joint and looked over at Lisa. They said nothing but just stared into each other's eyes for a few minutes. Doug reached out and held her again, but this time it was longer and tighter than before. Lisa started sobbing lightly and Doug stroked her hair to comfort her. Eventually they sat back into their seats and Doug started the truck. He drove back to her house and gave her a long, lingering kiss.

As Doug headed his truck back to his home he was left to ponder some very heavy thoughts. He was upset, confused and unsure of what to do next. In the midst of all of the unexpected events he had practically forgotten what he had done earlier that day. He had committed truancy, and he knew that this was the third time it had happened within a month. What he did not know was that he had a pair of very angry parents awaiting his return.

CHAPTER 9

DOUG THOUGHT ABOUT the responsibility of raising a child and some of the things he could teach him, such as sports, computers, video games and other activities Doug believed would hold a young boy's interest. Then it dawned on him. *What if the baby was a girl? What did he know about bringing up a girl?*

He exhaled in relief when he realized Lisa would be shouldering the majority of those tasks. The relief was short-lived. The more he thought about the situation, the more depressed he became. How could he even think about becoming a father? He was a struggling high school student with a low-paying part-time job and enough emotional problems to fill a shrink's notebook.

The reality suddenly hit him about how his parents would react to the news. They would not be pleased. So Doug decided he would say nothing about Lisa's condition that night. By the time Doug pulled his Silverado into the driveway it was well past ten.

Greg and Julie had been waiting up for him in the family room and heard him arrive. They wasted no time questioning him as soon as he stepped inside the front door. They both stood up and approached him as he entered the family room.

"Where have you been?" Greg asked in a very stern voice.

Doug tried to remain calm. With all of the things on his mind he did not want a confrontation. "I've been out."

Now it was Julie's turn. "What do you mean you've been out? Out where?"

"Just out. You know. Out and about."

"No, I *don't* know," Julie fired back. "What I do know is that your principal called to say you never returned for any of your afternoon classes. Now I want to know where you've been."

"I went to the park."

Greg angrily asked "Why? What possible reason would you have for going there?"

"I needed time to think."

"You needed time to think? Think about what?" Julie huffed. "We've spent most of the afternoon and evening trying to find out where you were."

Doug shuffled his feet and mumbled. "I just needed some time to think."

Greg was not buying his son's explanation and lashed out. "You needed some time to think? Really? It's more likely you needed time to do drugs."

Greg walked right up next to Doug so that he could detect any odor. The smell that Greg sensed made him furious.

"You've been doing drugs, haven't you?"

Doug tried to dismiss it as being a small matter, but started to sound defensive. "So I smoked some weed. What's the big deal?"

"What's the big deal? I'll tell you what's the big deal," Greg said. "Marijuana is illegal. It's a hallucinogenic. It warps your mind. It distorts your thinking. It impairs your judgment. It destroys your brain cells. It can cause cancer in your mouth. And it leads to harder drugs."

Doug was becoming increasingly more agitated. He shifted his weight from one foot to the other. Finally he responded in a low but terse tone. "It is not all of those things you say."

This only served to infuriate Greg all the more. Raising his voice again Greg shot back, "It's everything I said, and more? What do you think? That it's legal to smoke that crap?"

Doug looked right at his father and replied through gritted teeth, "No, I'm not saying it's legal, but it should be."

Greg could not believe his ears. "You think it should be *legal*?"

"Yes. Yes I do. Why not? It's not as dangerous or as additive as alcohol."

Greg sounded incredulous. "Are you crazy? Do you really think a person high on marijuana should be driving a vehicle?"

Not giving his son a chance to respond, Greg continued. "Of course they shouldn't be driving. I wouldn't want to be anywhere close to a driver who was high on that garbage. As to alcohol, it's not illegal to consume it if you're old enough. It does not lead to harder drinking. And it's possible to drink responsibly and still drive a car."

Doug was becoming more upset with his father's lecture and was desperate to win his argument. He raised his voice and shouted back, "You're just defending alcohol because you use it yourself. You'll never admit something is bad if you're doing it yourself."

Greg lowered his voice and squinted directly into Doug's eyes. "Don't you ever raise your voice to me like that again! Do you understand?"

Doug was starting to seethe but remained silent. Greg said in a firmer voice, "Did you hear me, boy?" Greg approached Doug and stood just inches from him.

"I heard you," Doug answered.

It was at that moment that Greg smelled the remnants of alcohol on Doug's breath. "Is that beer I smell on you?"

Doug seemed stunned by the question and mumbled a barely audible response. "What? Ah, no. Why?"

"Don't lie to me," Greg shouted. "You're nothing but a doped-up loser and a high school drop-out with no common sense, and no sense of responsibility. You are too stoned to even see what you're throwing away."

Julie had been observing the confrontation from off to the side and feared that it may start escalating out of control. She tried to calm things down by saying in a gentle voice, "Doug, you have a talented mind and you need school to develop it. We just don't want you to throw all of that away."

Doug took a breath to calm himself. "Mom, I just feel bored and out-of-place at school." His remark did nothing to calm Greg, who started shouting again.

"You need to start behaving like a responsible adult."

Doug shouted back, "I am acting like a responsible adult. I'm going to school, trying to graduate."

"You didn't go this afternoon, did you? You only go when you want and don't go when you don't. That's not acting responsible. You are almost eighteen. It's time you start acting your age or suffer the consequences. Based on your actions today there will be consequences starting now."

"What do you mean?"

"I mean that you're grounded for two weeks."

Doug was aghast and shouted back, "What? You can't do that."

But Greg stood his ground. "I most certainly can, and I will. The insurance on that vehicle is in my name and I control when and by whom that truck's going to be driven."

Doug was practically spitting nails as he shot back. "That's what it's all about for you, isn't it. You always have to be in total control. You're just not satisfied until you are controlling everyone's lives."

Julie was not about to let that comment go unchallenged. "Douglas, that is no way to speak to your father. He works hard for all of us."

Greg looked over at Julie as if to urge her to back off. "It's all right, sweetheart. I can defend myself against my own son."

Doug looked desperate and almost pleaded with his mother. "Mom, this just isn't right."

"What isn't right is the way you acted today," she said to Doug. "And it wasn't the first time this has happened. I think your father is correct."

"This is bullshit," Doug barked.

Julie was shocked by his response. "I've warned you about swearing around me. Never again. Do you understand?"

Doug took another deep breath and finally uttered, "Yeah, okay."

Greg held out his hand in a demanding gesture. "Give me the keys to your truck, right now."

Doug reluctantly reached into his jeans pocket and pulled out his key chain. It had several keys on it including his house key and two keys for his warehouse job. He stared at them for a moment before removing his truck key and handing it over to his father.

Greg turned the key over in his hand, put the key in his trousers pocket and then asked, "Where is the other copy?"

"What?"

"I know you have two keys to your truck. I was with you when we purchased it. It came with two keys. Now give me the other one."

"I don't have it on me."

Greg was losing his patience and questioned his son. "Stop playing games. Where is it?"

"It's hidden on the truck in case I ever lose the original."

"Well go get it, right now."

Doug walked out of the family room and headed outside to his truck. He passed by the kitchen where Michael was finishing up his homework. Michael looked up and called out to him, "Hey, Doug, can I talk to you for a minute?"

"Not now. I'm in a hurry."

Michael followed him out the door and down the steps. "It won't take long and it's important."

"All right, but wait here."

Michael didn't understand. "Why do I have to wait here? Why can't I just follow you?"

"Because I have to get the spare key that's hidden and I don't want you to see where it's located."

"Too late. I already know."

Doug wasn't sure whether or not to believe his brother and so called him out. "Where do you think it is?"

"It's taped to the inside of your fuel door."

Doug was surprised. "How did you find out? Oh, never mind. Anyway I have to get back inside right away. Dad's grounded me." The mere thought of that caused Doug to start feeling upset and angry again.

"Listen, I know you're in trouble right now. But I wanted you to know that Mom asked me if I noticed anything out of the ordinary with you lately."

Doug stared at his brother very suspiciously. "So what did you say?"

"Nothing. At least nothing serious. I told her you were showing off your new truck stereo to me. But I wanted you to know I didn't say anything about your knife. You're in enough trouble right now without having to worry about that. So I figured I'd tell you."

Doug stopped momentarily and just looked at Michael intently. Here was his little brother who normally was a nuisance now acting more like an ally and a confidant. With so much on his mind, especially the news Lisa had just laid on him, he was grateful.

"Thanks, bro."

"No problem. Good luck with Mom and Dad in there."

Doug just shrugged. "Yeah."

When Doug retuned to the family room, Greg and Julie were standing in the same place. He handed the spare truck key to his father. Then he made one more plea for some leniency. "How am I supposed to get to school?"

"Figure it out," Greg said firmly.

Doug sounded more and more frustrated. "But this makes no sense. I'm being punished for missing school, so you take away the only means I have of getting there?"

His father walked a purposeful step closer to Doug. Greg raised his voice as he instructed his son very sternly, "First of all, your punishment isn't just for missing school. It's also for all of the other crap you've been pulling here lately."

Doug interrupted. "Like what?"

"Like the drugs, like the lying about them, like the losers you hang out with."

"This is total bullshit."

That last remark caused Greg to almost lose it. "You've been warned about using that language." Turning to Julie he added, "Especially around your mother."

Julie tried to diffuse matters. "Doug, I can drive you and Michael to school for the next two weeks, and will try to arrange your rides home. You'll have to ask one of your co-workers for rides to the warehouse."

"Mom, even if I can get to school and work, how will I be able to see Lisa?"

Before Julie could utter any response Greg proclaimed, "The answer is you won't be able to, and that's probably a good thing. The less you see of her the better."

"What's that supposed to mean?" Doug's fists started to open and close.

"It means exactly what it sounds like. You need to spend more time with your books and less time with your drug buddy."

"She's my girlfriend, not my drug buddy. Do you get it? She's my girlfriend."

Greg was not about to back down. "Are you trying to say that you and she have never done drugs? I find that hard to believe. What else would the two of you have in common?"

"We have a lot in common."

Greg continued with the criticism. "Oh yeah. Drugs and being dropouts. That's all you two have in common."

Both men now were shouting at each other, prompting Julie to say, "Greg, maybe you should ease up a bit."

Greg barely lowered his voice as he glared back at Julie. "No I won't. And don't take his side on this."

"I am not taking anyone's side in this. But this shouting is getting us nowhere."

"Listen to you two. You say me and Lisa have nothing in common. We probably have more in common than you two."

The remarks incensed both parents. Julie spoke first. "You have no idea what you are talking about. And where do get off saying anything about your parents?"

Greg was even more forceful. "You sound just like a typical, foolish, know-it-all teenager. The drugs you're taking are making you talk nonsense. But beyond that it's disrespectful. I will not stand for this from any of my children, at any time."

Julie continued. "You have no business commenting on your parent's relationship. You are too young and immature to know anything about what real love is all about, or what it entails."

"My relationship with Lisa is deeper and far more mature than either of you realize. If you took the time to get to know her you would see that."

Doug looked away and tried to tune his father out. He cringed every time he heard his father refer to him, and especially Lisa. He kept thinking about Lisa not wanting to even smoke a single joint that night due to her pregnancy. He believed Lisa would not be doing anything dangerous or unhealthy for her baby, and that especially included any marijuana.

Greg continued with his loud lecturing. "You want to know what's likely going to happen to you? I'll tell you. You'll keep smoking dope, you'll eventually drop out of school, you'll keep making excuses for your fiascos, blaming everyone else for your failures, hanging around with loser dopers, including that Lisa girl. You will end up being a nobody, going nowhere, with no one except drug-using losers."

Finally, Doug could not take it anymore. His anger and short temper washed over him like a tsunami. Suddenly something in him just snapped. He lifted up the crystal Eiffel Tower off its wood table. To him, the wedding anniversary gift simply represented the artificial phoniness of his parents' marriage. He shifted the crystal to his right hand and drew his arm back.

Julie gasped. Greg yelled at him and ordered him to put it down. Doug hurled the crystal as hard as he could against the fireplace. It shattered with the ear-piercing sound of breaking glass.

Julie momentarily froze and then she started crying uncontrollably. Greg lunged toward Doug and shoved him to the floor. Greg then unleashed a nonstop tirade into his son's face.

"What have you done! You spoiled ingrate! I ought to rip your arms off, you drug-crazed moron!"

Michael heard all of the commotion and walked in. "Mom, what's wrong? What's going on?"

Julie took a minute to catch her breath and compose herself. "Your brother and your father had an argument about school and other things, and the argument got out of hand." Then she started sobbing again.

Michael went over to his mother and gave her a small hug. By now Greg had calmed down a bit and turned to Michael and said, "Why don't you help your brother clean this up? You can put it in the packing box that it was shipped in. The box is on the rafter shelf in the garage."

Michael glanced over at his brother who was slowly standing up. Michael was trying to get Doug's attention to show his brother he was trying to offer some moral support, or at least some eye contact. But Doug was looking away. So Michael walked out of the room, past his homework on the kitchen table and out to the garage.

Doug finally stood up and reluctantly retrieved a broom and dustpan from the closet just off the kitchen. He began cleaning up the shattered glass.

Greg turned toward Doug and watched him closely for a moment. "This isn't over yet. You will be in school tomorrow, on time and for the entire day, do you understand?" Doug hesitated for a moment and Greg raised his voice and asked once more, "Do you understand?"

Doug quietly answered, "Yes."

Greg then said, "Then finish cleaning this up and get to bed. I'll finish dealing with you in the morning."

Doug continued sweeping up the pieces of crystal. A few minutes later Michael returned with the large shipping box. He tried helping his brother gather up the larger pieces but Doug, in his troubled state of mind, was in no mood to be interacting with anyone. So when Michael offered him the box in which to put the broken pieces, Doug practically ignored him.

"I'm just trying to help," Michael informed his brother in a very gentle voice.

"I don't need your help. Why don't you just leave?"

"Well, Dad said I was supposed to help you. But if you don't want any help, then maybe I will just leave."

"Yeah, why don't you. I really wish you would."

Michael shrugged and turned to go. But as he took his next step he did not notice the one corner of the Eiffel Tower in his path. He stepped right on it and squished the part of the corner that had one of the four engravings of each member of the MacDonald family.

Doug heard the distinctive crushing sound of the glass. "What did you do?"

Michael looked sheepish. "Sorry. I didn't see it."

Doug was incensed. "How could you not see it? It was right in front of you. Are you half blind?"

Michael was puzzled by his brother's reaction. "What's the big deal? It was already broken."

"Why don't you just leave, like you said you were going to

a minute ago?"

Michael left the room and then gathered up his books from the kitchen table. Doug continued cleaning up the broken crystal. When he got to the shattered corner that Michael had stepped on, Doug noticed that parts of it had been practically ground into powder. He was able to decipher the name that had been engraved into the corner of the sculpture. He caught his breath when he realized the name was his own.

It figures, he thought.

CHAPTER 10

GREG AND JULIE had risen early in anticipation of the talk they would have with Doug. They enjoyed for the moment the pleasing aromas only a home-cooked breakfast could provide.

Julie had a cup of freshly brewed green tea that was giving off puffs of hot vapors. Her tea complimented a small pot of hot steaming coffee that had been automatically prepared for Greg with help from a pre-set timer. Julie had cooked bacon with scrambled eggs and the appealing scents drifted from the stove to the small wood breakfast table.

Doug and Michael entered the kitchen together. Michael looked very curious and Doug somber. Greg waited until all of them were seated at the breakfast table. He wanted to make sure everyone all heard the same message. He had already discussed with Julie what he intended to say.

"Douglas is grounded indefinitely."

Michael watched his brother slump in his chair.

"Your mother will arrange for your travel to and from school but you'll have to figure out getting to and from work. You can go nowhere other than school and work. Mom will confirm your weekly work schedule with your boss."

The rest of the breakfast was finished in relative silence.

///

Greg arrived at work shortly before eight. He checked his daily calendar on his iPhone. Greg sat for a minute feeling the smooth texture of polished glass under his fingers. Then he thought about all of the events of the past twenty-four hours involving his older son, and their impacts on the other members of his family. He looked back at the high-resolution display in his hand and the perfectly organized listing of meetings. If only parenting and child rearing could be as orderly and as predictable as the digital device he cradled in his palm.

Greg had four back-to-back meetings that would take him to lunchtime. He was glad his morning was filled up with intense work-related activities. Two of the four meetings he would be leading and the others would require significant participation on his part. This would take his mind off of the emotionally draining ordeal of the previous evening.

It was difficult for Greg not to dwell on it. Every time Greg thought about Doug smashing the Eiffel Tower sculpture he was consumed with conflicting feelings. He was naturally angry with his son for destroying such a special memento of his marriage and wedding anniversary. He also felt bad for Julie and how hard she cried at seeing her magical treasure end up shattered into so many pieces. He wondered what effect all of this would have on Michael. Greg was also angry with himself for letting things get so out of hand. He started berating himself for not having done more to defuse the situation. He felt strongly that his management training should have enabled him to handle the confrontation more effectively, and with less damage physically and emotionally.

Greg felt the need to discuss his various feelings of conflict with someone who could understand the situation, sympathize with his dilemma and yet demonstrate total discretion and confidentiality. There was only one person fitting that bill. That was Greg's good friend and police detective, Jim Barnett. As he punched Jim's number he took another sip of coffee. Then he set the cup down as Jim's line started ringing.

"Good morning. Atlanta Police Department, Detective Barnett speaking," Jim said in his familiar deep professional voice.

"Jim. This is Greg. I was wondering if you might be available for lunch today."

Jim noticed the tension in Greg's voice and replied, "Greg, is everything okay? You sound a bit stressed."

Greg decided to downplay the events of the past evening until he met with Jim in person. "Yes, I'm okay more or less. We had a bit of a confrontation with Doug last night. I'd prefer to discuss it with you over lunch if you're available today."

"Okay. Let me see where I'm at today." Jim swiped a few screens on his Galaxy phone that was standard issue for all Atlanta Police detectives. "It looks good for me today. I will be at an offsite for part of the morning. So it might be best if we meet somewhere."

"Sounds good to me," Greg responded. "Where will you be around lunchtime?"

"Well, just east of downtown. I'll be at Georgia Tech presenting my team's recommendations on campus security. The meeting will go to noon."

Greg thought and then suggested, "Let's meet at the Varsity around 12:15?"

The Varsity was renowned as one of the largest drive-in restaurants in the world. It was located close to Georgia Tech and had started some eighty years ago as a favorite spot for college students to chow down on a quick and inexpensive lunch. The restaurant offered a full lunch menu but specialized in hamburgers and hotdogs. Because of its great tasting food, quick service and affordable prices, the restaurant grew substantially over the past few decades.

"That sounds good to me. It's been a while since we've had lunch there. Why don't we say whichever one of us arrives first will get one of the tables in back?"

"Perfect. I'll see you just past noon. Good luck with your advisory report. Is it to the steering committee or to the full board?"

"Just to the steering committee. So hopefully it shouldn't be too bad," Jim responded. "See you this noon."

Greg hung up the phone and took another sip of coffee. He

savored the hazelnut flavor. Within minutes he unplugged his tablet computer from the charging cable and walked out of his office to his first meeting.

Greg's last meeting ended sooner than expected so he had a few extra minutes to spare before heading out to meet Jim. He decided to give Julie a call to see how her morning went with their two sons, and to have the latest updates on the situation to share with his friend.

"Hi honey. How is your morning going?"

"It came and went. Nothing out of the ordinary. I'll be having lunch with Jim Barnett today at the Varsity. How did it go with the boys?"

"It went okay. Pretty uneventful. Doug didn't say much of anything. Michael talked mostly about his English assignment. I'll be able to pick both boys up today and tomorrow. I'll have to come up with some other arrangements for the day after tomorrow. Is there any chance you could help out?"

Greg thought for a second. "The day after tomorrow? Let me see." He quickly scanned his calendar. "Right now it looks like I should be available. I definitely can take them in the morning. I will keep my schedule open for the afternoon, but let me know if you could pick them up."

"Will do."

"What about Doug's job?"

"I'm taking him today and he says his co-worker Elliott will be able to bring him home. I'm going to talk to both Elliott and Doug's boss today to get Doug's schedule for this week."

"Okay. It sounds like you have that part under control. We still need to come up with a better plan about handling Doug's behavior."

"I know. Maybe you and Jim can arrive at some suggestions."

"That's what I am hoping."

"So you guys are going to the Varsity, huh?"

"Yep."

"So what'll ya have? What'll ya have?"

Both of them chuckled at Julie citing the well-known catch phrase of the Varsity. It was so common it was offered on T-shirts and other mementos.

"Well, hon, I better get back. Have a good rest of the day."

"You too, sweetie. Tell Jim I said hello. I'll see you tonight. I love you."

"I love you, too. So long."

Greg ended the call and stood up to stretch. Then he headed out to his car. Ten minutes later he pulled into the crowded Varsity parking lot.

After a few minutes Greg saw Jim enter the restaurant. Jim greeted Greg with a friendly, "Not as crowded as it could be."

"No, not too bad. I got our drinks. They're on a table in back."

Jim grinned. "Good man. Diet Sprite for me?"

"Absolutely."

The two of them chuckled and then discussed some shoptalk while waiting for the patrons in front of them to be served. Soon the clerk behind the counter looked at Greg and growled, "What'll ya have?"

The two men glanced at each other and smiled at hearing the famous question. They knew it was considered poor etiquette to make the clerk ask twice. So each of them gave their orders quickly and clearly.

Within a few minutes of paying their orders they were handed their bags of food and jostled among the patrons to their table.

"So you said you had a bit of a clash with Doug last night?"

Greg sipped of his drink. "Well, it was more than just a clash. More like a major confrontation." Greg paused.

Jim was not sure if Greg simply was looking for the right words to use, or whether he was having second thoughts about discussing the details.

"So what was the major confrontation?"

Greg described the various aspects of the events of the prior evening. He also went into many of the details of Doug's recent behaviors, including the truancy, mood swings, likely use of drugs, general hanging out with undesirables, Doug's talking back to both his parents and showing little interest in school work.

"Has Doug always been this troubled?"

"Ever since he was about eight years old."

He proceeded to describe the numerous specialists who had worked with Doug over the years trying to treat his various ailments, but with little success. These ailments subjected him to panic attacks and feelings of fear, danger and insecurity.

Greg explained that at other times Doug could sound and act like a very intelligent person. During those times he could talk for hours about philosophy, quantum physics, the order of the universe, politics, religion, and world history. He could be especially knowledgeable in the elements of world history that involved warfare. Doug's interest in warfare also revealed a disturbing side of hyper-interest in violence. Variations of this type of violence could involve extreme and cruel human torture. Fortunately, Doug's interest in this was all limited to video games.

Jim had been listening to Greg's account intently. When Greg mentioned Doug's interest in violence, Jim asked, "Has Doug ever participated in any sort of torture or mutilation of animals?"

Greg seemed very surprised by the question. "Why would you ask that?"

Jim explained that one of the telltale signs of someone who may be prone to commit serious violence against another human is that they begin with violent acts against small, defenseless animals. It could start with mice, frogs or squirrels and then escalate to larger animals such as cats or dogs. Eventually it could lead to the ultimate acts of violence against humans.

Jim's explanation appeared to have made sense to Greg, who then said firmly, "No, Doug loves animals. Always has. He has never exhibited any animosity toward animals of any kind. In fact, quite to the contrary, Doug has loved animals of all types, shapes and sizes ever since he was a small boy."

Greg described how Doug had the usual variety of childhood pets including gold fish, hamsters and rabbits. These pets then led him to the more traditional variety of cats and dogs, including a Dalmatian, a collie and two Labrador retrievers, one black and one golden. He also developed quite an affinity for snakes, lizards and all forms of exotic reptiles.

"It almost seems as if Doug was two personalities, a gentle one for animals and a less than gentle one for some humans."

"Yes. He is definitely less than gentle at times. He has a very short-fused temper." Greg paused and then gazed. "Jim, I am really concerned about Doug. During the last several weeks his behavior seems to be escalating out of control. He is starting to have more frequent truancies. He has little interest in school. He shows no respect for either Julie or me. And lately he's been displaying some pretty harsh belligerence toward Michael."

Jim listened carefully as Greg described the troubling behaviors of his son. Jim then picked up his beverage cup and took a long slow drink. As he set his cup down he asked his friend, "Greg, have you ever heard of Tough Love?"

"One of Doug's counselors at school had mentioned it to Julie. I don't know much about it. Julie thought it was intended for gang bangers, and she wasn't sure she wanted Doug mixed in with those criminal types."

Jim raised his eyebrows a little and shook his head slightly as if to say those impressions were far from the truth. "Greg, first of all, Tough Love is not just for gang members. Those thugs are usually too hard-core to be affected by this program. It's really intended to stop otherwise law-abiding kids from becoming lawbreakers. It's meant to show parents how they can better manage out-of-control youths."

"Well, okay, what more can you tell me about it?"

Jim leaned in a bit and lowered his voice, "I can tell you that the Atlanta Police Department is a primary sponsor of the Tough Love program that is being run for the Atlanta area. I know the coordinator for the program. He is someone I think you and Julie should get to know. How about I set up an introduction for the three of you?"

"Can you tell me more about him?"

"Well, I know him fairly well. His name is Sgt. Timothy Mallory. He is a good man and a very good administrator. I know from others and from my own involvement that he is very effective at showing parents how Tough Love can be used to get troubled youths back on the straight and narrow. Sometimes it may be the only option."

"Julie heard that sometimes they encourage you to get physical with your child. Is that true? I do not want to engage in physical confrontations with Doug. A few years ago I wouldn't have hesitated resorting to physical force if needed. I'd like to think I'm more enlightened now."

"You are more enlightened these days. I know that from being around you."

"I'm also more practical. I understand Doug's volatile nature, and I realize Doug's size and strength could easily overpower me today."

"Well said, my friend, well said. I do think you and Julie should at least consider talking to Sgt. Mallory. Why don't you two think about it and let me know?"

"I'll talk it over with Julie and let you know in a few days."

"Sounds good, Greg." Glancing at his watch, Jim said, "Well, I better get back. Let me know what you two decide."

"Will do."

CHAPTER 11

GREG ARRIVED AFTER work to a fairly silent household. The boys had just finished their homework and prepared to sit down for dinner with their parents. Everyone dined quietly. After dinner Greg helped Julie clear the table and suggested she join him later in his office.

"I'll be there in about half an hour," she said. "I have to tie up some loose ends for a new client. It shouldn't take very long."

Twenty minutes later Julie entered Greg's room and sat on the sofa. Greg closed the door and sat beside her.

"I mentioned that Jim and I talked about a program called Tough Love. You said one of Doug's counselors had recommended it, correct?"

"Yes, that's right. His counselor mentioned it yesterday."

"Did she describe what it was about?"

"No, not really. But I'm not sure I want to put Doug into a program like that. I think it consists of severe police tactics. I feel that Doug needs as much compassion as discipline."

"Compassion?" Greg said incredulously. "How much compassion did he show last night when he shattered your anniversary crystal?"

Julie replied softly, "I know. I know."

"Not to mention his drug use and the disrespect he has toward us and Michael."

"I'm just not sure that putting him in with hardened criminals is the best approach."

"I had the same concerns, but Jim explained the program is less for repeat offenders and more for juveniles who may have gone sideways and need to be nudged onto a straighter path."

Julie trusted Jim in all matters involving police work and associated programs. If he said Tough Love was the way to go then Julie was inclined to try it. Plus the school counselor, whom Julie also believed in, had recommended it. After more discussion they agreed to go to a parents' introductory meeting on Tough Love in three weeks.

Greg and Julie also agreed they would closely monitor Doug's behavior. Julie put her organizing and logistics skills to good use. She became good friends with the parents of two of Michael's closest classmates. Among the three sets of parents Julie was able to ensure the boys were driven to school and returned home without Doug doing any driving.

Julie confirmed Doug's work schedule with his boss and re-arranged appointments so she could drive Doug to work when his co-worker Elliott was not available. Elliott had assured Julie he would bring Doug directly home after work. Julie felt she could trust Elliott to do so.

///

A week later at work, Elliot sensed Doug was in a tough spot and seemed very preoccupied. Ever since Lisa had mentioned her pregnancy Doug had thought of little else. He wanted so much to show her he would be able to support their child. Doug had approached his boss about working more hours. The boss told him that client orders were down and that his hours would likely be cut. When he saw Doug's disappointment he told Doug he would try to hold off the reduction.

Then Doug remembered his conversation with Dominic weeks earlier about going to work for him. Doug knew Dominic would likely be at Stephenson Park on Thursday evening. So he asked Tiny to drive him there during his lunch break. To avoid raising suspicion Doug told Elliot they would be looking at stereo equipment for Tiny's truck.

They arrived at the park twenty minutes later and Doug suggested Tiny stay put. Doug saw Dominic and Raven standing by their bikes.

"Well, it's knife-boy. What's up?"

Doug was nervous and shuffled his weight from one side to the other. He took a deep breath. "Uh, I'd like to earn some extra money."

Dominic looked at Raven who raised his eyes and shrugged his head. Dominic took a step closer to Doug. "Well, I'd like to earn some extra money, too." He glanced back at Raven who smirked.

Doug started to feel uncomfortable and his breathing had quickened. In an uneasy voice Doug began to walk away. "Uh, never mind. I shouldn't have come here. Sorry."

Dominic sensed Doug's tenseness and immediately walked toward him.

"Wait."

Doug turned around and Dominic stared at him for a second. "I'm just messing with you." Dominic put his arm around Doug and tried to calm him down. "Relax, dude." Dominic motioned over to Raven to step back a little to give him and Doug a bit more space. He pulled out a cigarette and offered another one to Doug, which he readily took.

As Dominic lit each of the cigarettes Doug remarked, "Nice lighter."

"Thanks," Dominic replied. "My ex-con Marine uncle got me this from Vietnam."

Doug relaxed a bit after taking a few puffs. Dominic then got down to the matter at hand. "You do weed?"

"Yeah."

"You know many tokers?"

Doug looked quizzically at Dominic and answered, "A few."

"Just a few? Or quite a few?"

"Uh, well, quite a few I guess."

"Good. How'd you like to earn some quick money selling weed to your friends?"

Doug thought about the question for a minute. "Well, yeah, I guess. How would this work?"

Dominic asked Doug how much his friends were paying for an eighth of an ounce of weed. When Doug told Dominic it varied but then gave him an average range thirty to forty dollars. Dominic smiled and said he could provide better quality at a lower price.

"I don't have any cash to get started."

Dominic smiled again. "I'll stake you an ounce that's worth a hundred green. You can easily sell it to your friends for double what I'll be selling it to you. Have your stake money back to me in four days. Agreed?"

Dominic extended his hand to Doug who was quickly doing a mental calculation in his head. He could make a hundred dollars in less than a week.

Julie had managed to convince Greg to allow Doug to have his truck back by the end of the week. That meant he'd be able to drive back and forth to see Dominic starting in four days. All seemed to be falling into place.

"Agreed," Doug replied.

He shook Dominic's hand and then had Tiny drive him back to work.

///

Soon Doug was making several hundred dollars a week selling high grade marijuana initially to friends and later to friends of friends.. Doug felt like an entrepreneur. He kept his weed well hidden in the locked glove and console compartments of his truck, and never took it inside the house. He also took pains to ensure his brother was unaware of the extent of his drug dealing.

His profits only kept increasing. During the third week Doug took a tiny sample of crystal methamphetamine that Dominic had offered him. That same week Greg and Julie had planned to attend an introductory meeting for parents about the Tough Love program. They told their sons they would be going to the civic center to attend a community affairs meeting.

Greg and Julie pulled up to the two-story community center where the Tough Love meeting would be held and walked into the main auditorium. Soon there were about twenty sets of parents taking their seats in front of a stage. Minutes later a gentleman walked onto the stage.

"Hello everyone. Thank you for coming. I'm from the Atlanta Police Department and I run the Touch Love program for Fulton County. My name is Sergeant Timothy Mallory, but to all of you I am simply Tim."

Tim was a large, gregarious, teddy-bear type of man. Julie instantly liked him. He seemed open, honest and very empathetic to the plight of parents with troubled teens. Greg was impressed with his large commanding presence.

Tim began his talk by telling them they were not alone in their dilemmas. He explained that many families faced problems of out-of-control teenagers. Parents of these troubled youths often feel helpless and alone.

Tim then explained what the minimum legal requirements were as parents. The meagerness surprised many of those in attendance. He emphasized that in this day and age of online communications, digital media and the ubiquitous social networks, most teenagers believed they were entitled to continuous access to such items as smart phones and the Internet.

Tim admitted that in today's digital society a parent might need to provide their teens with a computer, a cell phone and Internet access to be properly educated. He went on to say they do not need the most elaborate versions of these devices, nor do they need full access to the Internet and the various types of social media. He practically pled with parents to monitor their children's use of the Internet, Facebook, Twitter, Instagram and other forms of social media.

"I'm sure many of you are thinking there is no way you can monitor every email and text message that your child sends. You may be saying how can you keep track of which websites your kids are visiting? I assure you there are ways to accomplish this. We have an excellent cyber forensics group that can show you how. Your children should have no presumption of privacy. They are your legal responsibility until they are eighteen. Do not relinquish the responsibility you have for them, or the power you have over them."

His message seemed to resonate. He described the minimum standards a parent had for a child included three square meals a day, a roof overhead, reasonable clothing and no presumption of privacy. The roof overhead could even mean a room in the garage for extreme cases. Removing the door to a child's room could reduce privacy.

Tim told his audience he knew it could be difficult to take back basic creature comforts from children, but was often necessary to regain control over an out-of-control teenager.

"When you have an angry, out-of-control, irrational person the worst thing you can do is to start acting angry and out-of-control yourself. You must remain in control in order to re-establish order to the situation. I know that it is easier said than done, but you must try."

Tim told the group they needed to go home and establish clear and unambiguous guidelines with their teenaged children as to what will, and will not be, tolerated. He stressed that the most important part of this was to state specifically the consequences for non-compliance, and then to actually following through with the consequences when warranted. He also cautioned them not to make the consequences too lenient.

The parents then broke out into individualized groups for those whose children had similar emotional and behavior characteristics such as anger, theft, drugs, or violence. Discussions and handouts containing helpful tips and information were distributed to each parent. They were then all brought back for final questions and answers session with Tim. At the end he thanked them again for attending and wished them a good evening.

Greg and Julie agreed it had been a worthwhile session. As they drove home they discussed how they would lay down the law with Doug. They would establish ground rules and boundaries by which he would have to comply or face severe consequences. Then they rode in silence, each of them completely alone in their thoughts.

When they pulled into their driveway they could hear Doug's stereo blasting and pulsating. While Julie looked in on Michael, Greg ascended the staircase and walked the length of the hallway to the last door on the right. As expected, Doug had his door locked. Greg knocked, first gently, then with more force to ensure it was heard over the blaring racket emanating from inside.

"Who is it?" Doug yelled, in a voice dripping with annoyance.

"It's your father. Unlock the door."

"What do you want?"

"I want to come in and talk with you. Now open the door."

"I don't feel like talking right now. Just go away."

Greg's first impulse was to break down the door. But his cooler side prevailed as he remembered his comment to Julie about picking the lock. He strode over to the medicine cabinet in the master bedroom and retrieved the special key designed to open locked bedroom doors. Like a thief in his own house, he walked silently back to Doug's door.

The key slid flawlessly through the tiny circular opening, past several steel slots and stopped at the latch pin. In one quick, fluid motion, Greg twisted the key, turned the brass knob, and pushed open the door. Doug immediately turned and glared at his father.

"Get out of my room!"

Greg initially just stood his ground and said nothing. Once more Doug screamed at his father.

"I said get out of my room!"

Greg was about to yell right back at him. No child of his would be allowed to scream at a parent like that. Then he thought of the advice Tim had provided earlier.

"When an ill-tempered child causes a parent to lose their temper, both become irrational," Tim had cautioned.

And if the child has been using drugs, it's even more critical for the parent to remain calm. From the discussions earlier that evening, Greg suspected Doug was using crystal meth. He displayed several of the symptoms, including rapid heart rate, sweating, mood swings and irrational anger. As he turned down the stereo, Greg calmly stated, "No, I am not leaving. I am going to search *this* room of *my* house.

Doug glared at his father momentarily, but sensing Greg's determination, Doug stomped out of the room and raced downstairs. He was gone for no more than a few minutes. When he re-appeared in the doorway, there was something strangely different about his demeanor. He was more aggressive and arrogant. He walked toward his father in a forceful manner. Standing just inches from him, he was literally in his father's face. Their eyes locked as Doug spoke through gritted teeth.

"For the last time, I said get out of my room!"

He uttered these words as he pulled out a shiny, silver object from the front hip pocket of his jeans. With one quick flick of his wrist he opened the object's chrome-plated encasement, and revealed the five-inch stainless steel knife blade. As his hand continued on in one fluid motion, the encasement cover latched back to become part of the handle. Then he quickly reversed the direction of his motion to cause the razor-sharp blade to lock into place.

Greg's eyes widened in surprise as he said, "What is that?"

"It's my butterfly knife. Now get out of my room."

"Are you out of your mind? Put that away."

"Not till you get out of my room."

Greg grabbed Doug's right wrist that was brandishing the knife and pushed Doug back against the opened door of the room. Doug's expression changed into a lifeless determined stare. He knew he was taller and stronger than his father and he slowly started pushing his knife toward Greg's throat.

Greg almost panicked, but maintained some control. He started pushing back against his son's arm, but he was losing the battle. Slowly the deadly knife approached Greg's neck. When it was within inches of Greg's skin he yelled down to his wife.

Julie rushed upstairs to see what was happening. As soon as she saw her son threatening her husband with a knife she started screaming.

Greg yelled at her, "Call 911!"

Julie reached for her phone with shaking hands. She ran into her bedroom and with trembling fingers tried to dial 911. By now Michael had come upstairs. As soon as Julie saw Michael peering into Doug's room she ran out and pulled Michael back into her bedroom.

Greg and Doug had their eyes focused on each other like lasers. The knife blade started to pierce his skin. Blood started trickling down his neck and reached the collar of his yellow Van Heusen shirt. Greg's mind was racing. He could not believe his son was actually doing this. The sight of the blood only seemed to embolden Doug.

Greg took several deep breaths and then with all of the strength he could muster he slammed Doug's right wrist into the door behind him. The knife flew out of Doug's hand and close to Greg's foot. He immediately pressed his shoe on the blade handle.

He yelled to Julie, "Cancel the 911 call, now."

Doug felt a sharp stinging sensation shooting through the back of his hand. He doubled over in pain as he leaned down to pick up the butterfly knife. He knelt down next to Doug and helped him to his bed. Both were trembling.

Greg walked down to the master bedroom where Julie and Michael were still sitting on the bed. They both wiped away their tears and looked up at Greg. He put his arms around each of them.

He whispered to Julie, "I'm sorry."

"Me too."

"I'm going to walk Michael down to his room. I'll be right back." Julie nodded in agreement as she turned off her phone.

Greg put his arm around Michael's shoulder as they headed for his room.

Without looking up Michael asked, "Dad, what's wrong with Doug? Why is he acting like this?"

"That's what we're trying to figure out, son."

"I feel bad for him, Dad."

"I know."

As they entered Michael's room, he looked up and said, "I also feel bad for you and Mom."

Greg gave his son a big hug. "I know. But you know what. We're going to get this figured out. Now go to sleep."

"Good night, Dad. I love you."

"I love you too, son. Good night."

Greg walked back to the master bedroom. Julie looked at Greg's bloodstained shirt and wondered how this could be happening.

CHAPTER 12

THE EFFECTS OF the knife-wielding incident from Wednesday evening carried over into a tension-filled Thursday morning at the MacDonald household. Schools were not in session the following two days. Greg had called his mother, Francine, to come over and keep company with her two grandsons who would be out of school for two days. Greg had demanded both sets of keys to Doug's truck, again.

Before leaving for work Greg had called Jim and explained the events of the prior night. Greg and Julie had agreed that Doug needed to be enrolled in the Tough Love program as soon as possible. Jim offered to contact Tim about enrollment procedures.

Minutes later Jim called back and explained that Tim had suggested the four of them meet for lunch that day. Just before noon the four of them were seated in a corner booth of a popular chain restaurant just west of downtown. Tim remembered Greg and Julie from the night before. After exchanging some brief pleasantries, Tim turned to Greg and Julie and said quietly, "I understand there was an incident with your son last night."

"Yes, there was," Greg said. "We tried to talk to Doug last night after arriving home from your seminar. He quickly became out of control and attacked me with a knife."

"We think he was on drugs," Julie added.

Greg and Julie spend the next twenty minutes describing Doug's history of emotional instability, mood swings, rebellious nature and poor academic performance. Tim described for them some of the challenges of determining when questionable teenage behavior is due simply to the hormonal changes of puberty versus something more serious such as drugs or chemical imbalances.

Tim emphasized that Greg and Julie needed to have Doug sign a written contract as to exactly what would be expected of him while he participated in the program. More importantly, Doug needed to understand in writing what the consequences would be if he failed to comply with the requirements.

The requirements involved such areas as agreeing to attend Tough Love progress review meetings every other Wednesday evening, signing a contract with school counselors that outlined an academic improvement plan, and registering in an anger management program. The anger-management program consisted of Doug attending meetings for five weeks with other participants on Tuesdays and Thursdays.

Tim felt that it was critical that Doug understand the various elements of the programs, and his responsibilities that he would be expected to carry out. "Would you be interested in me helping you explain some of the aspects of these two programs to Doug?"

Julie and Greg looked at each other and both nodded yes. Greg then answered, "Definitely. That would help. Could you stop by tonight?"

Tim readily agreed and the three of them decided on the time. After finishing their lunch, the four of them left and anticipated what the evening would bring.

///

That evening a very somber looking Doug sat with his parents around the formal dining room table as Tim arrived. Out of habit Julie had lit two scented candles. Their warm glow and fragrance provided a softening effect that stood in stark contrast to the proceedings that were about to occur.

Tim shook everyone's hand in a very businesslike manner and then they all sat down around the oak dining table. Tim made a brief reference to the candles and correctly identified their scents, which impressed Julie. Just then Michael walked into the room.

He had been told in general terms what would be happening that night. But he wanted to see part of it. The thought of his brother being made to sign contracts with law enforcement seemed both curious and exciting. He stood silently for a second until Julie introduced him.

"This is our other son, Michael. He's in eighth grade." Then she turned to her younger son, "Michael, this is Sergeant Timothy Mallory from the Atlanta Police Department."

When Michael heard the description that a sergeant from the Atlanta Police Department was in their home, sitting at their dinner table and about to have his older brother sign papers of some sort, the entire experience seemed almost surreal to him.

Tim stood up and extended his hand saying, "Hello, Michael. It's nice to meet you."

Michael cleared his voice a bit and then shook his hand back. "Nice to meet you, sir."

The two stood silently for a few seconds.

"Michael, I think you have homework to do," Julie said, breaking the awkwardness.

"Not really. I finished it already."

Greg cleared his throat, causing Michael to look over at him. Greg twisted his head to the left, signaling Michael to leave the room. "Well, I better get back. I've got some reading to do." Then he glanced over at Tim. "It was nice meeting you."

"It was my pleasure to meet you, Michael. Have a good evening."

Michael walked out of the room slowly. As he passed by his brother he patted Doug's shoulder. Doug looked up surprised and then half-smiled with an expression of resignation. After Michael left the room the four of them addressed the issues at hand.

Tim looked over at Doug and explained the Tough Love program, and what it was intended to do. He stressed that the program was not intended to be a babysitter for Doug. For it to be successful, Doug would have to understand and perform his set of responsibilities. Doug would have to hold up his end of the bargain.

Tim then described some of the consequences that could happen to Doug if he chose not to live up to his part of the program, including juvenile court. Doug listened intently and seemed to comprehend the seriousness of the situation. He was fully engaged and started asking pertinent questions about his responsibilities.

"You know, Doug, threatening your father with a knife is assault, which is a felony and could result in jail time. Using and dealing drugs can also lead to prison. Do you understand the consequences of your action?"

Doug merely nodded.

"This program is intended to keep you out of the court system and jail. Do you understand?"

"Yes, I think so," Doug muttered.

Tim wanted to establish a good relationship with Doug but at the same time stress how he needed to take the program seriously.

"Douglas, you need to understand that this program will only work for you if you, and only you, live up to the commitments of this contract." Tim softened his expression a bit and then continued. "You have to commit yourself to the terms of this contract. You have to fully engage yourself in this. In other words, you have to be in this all the way."

Doug nodded slightly and then quietly. "I understand."

"Do you know what you become if you take you out of Doug being in this?"

Doug looked puzzled. He glimpsed over at his parents but they had nothing to offer. "No."

Tim grinned slightly as he said, "If you take *you* out of Doug you become a dog. And you don't want to become a dog, do you?"

Doug looked really confused now. He looked over at his parents who appeared to be grinning.

"Doug, I believe Sgt. Mallory is referring to your name," Julie said.

"Oh." Doug started to grin. "I get it."

"I was just trying to make it easy for you to remember that *you*," then Tim paused for effect, "and only *you* is what makes Doug truly Doug."

"That's pretty clever. Take the *u* out of Doug and you end up with a dog."

Tim grinned and then handed Doug Tough Love forms to sign that his parents had already done.

"Do you have any other questions about the Tough Love program, or your responsibilities in participating in it?"

Doug read over each of the clauses in the forms carefully. "No, I'm good." He then signed on the three lines requiring his signatures.

Next Tim went over the provisions of the anger management program. Doug would be drug tested each week. Any indication of drug use would result in immediate termination from both programs.

The four of them chatted briefly and then Tim told Doug he looked forward to hearing about his progress on each program. Doug shook Tim's hands as he stood to leave. As Tim left their house Doug went back to his room and pondered what the next few weeks would bring.

///

During the next week Doug exhibited model behavior. He was polite, respectful and responsible. His teachers noticed the change at school. He was more attentive and worked more diligently on his assignments. His warehouse boss noticed Doug's attention to detail and productivity had improved.

Doug's new behaviors were mostly an act. He knew that to get his truck back to continue selling drugs, he would have to temporarily do whatever was necessary. So Doug sat attentively at school, worked diligently on his assignments, attended his anger management classes on Tuesdays and Thursdays, and showed up at his first bi-weekly Wednesday progress review at Tough Love.

To accommodate his evening commitments, he had to reduce his hours at the warehouse. Instead of staying at work he arranged rides with Tiny over to Stephenson Park. There he would meet with Dominic who would provide him ever increasing supplies of high-grade marijuana. Doug would sell the weed to an ever-increasing number of high school students.

As word spread about the high quality and low cost of the grass, its demand increased. Doug began getting requests from students attending junior college and even junior high. Doug thought briefly thought about raising prices before deciding he did not want to alienate current customers.

///

By the middle of the third week Julie and Greg felt Doug was on the right path. So they allowed him to have his truck back. But it was only a temporary and conditional allowance. Doug had to sign an amendment to his contract that greatly restricted where and when he could drive. Tim had helped his parents with the amendment.

The first Wednesday that Doug had his truck back, he was scheduled to work. He fabricated an excuse why he needed a later and longer lunch than usual and took off for Stephenson Park. As he pulled into the parking lot he noticed Dominic and Raven's gleaming Harleys.

Dominic knew that Doug had reached an important decision concerning a proposal Dominic had offered to Doug the prior week. It came about in part because Doug had become more interested in earning larger amounts of money. Having a prolific dealer like Doug could accelerate Dominic's master plan to partner with Ramon Tartikov, the widely acknowledged drug kingpin of the entire Southeast region. Doug was moving several ounces of weed a week and could help Dominic exploit children and tweens in the Atlanta area.

The proposal consisted of Doug initially selling modest amounts of cocaine, ecstasy and crystal meth. Doug initially rejected the offer saying he was not interested in selling hard drugs to kids, but that was before he had thought long and hard about Lisa being pregnant and he becoming a father. The idea of being responsible for the raising of a child brought very mixed emotions to Doug.

One part of him felt excited about the prospect of being a father. He would think about witnessing all of the milestones in a baby's life, sharing with the child Doug's own peculiar set of values and how raising a child could bring Lisa and him even closer together.

Doug knew nothing about raising a child, but he had lived long enough to know that the one critical necessity was money. And that he did not have enough of it.

He had tried to get re-hired back at former employers but they were either unwilling or unable to offer him employment. His requirements with the Tough Love program and his anger management classes diminished his possibility to increase his hours at the warehouse.

When Dominic offered him the chance to significantly increase his earning power, Doug visualized the admiring look from Lisa. So he had decided to accept Dominic's offer.

"So, I've been thinking about what you said last week," Doug said.

"Yeah. Well dat's good. And what'd you decide?"

"Ah, that I'd like to try it."

"Good. Dat's very good. But you got the cash?"

Doug replied assuredly, "Yeah. I've got it. The full thousand."

"Let's see it."

Doug pulled a wad of cash out of his pocket that consisted of ten one hundred dollar bills. Dominic glanced down at the money and then back up at Doug who studied Dominic's expression. Doug noticed Dominic had an approving and mildly impressed look on his face, which pleased Doug immensely. The thought that he could gain the approval of a major gang leader had a profoundly satisfying effect on Doug. The fact that Dominic was willing to entrust Doug with a substantial amount of illegal drugs only served to heighten his satisfaction.

Dominic held his hand out. "Gimme dat."

Dominic then handed the bunched up bills over to Raven.

"Count it."

Raven quickly moved each bill from one hand to the other as if he were handling a deck of cards and then nodded.

"Get da package."

Raven walked over to his Harley that was parked about fifty yards away. With each stride he took his heavy motorcycle boots chomped on the broken pavement with the sound similar to broken glass being crushed under his feet. When he arrived at his bike he unlocked the left saddlebag that was attached to the rear fender. He looked around thoroughly in all directions and then slowly opened the saddlebag and pulled out a rectangular package. It was about a foot long and half as wide and a few inches thick. It was wrapped in plain brown paper.

Raven brought the package over to Dominic and handed it to him.

Dominic turned the package over a few times in his hands. "This is what you bought for a grand. It contains meth, ecstasy, and blow. You should be able to sell this for at least two grand, maybe even three." Dominic paused for a second to let Doug comprehend what he just said.

"For sure?" Doug asked.

"For sure." Dominic answered. He knew Doug would quickly start realizing just how far three thousand dollars could go. Then Dominic issued a stern warning. "But you never reveal to anyone who supplied this to you, understand?"

"Yeah, sure."

Dominic looked over at Raven whose expression had gone back to being stoic. Dominic then handed the package over to Doug. "Get on with it then. I'll be outta town for bout a week. I expect you to be ready for some more candy by then, understand."

"I understand."

///

Later that evening Dominic celebrated by partying hard and heavy with plenty of liquor. He finally collapsed on his couch in his office in the clubhouse. Raven dozed off under a blanket on a sofa just outside Dominic's door. Suddenly Raven felt a warm body snuggling against him, and a soft hand stroking his crotch. He roused himself awake and focused his eyes.

A sultry sounding woman whispered, "Hi, tiger, mind if I play with your gearshift?"

It was Tanya, wearing only tiny underwear. Raven immediately jumped up and wrapped his blanket around her.

"You fricking crazy? Gonna get us both killed."

"Nah. Dominic needs you. But his whiskey dick is no good to me tonight. How about you take his place?"

"Go. Now," Raven ordered.

As Tanya sashayed away, she teasingly dropped the blanket. Then she turned her head back and gave Raven a seductive look. Raven shook his head and muttered, "Damn."

CHAPTER 13

DOUG RETURNED TO the warehouse with time to spare. He was surprised there was less work left to do than expected, but time and work were not on his mind. He kept thinking about the possibility of earning so much more money. He could not wait to tell Lisa, and texted her about coming over. Doug knew she had not been feeling well the past week, and consequently the two had not spoken at length in several days. She texted back saying she wanted to see him, but he knew he would first need his parents' permission to drive over to Lisa's place.

After work he called his parents for their approval. Julie was okay with the idea because she liked Lisa and felt she was more good influence than bad on her son. Greg took a bit more convincing. Greg agreed, provided Doug visited only Lisa and would be home by ten-thirty. Doug was ecstatic. Ten minutes later he pulled into Lisa's driveway.

She greeted him silently and with a smile as she opened the door for him. Doug pulled her toward him and wrapped his arms around her. Doug softly kissed her forehead and then her lips.

"Hey," he whispered to her.

"Hey yourself," she said back.

"I've got some good news for you." Doug could not wait to tell her about his new source of income.

"Really? Well, let's go out back. I could use some fresh air."

The home had a large backyard. Among the many trees was a path that led from the back porch to a secluded area. The almost-full moon illuminated a crystal clear sky full of countless stars. The two of them walked out to the clearing and sat down on a comfortable wood bench.

"Do you mind if I smoke?"

Lisa shrugged and replied, "Go for it."

Doug lit up a cigarette and took a deep drag. As he slowly exhaled he looked up at the sky. "I've really missed not being able to come over to see you."

"I know. Me too. So how is that Tough Love program going?"

"It's all right, I guess. I had to sign an amendment to the original contract about where and when I can drive. I had to call and get permission to come over tonight."

"So, like, what do you do in Tough Love?"

"We share experiences with each other. They put us in groups with similar backgrounds. Sometimes college counselors come in and talk."

"You mean about what you're throwing away, that sort of crap?"

"No, just the opposite, about how much we have to gain, that structure, discipline, time management, all the shit we're forced to do now will come in handy later in life, like in college and stuff."

"I guess I can see that."

"But the cool part is when they bring in ex-cons to talk."

"You mean like scared straight?"

"No, more like 'there was a crooked man who walked a crooked mile.'"

"That's funny. But I get what you mean."

"Yeah, it hasn't been too bad so far."

"And what about anger management?"

"It's not too bad. I'm learning a lot of things."

"Like what kind of things?"

"Well, I learned that the make-up of my personality, like a lot of people with short tempers, tends to make me want to hang around and fight when I'm in a confrontation."

"Well, that sure sounds like what happened with your situations with your parents. So what do they say people should do?"

"They talk about the fight-or-flight syndrome. It means that when I'm in a situation where my temper is likely to erupt, I'm supposed to just walk away from the situation. That's the flight part. The only time I'm to consider the fight part is if my life or limb is threatened."

Lisa seemed impressed. "Well, it sounds like you're learning some good things there."

"Yeah, I am. The leader is a guy named Sam and he's pretty cool."

"How many are in your class?"

"Nine. Sam says they usually have between five and fifteen. This is a good size cause there's like a lot of different backgrounds."

"Are they mostly like your age?"

"Uh, yeah, I'd say about half of them are my age. There's this one fairly old guy who's pretty all right. We've been talking a bit about different things. He's lived through a lot of crap of his own over the years."

"Well, so, like, how old is he?"

Doug thought for a second and then answered, "Oh, he's old. He's like over thirty or something."

"Wow. That old, huh?"

Doug wasn't sure if Lisa was teasing. "Yeah, but he's cool." Doug gazed up at all of the stars and commented, "Quite a clear night, ain't it?"

Lisa corrected him softly. "You mean, isn't it?"

"Yeah, that's what I said."

Lisa just smiled and sighed. Then she extended her arm out and started lightly stroking the top of Doug's hand with her fingers. He looked over at her with an expression that told her he wanted to tell her something important.

She gradually stopped stroking his hand and moved her arm back. Then she asked him, "So you said you had some good news?"

Doug sat up straighter. "Yeah. I've been thinking a lot about your condition."

Lisa raised her eyebrows slightly and looked a bit more serious. "Okay."

"And I just want you to know that I would really want to help raise the baby with you."

Lisa sat motionless and stared at him without uttering a word.

"I mean, I'd like to be a part of the baby's life." He paused for a second and then added, "You know, be a father to our baby."

"But sweetie, there's no way you have any means of supporting a child. You barely make enough money for yourself. You're only working part-time at a warehouse."

Doug turned his upper body toward Lisa and held her shoulders tenderly. Lisa looked into his eyes and saw an expression of confidence like she had never seen before.

"Baby, that's the good news I have to tell you. I have a new job. I have a new source of income. And it's gonna make us enough money for the baby."

"So just what is this new source of income?"

"Well, do you remember when we were at the park a few weeks ago and I pulled that drunk off of the girl?"

"You mean the girlfriend of the gang leader?"

"Yeah."

"Uh, yeah, I remember. Her name was Tanya I think. And what was his name? Oh, wait, I think it was Don Williams, right?"

"Close. It's Dominic Williams. And he heads up the motorcycle gang known as the Raptors."

"So what does that have to do with you earning money?"

"It has to do with working with the gang leader."

"What? How?"

"The dude's motorcycle gang is actually a front for their drug dealing. I've been selling some weed for him for a few weeks. It brings in a little money but not all that much. So he's offered to let me sell some slightly harder drugs that will bring in a lot more money for us."

"Are you serious?"

"Yes. Of course. It's a lock. Every week I will be bringing in . . ."

"Stop!" Lisa shouted. "Are you crazy? Don't you know how illegal that is? What were you thinking?"

Doug looked surprised. "I was thinking this is a way to get us started so that we can raise our child. I have thought this through."

"What do you mean you have thought this through? What exactly have you thought?"

"Look, we both believe that cannabis in all its various forms should be legal. You and I and all of our friends all do weed. So if you have no problem with using weed, you shouldn't have any problem with me selling it."

"Using it is one thing. Selling it is altogether different."

"Well, I don't think so. And besides, if I don't sell it to those who want it then someone else will. Why shouldn't I be their supplier and get the profits? I know enough people wanting weed so that the number of buyers will only keep increasing."

"But you won't be selling just weed now. You said you were going to start selling harder drugs, right?"

"Well, yeah."

"What kind of harder drugs?"

Doug tried to sound as nonchalant as he could as he replied, "Just some ecstasy and other stuff like that."

Lisa sensed that he was not revealing anything close to the entire story. "What other kind of stuff?"

"Just stuff. Like meth and blow."

"Are you out of your mind?" She caught her breath. "You plan to sell cocaine and meth to kids? That is just so wrong. Not to mention how illegal that is. That's a major felony if you get caught."

"That's the beauty of it. I won't get caught. And it will bring in up to a thousand dollars a week for us. Think about what that could buy us. Think about what that could buy for the baby."

Lisa was shaking her head in disbelief. Then she decided to calm down a bit and try to reason with her boyfriend.

"Sweetheart, listen to me. This is not the way to go. Surely there are other more legal ways to earn money."

Doug sighed. "Trust me. I have tried the other ways. I really have. I asked my boss at the warehouse for more hours but he said a major contract that would have provided more hours for everyone did not go through. I tried going back to Video Town to try to get some part-time work but they were not hiring."

Lisa could see that Doug was talking sincerely and really believed he had tried his best at finding other employment. "I even went back to the pizza joint. And several other sandwich shops. None of them are hiring. That's why I think this job is the only way to earn an income."

He paused briefly and was practically pleading with Lisa. "And it's really good money. It will be money for us. It will be money for the three of us. So that we can bring our child up right. Can't you see that?" Doug was almost starting to sob as he said, "I thought you would have been pleased with my efforts."

Lisa looked deeply in his eyes and saw a person who more than anything else looked sad and resigned. She realized that in his own twisted way he was simply trying the only way he knew how to provide some support for his girlfriend and their love child.

She thought for a moment about all of the special moments she had spent with him the past year. She recalled all of the long nights they spent talking over every bit of their young lives. The thoughts of all of their emotional highs and lows came flooding back to Lisa. This included the occasional triumphs of finding a job or of passing a test. They also involved a number of disappointments such as failing an exam, cutting back on work hours, losing a job and never seeming to have enough money.

Lisa put her hand behind his head and lightly stroked his thick brown hair. She lowered her eyes for a second and then looked back up at Doug.

"Sweetheart, I know you were only trying to do what you thought was best for us. And I really appreciate that."

Doug temporarily regained his composure and looked expectantly back at Lisa.

But his hopeful feeling was short-lived and her voice did not make him feel in the least bit optimistic. "But I just can't support you selling drugs as a means of earning money. It's not right. And it certainly isn't legal." This was not the kind of news Doug was expecting to hear.

Lisa placed her hands back on her lap and inhaled deeply. She was going to have to give Doug another dose of bad news. But she was concerned that this news might be more than he would be able to take. She knew all about his various dysfunctions. And even though he appeared to be making some progress with his anger management, she feared he may still have an explosively quick temper. But she knew she had to tell him.

"Listen, babe, I need to tell you something."

Doug noticed the subtle change in Lisa's voice.

"What is it?"

"Well, there's no easy way to say this. Look, just like you, I have been doing a lot of thinking about my baby." She paused. "I mean our baby. I've been thinking long and hard about our baby's future."

"Babe, what's going on? What are you trying to say?"

"I've aborted the baby."

"What!" Doug could not believe his ears. "Why? When?" A dozen questions started flooding his brain.

Lisa started breathing heavily. She moved her fingers back on top of Doug's hands. "Baby, I am so sorry but this was a decision I had to make alone."

"Why? Why didn't you call me so we could talk this out together?"

Tears welled up in Lisa's eyes. She momentarily turned away from her boyfriend and then returned her moistening eyes back to his gaze. "Because." Lisa paused again and drew a deep breath.

"Because I had sensed by some of the things you were saying lately that you might want to keep it. Once your mind is made up you can be so damn persuasive."

"Would that have been so bad? Would it have been so terrible to have kept the baby?" He had begun to sob as the full realization washed over him that his potential child no longer existed.

Lisa made her voice as soft and gentle and as sincere as possible as she tried to explain. "Sweetheart, the way I saw it I had three options. I could keep the baby; I could abort it; or I could put it up for adoption. The thought of carrying a living being for nine months and going through the pain of childbirth only to give the child away to parents I could never meet was more than I could handle."

"Okay. I get that. Adoption is not something I would have wanted either. Besides never seeing the child again, there's no way of knowing what kind of parents they would be. We would have been totally at the hands of the government adoption agencies, and you know how I feel about government agencies."

"I know. So we agree that adoption was not really an option for us, at least not for this baby."

"I still don't understand why you didn't think we could have raised this child. I would have found a way to earn the money somehow."

"It's not just a matter of the money."

"Then what else is it?"

"I don't want to bring a child into this world until its biological parents are mature and responsible enough to care for, raise and nurture it into adulthood."

"And you don't think we are? We're both mature, we're both responsible, and I told you I now can bring home the money."

"No, sweetheart, we are not mature and we are not responsible. I love you for all that you are, but one thing you are not is mature and responsible. In some twisted crazy way, that's one of the things I love about you. You are the ultimate rebel, the ultimate non-conformist. The way you are so anti-establishment, anti-authority and anti-government is very endearing to me. I think it's endearing."

She took a deep breath and continued. "There isn't any other man I would rather have to father my children, when the time is right. I hope and pray you can see that the time is not only not right, it's just so totally wrong. For so many reasons. We are still in a special needs high school. One of us would likely not graduate while raising a child, and maybe neither of us would. Then what would we have? And the thought of my baby's father being a drug dealer frightens me. It should frighten you too. The fact that it doesn't just tells me how immature you are. Can you see what I'm saying?"

Doug took his last puff on the cigarette and then crushed it out. "I don't know. I was trying so hard to make this work. I thought you'd be pleased that I had a way to make an income. I've just got to think this all through."

Not much more was said as they both stood up and headed back toward the house. As he got ready to leave, the two of them hugged for one more time. Lisa kissed him tenderly on his forehead and tears started forming again in each of their eyes.

Doug then turned and walked toward his truck.

He drove home slowly with his mind in a mental fog. He was understandably upset, disappointed and angry. He fought to control all of these conflicting emotions. Quietly he started sobbing again. Just when he felt he had turned a corner and things were starting to improve, he now felt like his whole world was caving in on him.

///

At 10:30 Doug pulled into his parent's driveway. His eyes were red from all the tears he had cried the past hour. He went directly upstairs and passed by Michael's room on the way to his own. Michael was still up listening to music on his iPod while reading a novel for his English class. He noticed Doug walk by and that he was very distraught. Michael had never seen his normally confident brother look so downtrodden. So he followed Doug into his room.

Doug turned around as he reached his room and said to his brother. "What do you want?"

Michael saw how red Doug's eyes were. "Doug, what's wrong?"

"Nothing."

"Then why are your eyes so red?" Doug said nothing. Michael felt a trace of fear from seeing his usually self-assured brother seem so vulnerable. Michael thought of his grandmother telling him to offer Doug the most support when he seemed to want it the least.

"Hey, Doug. Look, I know something's really wrong. And I know you probably don't want to talk about it. Especially to me, but remember I never told Mom or Dad about your knife."

Doug raised his eyebrows slightly at this comment. He thought to himself Michael was right. Maybe his brother was becoming more trustworthy.

"I also never told anyone about the grass you're starting to sell."

"What do you know about me selling weed?"

"Hey, it's no big deal. Some friends of some of my friends heard you might be a supplier for grass. It's no big deal to me. Is that what's bothering you? Are you in some trouble for selling weed?"

"No. It's not that."

Michael patted his brother's shoulder. "Well, whatever it is, if you ever want to talk about it I'm here for you."

Doug half smiled as he thought about the ironic juxtaposition this whole situation was presenting. Here was his brother, younger in age by over four years, offering him help and support. Then again, he thought, who was he to question it? Doug sat down on his bed and motioned to Michael to join him.

Doug looked at his brother. "Listen, I'm going to tell you something but you can't tell a soul, understood?"

"I understand. Your secret's safe with me. I think I've proven that to you already."

Doug told Michael about Lisa having been pregnant and then aborting the baby. He started tearing up as he explained to his younger brother that he had lined up a way to earn more money so as to help raise the child.

"How were you going to earn more money?"

"I'd rather not say right now. Maybe down the line I will."

Michael was not about to press the issue. Doug had already divulged far more to Michael than he had ever expected. If Doug wanted to hold off on some of the details, Michael was fine with that. "I understand."

"Thanks, bro."

"No problem. But when or if you want to talk some more about any of this, or anything else for that matter, just let me know."

"Okay. I might ask your advice on some outfits sometime. You seem to have a little better taste in clothes than me."

"Yeah. I guess so. Anytime." The two remained silent for a few minutes. Then Doug said, "Well, I guess we better turn in. Thanks for listening."

They both stood up at the same time. They took a second, and perhaps for the first time, really looked closely at each other. Without saying a word they hugged each other. Then Michael took a step back and headed toward his room. The physical distance between Doug and his brother increased with each step, but their emotional distance was shrinking.

CHAPTER 14

WHEN DOUG AWOKE on that first Thursday in December, he was still as confused, disappointed and as angry as he was the night before. His bed blankets were tangled and scattered from a restless night.

Doug tried to disguise his anxiety during breakfast, but Julie noticed something was wrong. Before saying anything she set a hot batch of pancakes on the table and their fresh aroma filled the kitchen.

"Is everything okay, Doug? You look a little down."

"Yeah, I'm alright. Just tired. Didn't sleep too well last night." He shot a glance over at Michael who wisely remained focused on his cereal and fruit.

"Well, don't forget about your anger management class tonight."

"I know."

Doug started to see some benefits from participating. He understood the sources of anger had more to do with how the instigator felt about himself instead of how he felt about the target. The program had started three weeks ago and consisted of ten sessions. It required him to attend a two-hour evening class from seven until nine each Tuesday and Thursday. This would be Doug's fifth meeting.

The boys finished breakfast and left. On the way Michael thought about his conversation with Doug the night before. "So how're you really doing?"

"Bummed out. I didn't sleep much last night."

"Will you be okay for your anger class tonight?"

"Yeah, I'll be good. These classes aren't bad. They're actually kinda educational, at times even entertaining and funny."

"Really?"

"Yeah. Somewhat. A couple of guys are kinda cool."

Michael nodded. "Well, if you ever want to talk about it, or anything else, I'm here for you."

"Got it. Thanks." Doug looked over at his brother. "And thanks for last night. I was glad we talked."

"No problem."

The two brothers smiled at each other. They agreed on a radio station and rode the rest of the way listening to some new-wave music. Doug dropped his brother off at his junior high school and then drove over to his continuation school. He looked for Lisa but she had called in sick. Doug was not surprised. He focused what little attention he could muster on the anger class he would be attending that evening.

The day dragged on until it was time for Doug's anger class. Doug smiled at Sam Philips, who headed up the program.

Sam stood behind the sign-in table. "Good evening, Doug. How are you doing tonight?"

Doug shrugged. "Doing okay. I'm back to driving my truck again."

"Well, that's good. You be safe out there, okay?"

"I know. Thanks."

Doug walked to the balcony and quickly lit up a cigarette as he popped open a soda. He looked out at the countless office lights flickering from random floors of several tall buildings. He thought about recent events in his own life, and how flickering and random they also seemed.

He was glad to be there. He had much to sort out in his life and in a bizarre way found this strange combination of misfits to be a safe haven for him. Each had their own story of anger and rage and difficulties with coping. Hearing their episodes made Doug feel he was not alone with his struggles. He especially found comfort and solace in his private conversations with Sam and one other participant, Carl Thomas.

Besides Doug and Carl, there were seven others registered for this class. The typical size of an anger management class was twelve. Carl was the oldest, at thirty-one, with the youngest being sixteen. Doug saw how out-of-control anger could have more serious consequences the older a person becomes.

Sam announced the meeting would start shortly and suggested anyone so inclined grab more coffee or soda. He also reminded everyone there would be no class on the following Tuesday. Doug used the time to think back over the first four sessions of this program. During the first meeting he had felt nothing but resentment at having been coerced to attend. After the second session Doug started liking the idea of listening, sharing, growing and maturing.

Doug recalled how Sam had asked each one to identify the triggers that set off their anger. It could be a word, a phrase, a tone, a situation or any combination of these. Doug had thought long and hard about this and determined that his trigger expression was being called an entitlement loser. Some classmates at the private junior high school Doug had attended previously put that label on him when word leaked out that he would be transferring to a publicly funded continuation school.

Unenlightened parents of these classmates believed the continuation schools were a waste of tax dollars, and only benefitted parents and students who felt entitled to such subsidies. The label triggered Doug's rage on more than one occasion because it implied that both he and his parents were essentially slugs on the public dole. He knew nothing was further from the truth.

Next, participants were asked to explain the events that had landed them in this program. Doug was struck by the varieties and severities of what they described. Three of them were recovering alcoholics. Two of them had been arrested for domestic abuse and others were charged in juvenile court, placed on probation or issued temporary restraining orders.

The story of Carl Thomas had the greatest effect on Doug. Carl told how this program coupled with alcohol treatment had literally saved his life.

"I was about to turn thirty. My wife had left me after two years due to my constant drinking and temper. I had been arrested for drunk driving, twice. It was just a matter of time before I sought out drug dealers and was doing lines of coke. After my divorce in my darkest hours I started experimenting with heroin."

Sam gently coaxed him to continue by asking why he was there.

"There actually were two related events that brought me here."

Doug had been sitting next to Carl. Doug remembered how Carl's hand was shaking as he lifted his coffee cup. He took a long sip, then set the cup down not far from Doug's elbow. He smelled the strong aroma of the dark black java and faint steam rising from it. The room grew stone silent with everyone focused on Carl.

"The first event was the death of my younger brother last year." Doug lifted his eyebrows and caught his breath. Carl hesitated for a second. He cleared his throat and then continued.

"He was killed by a drunk driver. That brought about a major attitude adjustment for me. I had just started another round of forced alcohol treatment due to my second DUI. We were pretty close and this hit me hard. So I decided then and there to never have another drink. I've been going to AA meetings every week ever since. Then last month some court-ordered newcomer attended."

Doug recollected how Carl had glanced over toward him as he took another sip of coffee. "This newbie and I are chatting at break, you know, fairly casually when all of a sudden he starts defending drunk drivers. When I tell him about my brother, this guy says something about maybe it wasn't entirely the driver's fault. Like maybe my brother somehow had something to do with it. Well, I just lost it. Before I know it people are pulling me off this guy whose face is all bloody. My fists have some of the same blood on them. Next thing I know I'm being sent to this anger management course."

At that point Carl had looked up at Sam and told him he knew he belonged here. He knew he had a destructive short-temper and needed to do something about it before it caused him, or someone else, damage that could be serious, permanent or even fatal.

Carl had sought Doug out during the mid-session break that night, asking several questions about the sources of Doug's anger. Carl listened and showed a kind of empathy that Doug had not experienced before. It seemed as if for the first time Doug had found someone who understood his demons and could offer constructive suggestions about dealing with them. Carl was also smart enough to know when he was getting in over his head with Doug, and wisely brought Sam into the discussion whenever appropriate.

Doug ended his brief walk down memory lane as Sam stood in front of his desk. The tall former marine was still trim and fit, and easily garnered their attention. Although almost fifty he appeared years younger. While he normally projected an all-business attitude, especially when cautioning his participants about the dangers of out-of-control anger, he could also be warm and friendly.

"All stand for the pledge of allegiance," he commanded with a strong voice. After the recitation Sam asked everyone to be seated. Next was the standard practice of Sam reviewing several anger management techniques and asking each person to describe an incident since the last meeting. When it came to Doug, he cleared his throat. "Ah, well I found out my girlfriend was pregnant."

Everyone looked up. A few made comments under their breath saying news like that would definitely get them angry. Doug overheard the remarks and quickly clarified an important point.

"No. I mean, that's not what the big deal was." Those in front turned around to face Doug. Everyone's eyes were riveted on his, waiting and wondering what would come next.

"My girlfriend aborted the baby." Doug paused for a moment and collected his breath. The room grew eerily quiet. There was absolute stillness. "I didn't know she was doing that. I started thinking about raising a child, and all it entailed."

No one spoke. Finally, Sam asked in a very soft tone, "How did you feel when she told you that, and what did you do?"

Doug blinked his eyes a few times and adjusted his position in his chair. "I first felt numb, and then, I felt a whole bunch of things. I felt surprised. I felt confused. I felt betrayed. I felt disappointed. I felt hurt. "

He hesitated for a second. Sam had grown concerned about what Doug might have done and gently asked, "Did you feel any anger? Did you act on it?"

Doug shifted his head to look straight at Sam. "No. I was feeling a lot of things, but anger wasn't one of them. Disbelief was probably the strongest thing I felt. I just couldn't believe she could have done that without talking to me first. I know in the end it was her decision to make. But I really thought she would have told me before."

He glanced around, then looked back at Sam. "But no, I didn't feel any anger toward her. It never even crossed my mind to yell at her, or to lose my temper, or to strike. Sure, I was upset and hurt, but I wasn't angry."

Sam leaned back on the front edge of his desk in a half sitting position. He dropped his hands to either side and grasped lightly the edge of the surface. "That's a heavy load to bear. So what did you do?"

"We talked for a while. My mind was just spinning. Not much of what she was saying was making any sense to me. So after a while there wasn't much more to say. We decided to call it a night. I went home trying to figure this all out. But you know what? It's been twenty-four hours and I'm just as confused now as I was last night. But I'm not feeling anger. Disappointment? Yes. Hurt? Definitely. But not anger."

Sam nodded. "Well, that's good, Doug. A person could have easily gone off the deep end with news like that. I'm glad you didn't. It sounds like you handled it the best you could."

Sam paused. He squinted his eyes slightly. "If you don't mind me asking. Did you happen to mention this to anyone else? As we talked about, sometimes managing your anger involves sharing the sources of the anger with someone you trust and confide in."

Doug thought for a minute. "Well, I can tell you who I didn't tell. That would be my parents." There were some nods of understanding from those around him. "I'm not sure who would have killed me first, my mom or my dad." This brought about some light-hearted chuckling. Even Sam smiled at the remark.

"There was someone I shared the news with. That's my brother. He's a few years younger than me so I wasn't sure that was the right thing to do. He saw how upset I was and wanted to offer support. He had proved he could keep a secret. So I told him about this. It actually seemed to help. He's the only one I've told. Now I've told all of you."

"Doug, thanks for sharing this. I'm sure it could not have been easy," Sam said.

Doug nodded back in agreement. Before Sam went on to the next person Carl turned around to Doug and said, "See me at break, okay?"

Doug looked surprised but immediately replied, "Okay."

The final member was twenty-four-year old Fred Beckers who was a former college football linebacker. Every time Fred spoke Doug could not help but recall the first evening when Sam orchestrated an amusing exchange. It had stemmed from Fred having boasted to the group that after some victorious college games he would go out and drink his teammates under the table. This naturally only exacerbated his drinking problem.

Because Fred partied hard with fellow players, Sam tactfully had asked him if he had ever had relations with a man. Fred was clearly offended. His response was quick and adamant. "Of course not. How dare you. What do think I am, a faggot?"

Sam then asked Fred if he had ever become so drunk that he blacked out. Fred sheepishly admitted he had once blacked out after a very long night of heavy drinking. Sam calmly said that if Fred was truly blacked out, he would have no way of knowing whether he ever had homosexual relations. Doug smiled as he thought about how the group had chuckled as Fred squirmed uncomfortably when he realized the logic of Sam's comment.

Sam distributed some case studies on anger management, and a clinical analysis of some of the biological effects of anger such as heart rate, shortness of breath and increased blood pressure. The conclusion of these discussions took them up to their first break.

"Okay, everyone. Let's break. Be back in fifteen minutes."

Doug went outside to smoke. He walked up to Carl. "You wanted to see me?"

"Yes. Sorry about last night."

"Yeah. It came totally out of the blue."

"You said you talked to your younger brother about it?"

Doug nodded as he lit up.

"Well, I think that's neat you confided in him. I really miss my younger brother. It's easy to take a sibling for granted. I started doing that. If you feel trusting enough to confide in him about such a private matter, that's really cool. I'd suggest you keep building on that. You know what I mean?"

"Yeah. I understand. You're right. It's easy to take a brother, especially a younger one, for granted."

"You said your brother proved his trust to you?"

"Yeah."

Carl took a drag. "Well, how'd he do that?"

"He could have blabbed to my folks that I have a butterfly knife."

"A butterfly knife, huh? You know those are illegal, right?"

"Yeah, I know. I just wanted to have one."

"I get it. Just be careful with that out there, okay?"

"I will."

"Getting back to your girlfriend. You said that you were considering raising the child. Had you thought about how you'd do that?"

"Well, yeah. That's what I tried to tell her. I had a plan to earn money. But she didn't go for it."

"What was your plan?"

Doug crushed out his smoke, looked around to ensure they were out of earshot and lowered his voice. "I made a deal to sell some grass."

"Grass, huh." Carl sounded unconvinced. "Can you make much selling weed?"

"Well, I'm expanding it to other drugs."

"What? Are you crazy?" Carl tried hard not to raise his voice. They noticed it was time to return. "Listen, man, I want to talk to you some more about this. Can you stay for a few minutes after the class?"

"Uh, yeah. I guess so. For a few minutes,"

"Good. It's important you do so." Carl noticed most everyone was back. "Come on. We better get back inside."

Doug and Carl took up their seats along with the rest of the group. The next part of the meeting involved a thirty-minute video on some of the more common causes of and responses to anger. Sam then led a spirited discussion about the film in which everyone voiced their viewpoints on the parts of the video with which they agreed or disagreed. Their opinions took them up to adjournment.

As everyone filed out, Doug noticed Carl speaking to Sam. When Doug approached Carl he pulled Doug. "Listen, we all agreed to be open and honest here. So in that spirit I mentioned to Sam what you told me about your drug dealing. Do you mind if he joins us for a minute?"

Doug shrugged. "No. Sam's cool. That's okay."

Sam walked over and joined the two of them. He looked Doug directly in the eye. "Doug, don't do it."

"Uh? Don't do what?"

"Don't sell drugs. You've got to know that's not the way to go."

Doug shot a glance over to Carl and then back to Sam. "If I don't do it someone else will. At least with mine they know they're getting good stuff."

Sam's voice grew stern. "Look, I know you started out selling some weed. I don't condone that, but I know kids are going to smoke it one way or another. States have started legalizing it, and that's likely to continue. In your case, though, you're selling weed illegally to under-aged kids. Now selling hard drugs, that's a whole other ball game."

Doug started fidgeting. "Listen, kid, I know what you're going through. I've been there," Carl said calmly. "Parents who don't understand. Teachers and cops who have it out for you. No one willing to give you a break. And now you feel betrayed by the girl you were willing to do anything for, right?"

"Well, yeah, something like that."

"I get it. We both do. But this is not the way to go."

"Look, Doug, I've only known you for a few weeks," Sam added. "But I've been doing this a long time. I'm pretty good at reading people. I can tell you're smart, and I can tell you respect loyalty, correct?"

"Probably more than anything else."

"Well, then, think about the people who have been most

loyal to you over the years. Do you think it's this drug dealer?"

"Probably not. I don't know that anyone has really been totally loyal to me lately."

"That's the point, dude. Loyalty isn't just about the last few days. It develops over years," Carl said. "Your parents sound like good people. Haven't they been loyal to you over the years? Have they ever abandoned you?"

"No."

Carl continued. "Have they ever beaten you?"

"No"

"Or abused you?"

Doug raised his voice slightly. "No. I get your point."

"It's not just your parents," Sam said. "Didn't you say you had a grandmother who is always supporting you?"

"Yeah. My Dad's mom. She's pretty good."

"And what about your brother?" Sam asked. "Didn't you say you and he were growing closer? Not to mention your girlfriend. Wouldn't you agree all these people are loyal to you?"

"Yes. I suppose. I mean, yeah I'd agree they're loyal to me."

"Doug, my point is all these people supported you loyally in the past, and will continue to do so in the future. Why jeopardize that? Your drug dealer won't be around in the future."

Carl added, "In all likelihood he'll be in jail sooner rather than later. Take it from me, kid, it just isn't worth it."

Doug sounded sullen. "I know."

Sam looked at his watch. "I need to be locking up. Doug, I hope you will consider what we said. You're heading down a dead-end road. Only you can change your direction. Now is the time."

Doug nodded. "I know. You've given me things to think about." Sam locked up and the three of them walked out to their vehicles and said good-bye.

Sam called out, "Remember there's no class next Tuesday. I'll see you on Thursday."

"Okay," they both called out.

Doug climbed into his truck and headed home in his normal manner, but there was nothing normal about the flood of conflicting thoughts bombarding his brain as he drove home.

CHAPTER 15

DOUG ARRIVED HOME forlorn. He needed to discuss important issues with Michael, his father, Lisa, and especially Dominic, but was unsure how to do so. Then he recalled an article he had discussed with Greg about how restful sleep helped the brain refresh itself much like a computer. Conflicting decisions and unsolvable problems were sorted out and re-organized resulting in orderly solutions, particularly if the problems were dwelled on just before sleep. So Doug thought only about his issues as he dozed off.

He awoke early and felt surprisingly refreshed. Doug knew what to do and for the first time in a long time felt excited and confident.

Dawn had just broken and faint rays of daylight streamed in. Etched on the horizon was the most brilliant sunrise Doug had ever witnessed. It was as if a painter had dipped a giant brush into different colors and flicked the wet brush several times against the sky. The explosion of light and color made Doug feel it would be a very good day.

He dressed for school and walked past Michael's room.

Doug poked his head in. "Morning, guy."

"Oh, hey, how ya doing?"

"Okay. Hey, are you still interested in learning a little bit about World of Warcraft?"

Michael's eyes widened. "Well, duh, yeah. Like are you serious?"

"Totally. How about tomorrow afternoon?"

"Ah, yeah. Cool."

Doug bounded down the stairs feeling very content as he entered the kitchen. His mother had just taken her flapjacks off of the stove and was feeding their golden retriever, Goldie. His father was pouring a cup of coffee for Julie and himself.

"Hi mom. Hi dad," Doug said briskly.

"Well, good morning to you. You sound pretty chipper," Julie said.

"Yeah, I guess. I slept pretty well last night."

"Well, that's good. Restful sleep works wonders," Greg said.

Doug walked by his dad and asked quietly, "Do you think we could go out to eat tonight? Just us? I'd like to talk about some anger-class stuff. Some other things too."

"Weren't you planning to see Lisa tonight?"

"Yeah. But her mom needs her to babysit for a close friend. We're going to hang out tomorrow."

"Well, don't get me wrong. I'd love to spend time with you, but don't you think we should include your mother?"

"Well, normally, yeah, except tonight I'd rather speak to you alone about some things."

Greg looked quizzical. "Well, now you have my interest. You surely know whatever we discuss I will eventually share with her. We don't keep secrets. I'll have to tell her before I agree."

"I understand."

Greg briefed Julie on Doug's request for a boys' night out. Julie thought it was a great opportunity and readily approved. She said she'd rent a movie to watch with Michael and see if Francine wanted to join them.

///

Greg arrived home from work just after five o'clock. He dropped his briefcase off in his office and then freshened up in the bathroom. Later Julie joined him in the kitchen where they kissed.

"Hi honey. You're home early."

"Yeah. Traffic was lighter than normal. Is Doug ready?"

Before she answered, Doug came down the stairs. He greeted his dad with a grin. Francine and Michael joined them and everyone chatted briefly before Greg suggested Doug and he head out.

Fifteen minutes later they arrived at the Pizza Palace. They enjoyed the aroma of fresh baked bread as they found a corner booth in back.

They had barely seated themselves when a friendly young male server took their drink and food orders. The server brought Greg a beer and Doug a lemonade-iced tea drink.

"Your pizza will be up in fifteen minutes," the waiter said.

Once they were alone, Greg looked at his son. "Before we talk why don't we just enjoy our drinks for a minute first."

"Right on, Dad."

Greg raised his beer bottle and Doug did his glass. As their containers touched Greg said, "To fathers and sons."

Doug nodded his head as they took a swig of their drinks. They talked on a variety of subjects for the next twenty minutes, talking and chewing their food. The topics included computers, work, video games, women and even sports. The content was less important than the process. More than anything, they were communicating as men and bonding as a father and son.

"Son, whatever you wanted to talk about, I'm glad you decided to do it here, with just the two of us. It's been a very emotional few weeks, but I hope the worse of it is behind us. I feel like it might be."

Doug took a deep breath and scanned the restaurant as if looking for some source of enlightenment. He knew what he wanted to say. He just was not sure how to say it.

"Dad, I'm sorry for all of the crap I've caused you and Mom."

Greg replied softly, "I know, son."

Doug told his father the anger classes were helping. He described the insights he had gained and explained how the real-life experiences of people like Carl Thomas made Doug want to make something of himself. Doug felt comfortable confiding with his father, and talked about some of the other participants in his group.

"Dad, there's several alcoholics there who say they are sick and tired of always feeling sick and tired. That's sort of how I feel."

Greg sat motionless taking in every word. He knew this was not easy for Doug, but sensed more would be revealed.

"I know I'm messed up and that I've screwed up even more."

Greg studied his son carefully and silently.

"Dad, I got Lisa pregnant."

Greg swallowed hard, bowed his head and closed his eyes for a few seconds, telling himself to remain calm.

"When is she due?"

Doug's voice was low and somber. "She isn't. I mean she's not having it. She aborted it."

Greg watched Doug's eyes moisten. "She aborted it, Dad. She aborted it without even telling me."

Doug paused to catch his breath. "She said there was no way we could raise a child. What she meant was there was no way I could raise a child with her. I don't have much of a job. Barely have an education."

By now there was a tear coming down his cheek, which he wiped away. "She said I'm not mature enough and not responsible enough."

Greg reached across the table and held onto his son's arm. "I'm sorry to hear what you're going through. Words may not help much, but let me try."

Doug had an intense, hopeful expression on his face. He was looking for something, anything, to comfort him.

"The fact that you're willing to tell me this shows you're maturing. Lisa was honest with you, and I presume you were honest with her without flying into a rage, correct?"

"Yeah, but I practically cried, Dad. Practically cried. How mature is that?"

Doug felt the onslaught of a panic attack. His breathing grew rapid and deep. Then Greg grabbed Doug's arms with both his hands and shook them lightly for emphasis.

"Listen to me. What you did was mature. You were feeling the loss of your baby. What parent would not shed tears at the death of their child? Do you think your mother and I would not cry if something happened to you or Michael? Of course we would. What you showed was maybe the ultimate expression of maturity, a parent mourning the loss of his offspring."

The two of them just looked at each other. Greg's words soothed Doug whose breathing gradually slowed and the pangs of a panic attack subsided. Doug felt relieved he had shared such a private matter with his father. Now he wrestled with sharing another secret.

"Dad, there's something else I want to tell you."

Greg slowly pulled his hands back. "Okay."

"I've been selling weed to make extra money."

Greg widened his eyes but kept his voice low. A dozen questions flooded his brain, but he started out with just the basics. "For how long? And to whom?"

"A little over a month. I've been selling it to my friends."

"Where are you getting it from?"

"From a supplier in Stephenson Park."

"You mean a drug dealer?"

Doug's breathing starting to hasten, and he quickly tried to apply some of the techniques he learned at his anger class about deep breathing and remaining calm.

"Dad. Yes. A drug dealer. But what I wanted to tell you is that I'm not doing it any more. I'm not selling any more weed, and never will. Okay?"

Doug decided not to divulge everything about his drug dealing. At least not yet. At some point Doug would tell his father about Dominic and Raven and the offer to sell hard drugs. "You know what you're doing is illegal."

"Was doing, Dad. Was doing. I'm not doing it anymore, and never plan to again."

Greg thought about what his son was saying. He thought about how Julie would react to the news, and his best friend, Jim. How could he tell them his son was a drug dealer?

Still, Doug had shared this all in total sincerity. It was marijuana, not hard drugs, and many felt Georgia soon would legalize it. Several states already had. Considering what Doug had been through in recent weeks, maybe this was not such a major calamity.

"And you are telling me this why?"

"Because I want to be honest with you. Keeping secrets just adds to my problems. During the past three weeks I've heard countless stories from those in my anger class about how deception just feeds on more deception. I don't want to keep secrets anymore."

Greg looked at his son and smiled. "Fair enough. Let's drink to honesty." With that the two of them touched their bottle and glass.

Doug smiled. "To honesty."

By the time they finished their pizza they decided to drive out to a popular dessert bar where they talked some more. They ended the evening with a better understanding of each other than they had ever had before. It was just past nine when they arrived home. Doug chatted briefly with the other family members before going to his room.

Later, both he and his father fell asleep with renewed hope that the future would indeed be brighter for them. Their bond had never been stronger. Their relationship had never felt closer.

///

For the second consecutive day Doug awoke up feeling rested. The day was bright and clear and reflected the state of Doug's mind. He was looking forward to spending time with his brother and then having dinner with Lisa.

Michael arrived home from soccer practice just after noon. He ran up the stairs and found Doug's door locked. He knocked and could hear Doug shuffling around inside. It sounded like he had been putting something back in his safe.

Doug called out from behind his door, "Just a minute."

"Okay. Dude, I'm ready to learn about World of Warcraft."

Soon Doug opened the door and welcomed Michael in. In no time Doug had brought up his WoW account and had created one for Michael. For the next hour Doug taught his brother all about the intricacies of WoW. Michael absorbed the information like a sponge, which pleased Doug.

They went over the different characters, weapons and levels. They discussed how money could be collected and distributed. Doug explained how unsuspecting beginners are tempted to acquire articles from the auction house that are too costly and easier to earn with little effort.

Doug envisioned Michael eventually assisting him with his WoW consulting ventures. That meant potential income for Michael and additional revenue for Doug. Finally they agreed that they had covered enough for the first session.

Doug praised his younger brother. "You did awesome. You picked up on the moves a lot quicker than I thought you would."

"Yeah, not too bad," Michael responded, trying to sound modest.

"Plus you avoided getting merc'd," Doug said, referring to a major loss of points or money.

"So, I'm, like, wondering if there's anything I can do for you," Michael said.

Doug was surprised by the request. "Well, you know I'm taking Lisa out to dinner tonight. I could really use a new outfit. How about helping me pick something out?"

Where Doug leaned toward basic jeans and T-shirts, Michael favored a more layered look with pop culture shirts and sleeveless vests.

Michael felt honored but uncertain he should take on that responsibility. "Uh, I'm not sure I want to do that. What if Lisa doesn't like it?"

"Well, duh, I trust you or I wouldn't be asking. I'm sure Lisa will like it. She's always saying how swaggy your clothes are. Tell you what, how about I sweeten the deal."

"What do'ya mean?"

"Well, you know Dad's gun safe?"

"Ya, so what about it?"

"Well, I happen to know he keeps ready cash in it along with his loaded gun. I know the combination."

Michael sounded confused. "You're telling me this, why?"

"Look. I know you don't steal, but if you ever need some quick cash that you could pay back, it's there. I know Dad keeps around a grand in hundreds and twenties there for emergencies, and he's never used it"

Michael seemed interested. "How'd you get the combo?"

"I overheard Dad give it to mom when they didn't know I was listening. It's seven-one-three. I know it works because I opened it and found my butterfly knife hidden inside."

"Well, I doubt I will ever break into it, but if you'd like me to help you pick out some threads I guess I could do that."

"Now you're talking."

They soon left for Michael's favorite clothing store. After looking at and trying on a few selections Doug decided on olive green khakis, a light-green mock turtle sweater with splashes of color on the front and a tan vested coverall. Doug really liked the look and told Michael he appreciated his help.

They returned home by four-thirty. Doug showered, dressed and was soon off to pick up Lisa. She greeted him at her door with a short kiss.

"Wow. You look great. I like the duds."

"Thanks. Glad you like them. Are you ready to go?"

"All set."

They had six o'clock reservations at an upscale restaurant and arrived a few minutes early. A pleasant hostess seated them in a side booth on the quieter side of the place. They placed their orders and soon enjoyed two delicious entrees.

During dinner Doug talked sincerely about many of the same topics that he had covered with his dad the night before. Lisa was quite moved by Doug's seemingly quick growth spurt of maturity. She was not quite sure if there were factors other than anger management contributing to this sudden display of responsibility, but whatever they were she was thankful for them.

Lisa agreed to support Doug in his new endeavor to straighten out his life. He was not yet ready to turn everything around. He admitted he would still smoke cigarettes, the occasional weed, and would frequently play WoW.

Doug was committed to improving his life and desperately wanted Lisa to believe him. He described the actions he had planned to take. These included giving up drug dealing, hanging out less with dopers and tweakers and more with those interested in school and college, applying himself more to his school work, controlling his temper, utilizing anger management techniques, taking his medications and agreeing to attend and apply his counseling sessions for his various emotional conditions.

After a leisurely and romantic two-hour dinner the two of them headed back to Lisa's. The couple hugged on her doorstep and then Doug planted a long, soft, sensual kiss. Lisa was quite taken with his intoxicating combination of gentleness and passion. She regretted he could not stay for the night, but was confident the appropriate time would come soon.

After another long kiss, Doug asked her to join him on the following Wednesday night at his two-week progress meeting for Tough Love. Lisa quickly said yes. After the session he planned to meet and tell Dominic he would no longer be selling drugs for him. They kissed some more and then whispered their final goodnights. As Doug drove home, he felt happy, satisfied and content.

CHAPTER 16

THE NEXT SEVERAL days were among the most emotionally satisfying for Doug. The people in his life noticed how calm and content he seemed. He treated his parents with a respect and politeness they had seldom seen. Michael enjoyed a few more tutoring sessions on WoW, although Michael often found Doug behind his locked door as if working on some secret project.

Wednesday was the second two-week progress meeting at Tough Love. Enrollees were encouraged to bring a non-parent close friend. Doug felt good that Lisa had agreed to join him. He also felt apprehensive about his planned meeting with Dominic.

Before leaving Doug retrieved from his safe the package of drugs he had acquired from Dominic. He slipped on his leather jacket and shoved the brown wrapped bundle of drugs inside his coat making sure the package was completely concealed. Before leaving he snuck into Greg's office and retrieved his butterfly knife from the gun safe. He did not expect to use it but he felt safer with it. He tucked it in his jeans, bolted down the stairs and hopped into his truck. He placed the drugs in the glove compartment and locked it. Then he headed out to Lisa's home.

Lisa was waiting when Doug pulled into her driveway at 6:30. He looked into her eyes, cupped her face and kissed her lips.

"Thanks for agreeing to come with me tonight," he whispered.

"I'm glad you asked me along to both outings," she replied, referring not only to the Tough Love session but also to Doug's meeting with Dominic.

"Are you sure you want to go to the park with me afterward?" Doug asked.

"Absolutely. Tonight marks the start of a new chapter in your life. I want to be there with you."

///

They took their seats just before Sgt. Mallory called the meeting to order. He welcomed the dozen or so guests. A behavioral scientist professor gave an entertaining yet informative talk on the challenges of communicating effectively between generations, and some techniques for improvement. Doug was surprised to see Lisa so engrossed in the talk.

Afterwards, the participants were split out into smaller groups according to age, gender and degree of emotional instability. Doug's group consisted of three others with similar issues as himself. A counselor led a discussion among the members of the group and invited input and feedback from the guests. Lisa talked about peer pressures and unrealistic expectations.

All of the attendees were eventually brought back into the main meeting room. Sgt. Mallory addressed the group and reminded the participants that they needed signatures attesting their attendance. Doug also had to provide evidence he had attended his anger management classes and passed drug tests. He presented this to Sgt. Mallory who congratulated him on his progress and improved attitude. Sgt. Mallory also thanked Lisa for having attended and wished her a good evening.

Doug and Lisa walked down the metal stairs to his truck. He helped her climb inside. She sensed Doug was becoming nervous.

As he turned on the ignition, Lisa reached to his hand. "Sweetheart, are you sure you want to do this?"

"What do you mean?"

"I mean confronting Dominic. Couldn't you just walk away from him?"

"No way. I mean, it's like, I still have all his drugs. He's going to be expecting me to purchase more. If I don't show up he'd just send Raven after me, that hair-slicked guy. He's not someone I want to tangle with. I hear he's already killed one guy, and maybe more."

"I guess you're right," Lisa said. "Better to just end this thing tonight."

"Oh, I know I'm right. I have to return his drugs, tell him I'm done slinging dope, and ask for my thousand bucks back."

Lisa saw Doug's determination and felt hopeful that Doug's newfound maturity and responsibility would bring them closer together than ever before.

Doug pulled into the park and drove toward the corner where Dominic hung out. The far end of the paved lot was roped off for maintenance, so Doug took the first available spot near the entrance. He noticed the two familiar Harleys parked nearby. Doug unlocked the glove compartment and pulled out the large, brown package. Lisa's eyes widened as she realized what was inside. He stashed the bundle inside his jacket and walked around the truck to help Lisa out.

They sauntered toward the dimly lit end of the lot. Half way there Doug noticed Dominic standing close to Raven at the far side.

"Did you bring the next bundle of candy for our friend here?" Dominic asked Raven.

"Sure did, boss."

"Were you able to get the headies?" Dominic inquired, referring to even higher quality marijuana they were able to obtain from a contact from Ramon Tartikov.

"All wrapped up nice and neat along with meth and blow."

"Good. Bring it out."

"Will do. I'll hit the head on the way. That Cajun food's not being agreeable."

Dominic chuckled. "Still getting used to Southern cooking."

"Guess so."

Raven started walking toward the restrooms.

"That guy scares me," Lisa whispered.

"He scares a lot of people."

As Doug and Lisa approached, Dominic called out.

"Hey, bro."

"How ya doing?" Doug replied.

"The question is, how you're doing?"

"We're doing okay. Don't know if you remember my girlfriend. This is Lisa."

"Yes it is," Dominic joked. "I may not remember the name, but I never forget a face."

"Right."

"She was here the night you pulled that drunk off of Tanya," Dominic recalled.

"Right on."

Dominic gave Lisa a forced grin and then immediately turned his attention back to Doug.

"I guess we all had some extra walking to do tonight with the lot being torn up. We saw your bikes parked at the other end."

Lisa decided this might be an opportunity for her to pay him a compliment. "Your bikes look beautiful. All that polished chrome's really impressive."

Dominic grinned, not expecting the compliment.

"We saw Raven heading back the other way," Doug said.

"Yeah. He's going to pick up the next buddle of candy for you. You sold all of your first batch, right?"

Doug hesitated for a minute. He looked over at Lisa who had a very concerned look on her face.

"Well, not exactly," Doug said quietly.

"Maybe not all of the hard stuff but you were able to move all the weed, yes?" Dominic asked.

Doug shifted his weight from one foot to the other. His eyes moved away from Dominic and scanned the surrounding area for a second. Dominic was growing suspicious.

Finally Doug spoke. "Well, the fact is I didn't sell any of it."

"What?" Dominic sounded incredulous.

"I've decided I won't be slinging drugs anymore."

Dominic's voice was dripping with sarcasm as he growled, "Oh *you've decided*, have you? Well, a deal's a deal, dude. There's no backing out."

Doug tried to explain. "I've been in a lot of trouble at school and at home, and this just isn't a good time."

Dominic was seething. If word got out that a key dealer

pulled out on his own, Dominic's reputation, and his plans for expanding his drug empire, could be damaged. He was not about to let that happen.

Dominic stepped forward with his face only inches from Doug's as he gritted through his teeth. "Oh, this isn't a good time for you?"

Dominic paused as if for effect and took a deep breath. Then he continued literally in Doug's face. "Well, you have no idea. This is definitely not a good time for me. And when it's not a good time for me it means that's a real problem for you."

Doug was just staring at Dominic who then raised his voice. "I've got shipments coming in based on your estimates, you crazy little bitch. Why would you even think that you could back out now?"

Doug took a few steps back and tried one last time to reason with Dominic. He opened his jacket and pulled out the package of drugs.

Doug spoke quietly and hesitantly. "Here, I really need to give this back to you. And I really need the thousand dollars back."

Doug tried to hand the package to Dominic, but he would not extend his arms, so Doug laid the bundle on a nearby bench.

Dominic almost chuckled as he replied, "Oh, you think this deal had a money-back guarantee or something?"

"Please."

"Are you out of your mind? No way, man, a deal is a deal. I've already ordered that new shipment. You think I can just cancel this?"

Doug was losing patience and fired back, "I think for as long as you've been dealing drugs you ought to have some say in cancelling an order."

No one had spoken to Dominic like that in years, least of all an unproven teenager.

Doug felt his confidence, and his anger, grow as he scoffed at Dominic. "Otherwise, maybe you're not as big a drug king as you think you are."

Doug applied the techniques he had learned at anger management, taking a deep breath and clearing his head by thinking of more pleasant memories. Lisa was growing concerned that the arguing would escalate.

Dominic grabbed Doug by the zippered edges of his open leather jacket and shoved him. "Why, you ungrateful, stupid bitch."

Lisa moved toward them and said to Dominic, "Please. Could you just give him his money?"

Dominic kept staring at Doug and sneered, "Oh, so what, now your skank does your talking?"

Doug was just about at his boiling point. "Leave her out of this."

Doug's mind was racing. He wanted to lash out at this thug who was bullying him and his girlfriend, but he knew if his fast-growing anger turned into full-blown rage it could lead to something much worse.

Doug started taking deep breaths. The gulps of oxygen slowly worked their effects like a magic tonic. Calmness began permeating his body. He glanced over at Lisa as if to reassure her and then turned back to Dominic.

"I just want my money back, okay? I've brought your drugs back untouched. The package has not been opened. I really need the cash."

Dominic stepped forward and once more was just inches from Doug's face. Dominic grabbed Doug's jacket again and spoke in a mocking voice, "So you just want your money back, is that all you want?"

Doug remained silent. Dominic released his grips on Doug's jacket. Then he used a menacing tone to say again, "I asked you a question. Are you deaf as well as stupid?"

Doug almost reacted instantly and felt his fury boiling. "I just need my money back."

"Yo, wrong on both counts, bitch. First of all, it's not your money. It's my money, for me to do with as I please. And second, you're not getting it back. If you need more money, here's an easy way to do it." Dominic moved a few steps to his side and picked up the brown wrapped package and shoved it into Doug's chest. "Sling your drugs."

Doug forcibly shoved the package back at Dominic. "I said I'm not doing this anymore."

"Oh, so you just think you are entitled to walk away? Is that what you think?"

Lisa sensed things were escalating and grabbed Doug's arm. "Come on, Doug. Let's go."

Dominic heard Lisa's comment and mockingly said to Doug, "You think you can just up and go because your slut of a girlfriend tells you?"

With his left hand Dominic grabbed Doug around the neck while using his right hand to pull out his gun. He pressed the barrel against Doug's temple. "You think you're entitled to walk out on this? Well, you can't. You're a loser and she's a whore. You're gonna own up to your end of the bargain or your whore will be picking up your splattered brains."

All of the pent up rage that Doug had tried so hard to suppress came bubbling up to the surface. It caused him to instantly but temporarily snap. Focusing all his strength to his right hand, he grabbed Dominic's wrist and smashed the back of it onto the top of the picnic table. The gun went flying underneath the table and landed in a small hidden crevice. Then he pushed Dominic backward with a powerful thrust.

Dominic was momentarily stunned by the action. He looked into Doug's eyes and had never seen such rage or hatred staring back at him. As Dominic tried to comprehend what was going on, Doug reached into his pocket and pulled out his butterfly knife. In one swift fluid motion he opened the knife, exposed its deadly blade and locked it securely in place. Never before had he unlocked his weapon so quickly and so expertly.

Doug pointed the knife up at Dominic's throat. "Give me my money, now."

He intended only to frighten Dominic into giving his money back, just as Doug had intended only to scare Greg weeks earlier. But Dominic anticipated Doug's move and deftly intercepted the motion by grasping Doug's right wrist that was holding the knife. Dominic tightened his grip on Doug, but Doug held onto his weapon as if it were locked into a vise.

Dominic hissed. "So what, bitch, you think you can stab me for your money? I don't think so."

With a huge surge Dominic twisted Doug's forearm back to where the knife was now pointing at Doug's ribcage. Doug countered with a move that pointed the knife out and away from him. What Doug did not know was that Dominic had mastered a few martial arts moves and would be able to work Doug's leverage against him.

"Stop! Stop, please," Lisa cried out desperately. Her phone was in her purse back in Doug's truck but she did not want to leave. She could not believe what she was witnessing. She tried looking for the gun but could not find it. She so much wanted to do something, anything but she felt utterly helpless.

The blade slashed the left side of Doug's abdomen. He ignored the stinging sensation but realized he now was fighting for his life. He gathered all his strength to thrust the knife toward Dominic. Acting on instinct, Dominic turned slightly. The blade cut threw Dominic's jacket and left a three-inch gash in his right forearm.

"Son of a bitch!" Dominic yelled. He used all of his know-how and brute strength to twist Doug's wrist back. Dominic then plunged the knife deep into Doug's mid-section and snarled, "You stupid little bitch."

Doug let out a blood-curdling scream. He felt the knife penetrate his skin. The razor-sharp blade severed arteries and organs in its path. The pain was unbearable. It shot through his body like hot scalding liquids. Blood poured through his shirt and jacket as his knees buckled and hit the ground.

"No!" Lisa screamed. She stood frozen, unable to think or feel anything.

Dominic looked satisfied as he pulled the knife back out of his victim. Doug groaned and pressed his hands against the wound, trying to stop the bleeding. He felt faint and cold as his heart raced. His legs buckled as he collapsed. Lisa ran over to him screaming for someone to help. Blood oozed from his stomach and from beneath the back of his head.

"Why did you do this? How could you do this?" Lisa cried out at Dominic.

"The little bitch got what he deserved," Dominic said as he walked away.

Raven rushed up to Dominic with his gun pointed toward Doug. "What happened?"

"The dick pulled a knife on me. You believe that?"

"Really. He dead?"

"Probably," Dominic replied. "I shoved his own blade straight up his gut."

Raven cocked his gun. "Well, if he's not, how about I finish him off for you?"

"Don't bother."

"What about the girl?" Raven wanted to know.

"What about the whore?"

"Didn't she see everything?" Raven wanted to know.

"She's hysterical. I'm not sure what exactly she saw, or what she will remember. Besides, Tanya is my alibi tonight." Dominic smiled at Raven. "She'll say I was with her all night."

"Okay." Raven noticed the bloody knife still in Dominic's hand. "Better give me that. I'll take care of it. Here's your gun. I found it under the table."

Dominic handed him the bloody knife. Raven gave him his gun and pulled out a handkerchief and quickly wrapped the weapon several times over in his linen. They both glanced over at Lisa who was now kneeling over Doug and wailing loudly.

"You need to bounce. I'll take care of this," Raven said.

"Okay. Meet me back at the clubhouse in about an hour."

"Later," Raven replied.

Dominic walked quickly toward his Harley and was gone seconds later. Raven ran over to Lisa. She had tried to place Doug's hands over the wound that was still oozing blood. When Raven approached she cowered.

"Shut the hell up," Raven commanded. Lisa was so startled by his authoritative order that she momentarily lost her breath. He knew he had to calm her down and keep her quiet. So he pulled out a black scarf from inside his jacket and placed it in her hands. Then he pushed her hands and scarf firmly on the gaping hole in Doug's abdomen.

"Keep pressing on this, hard, like this." She hesitated so he pressed her palms down on the scarf to cover the wound. Lisa could feel the deep gouge in Doug's stomach as blood flowed between her fingers. She started crying uncontrollably. Her eyes kept moving from the scarf to Doug's face, which looked tortured.

"Baby, come back. Don't give up. Come back. Come back, baby. Please come back."

Raven knew he needed to quiet her down. "Help will be here soon. You need to calm down. I've got to go."

Raven retrieved Doug's smartphone and the drugs and then ran to his Harley. Moments later the motorcycle roared; he was gone.

Doug slipped in and out of consciousness. His eyes rolled back as Lisa kept talking to him. Suddenly she heard sirens in the distance. She saw the flashing lights of an arriving ambulance and a medical vehicle. Never had she been so relieved to experience sirens and blinking red lights.

Lisa pointed to the stab wounds and the medical technicians immediately applied pressure and checked his vital signs. One of them gently lifted his head and inspected it closely. Lisa noticed that he had a sudden look of concern.

"Clark," he said to his medical partner. "Call emergency and tell them we're coming in hot."

CHAPTER 17

IT WAS JUST past ten o'clock on Wednesday evening when the telephone rang. Michael was upstairs playing WoW. Greg was in his home office watching the evening news. Julie was in the family room enjoying a romantic movie while going through emails.

As Julie answered, she half expected it to be Doug asking if he could stay out later. The voice on the other end of the line was definitely not her son's.

"Mrs. MacDonald?"

Julie heard sobbing. "Yes? Who is this?"

"This is Lisa, Lisa Gilbert."

"Oh, yes, I know, Lisa," Julie said. "What is wrong? Are you and Doug okay? Is everything all right?"

"No, Mrs. MacDonald," Lisa answered but then was interrupted by an outpouring of her sobbing. "We are not okay. Doug was stabbed. It's really bad. They're taking him to the hospital."

Lisa had been talking so fast and crying so hard that Julie could barely understand her.

"Lisa, slow down. What are you saying? It sounded like you

said Doug was grabbed."

"No," Lisa kept crying. She took a few deep breaths to compose herself. "He was stabbed. He was stabbed in his stomach. Twice."

"What!?" Julie slumped and shouted back into the phone. "Where is he now? How is he?"

Julie's voice was so loud that Greg heard her clear back in his office. He rushed out to the kitchen. Julie's distress was obvious. He tried to communicate with her, but she was trying desperately to calm Lisa down to get more information. Finally, Julie looked at her husband and said, "Doug's been stabbed."

"Where was he? Who did it? Why? Who are you talking to?"

"To Lisa. Let me talk to her," Julie pleaded with Greg. Then to Lisa she asked, "Where did they take him?"

Lisa replied between sobs, "Atlanta General."

"Where are you right now?"

"Stephenson Park. I tried to go to the hospital with Doug, but they wouldn't let me ride along."

Julie passed the information on to Greg. "That park is very large. Does she know what part she's in?"

"You take Parkway Drive into the entrance, past the Southeast Portal and turn right. I'm in Doug's truck at the start of the parking lot. I've got his keys. Would it be okay if I drove Doug's truck over to the hospital?"

"Stay there. We'll pick you up on the way to the hospital," Julie said. "Have you talked to your mom?"

"I sent her a text message."

"Well, you should keep trying to contact her. Use your phone and email in case her texts aren't getting through. Stay right where you are. We'll be there as soon as we can. And have your mom call us as soon as you hear from her, okay?"

"Okay."

As Julie ended the call Michael walked in and asked, "What's going on?"

There was no easy way to tell him so Greg just said, "Your brother was stabbed at Stephenson Park and was taken to Atlanta General."

Michael froze and shot a quick glance toward his mother. "Seriously?"

"I'm afraid so," Julie said softly. "Your father and I are getting ready to leave."

Michael looked frightened and near tears.

"We're going to the park to pick up Lisa and get Doug's truck on our way to the hospital," Greg explained.

"Well, I'm going, too. He's my brother. I want to see him as much as you do."

Julie could see the anguish on Michael's face and knew she could not refuse. She nodded toward her husband who reluctantly agreed.

///

Before leaving Greg checked his gun safe. He was relieved to see his firearm but immediately noticed the knife missing. As the three of them walked out into the garage and climbed into the family Lexus, Michael asked, "So, like, who did this?"

"We don't know yet," Julie responded.

"Was Lisa there when it happened?"

"Yes," Julie again responded to her son.

"Well, so, like, whoever did it, do we know why?" Michael persisted.

Greg could tell that his wife was starting to grow impatient with all of their son's questions. So he decided to intervene, gently but firmly.

"Michael, you are asking good questions. We all want answers, but we don't have any yet. Let's wait until we pick up Lisa and see what more she can tell us. I plan to call our detective friend Jim Barnett and ask what he can find out. For now let's just hope you're brother is okay."

They arrived at the park and rushed over to Lisa now outside the truck. They hugged as Julie tried to soothe her, while struggling to remain calm. Everyone wanted to get to the hospital immediately.

Greg decided he would drive his son's truck to the hospital and that Julie would drive the family car.

"Michael, you ride with your mother. Lisa, you come with me."

They quickly drove off and within seconds Greg asked for details.

"So, tell me what happened, everything."

Lisa drew in a breath. She was reluctant to reveal Doug's drug dealing but felt compelled to tell Doug's father the truth. She recounted her experience of barely an hour earlier and described the attacker. She believed his name was Dominic and may have led a motorcycle gang. She described Dominic's unnamed bodyguard as being really scary and vicious.

"It was horrible, Mr. MacDonald. He put a gun to Doug's head and then they were struggling with the knife. I think Doug may have cut Dominic's arm, but not too deeply. Because Dominic was able to shove the knife into Doug. He screamed in so much pain. Then he fell back to the ground."

Lisa started crying uncontrollably. Greg tried to console her.

"Take it easy. It wasn't your fault. Let's just hope he's okay. My God, what a nightmare."

Greg called Jim after Lisa calmed down. The detective was surprised to hear from his friend so late into the evening.

"Greg, how are you? Is everything okay?"

"Jim. I'm sorry to be calling you so late, but Doug was just stabbed at Stephenson Park."

"Oh my God. How is he?"

"Julie and Michael are in my car and I'm in Doug's truck with his girlfriend. We're headed to Atlanta General. It sounds bad, Jim, real bad. Lisa was with him. She told us the paramedics were very concerned."

"Did Lisa know the attacker?"

"She thought his name was Dominic and may head up some gang."

"Sounds like Dominic Williams," Jim said.

"You know him?"

"The guys in the gang unit know of a banger by that name. He leads a motorcycle gang called the Raptors."

"Damn."

"Well, we can't be certain until we get a positive identification."

"Are you saying you need Lisa to identify this thug?"

"The sooner the better, Greg, while it's still fresh in her mind."

"Really? You mean tonight?"

"That would be best. Tell you what. I'll head down to

headquarters and pick up some photos for her to view at the hospital. It'll take me an hour."

"You're sure you need this done right now? It's almost eleven o'clock and Lisa is still pretty shook up."

"Greg, I not only need to do this. I want to do this, and not just to get the photos to Lisa. I want to be there for you and your family. I can only imagine what you're going through."

"Thanks, Jim. I hope you can re-connect with your own son, sometime soon."

"See you shortly, buddy. Drive safe."

///

Atlanta General, with fully staffed trauma centers, was the best-equipped hospital in the region. Both Michael and Doug had been born there. The four walked into emergency together, expecting few people to be inside. They were surprised to see several dozen patients and family members sitting throughout the large seating area.

Greg strode up to admissions and a receptionist at the counter smiled and asked pleasantly, "May I help you?"

"Hi. I understand my son, Doug MacDonald, was brought here a short time ago."

"Okay. Let me see." The woman entered a few commands into her flat-screen computer, waited a second and then entered another. "Is it 'Mc' or 'Mac'?"

"Mac."

"Here it is. Douglas MacDonald, age seventeen?" she asked.

"Yes," Greg replied. Julie stood next to him with Michael and Lisa right behind.

The receptionist's face changed from cheerful to serious. "He's in our trauma center. I'll get an attendant to escort you." A hospital technician led them down a long hall and then turned left a short way to a small waiting room.

The attendant motioned to a nurse who was standing behind an open counter to come over and assist them.

The nurse put down her papers and walked around the counter.

The nurse looked over at Greg and Julie, and then glanced over at Michael and Lisa who were standing behind them.

"Hello. I'm Amy Johnson. The doctor and others are treating your son right now."

Greg sounded worried. "Can you tell us about his condition?"

"The doctor will be able to brief you shortly."

"Mrs. MacDonald, why don't we all sit down for a minute?" She led them over to a couch and three stuffed chairs around a coffee table off to the side of the room where they all took a seat.

She glanced over at Lisa and Michael, and then looked directly at Greg and Julie.

"Your son has suffered deep stab wounds to his abdomen. The wound is very serious and requires emergency surgery. He's lost a lot of blood. Dr. Martello is treating him right now. He'll be able to tell you more of the details. Why don't you try to make yourselves comfortable? If you would like some coffee or other beverages, there is a machine just off the main lobby."

///

Nearly an hour had elapsed when Greg's cell phone started vibrating. It was Jim calling to say he was pulling into the hospital parking lot. He wanted to know where Greg and Lisa would be located. Greg told him where they were and gave him instructions on how to get there.

A few minutes later Greg was shaking the hand of his best friend. "Hi, Jim. Thanks for coming."

"Of course. How is Doug?"

"Not good." Greg took a deep breath. "The doctor is supposed to brief us any minute."

Greg saw that Jim was holding a manila folder and presumed they were the photographs he said he would bring along for Lisa to look at. Realizing that the two people had likely never met, Greg introduced them.

"Jim, this is Lisa Gilbert. She's Doug's girlfriend who was with him tonight when it happened." Then, turning to Lisa, he said, "Lisa, meet Detective Jim Barnett of the Atlanta Police Department. He is a trusted friend of the family."

The two took a step forward to shake hands with each telling the other it was nice to meet. Greg had arranged with the nurse for a small private room for Lisa and Jim where Lisa could try to identify Dominic from four photographs. Jim led Lisa into the room and closed the door.

Ten minutes later Jim and Lisa walked back to the sitting area. Lisa looked distressed. Greg glanced at Jim who appeared somber. He shook his head side to side. Greg sensed Lisa could not positively identify Doug's attacker. Julie saw how troubled Lisa seemed and walked over to give her a slight hug. Instinctively, Michael came over and tenderly held Lisa's hand. She was surprised at Michael's gesture, but clearly appreciated his kind action.

For a few minutes the five of them stood soundless and motionless. There were no other individuals close by and the stillness brought an eeriness to the situation. Suddenly the silence was broken with the pounding sound of the opening of the two heavy swing doors leading into the trauma center.

All five turned to watch as a middle-aged doctor walked through. He was tall and slim and wore wire rim glasses. His light-blue scrubs still had splotches of blood on them. He surveyed the scene in the waiting room and quickly surmised that Greg and Julie were the parents of the patient he had just treated.

"Hello. Are you the parents of Douglas MacDonald?"

"Yes," Greg replied.

"I'm Doctor Dennis Martello. My team and I have been treating your son. We have been able to repair some of the damage to his internal organs, but he is still in critical condition. He has sustained two major lacerations to his abdomen and lost a substantial amount of blood. He has received several blood transfusions and is on IVs."

As the doctor paused, Julie asked, "Doctor, will he make a full recovery?"

"It's too soon to tell."

Julie and Greg were stunned. Julie grabbed Greg's arm and asked, "What do you mean?"

"Your son experienced an extradural hematoma, a severe traumatic brain injury. Something struck the back of his head with significant force and it caused a buildup of blood between the outer membrane of the upper spine and the inside of the skull. We will have to monitor this constantly for the next few days. The buildup of blood could increase pressure on the intracranial space that may compress delicate brain tissues and cause the brain to shift. That could cause critical problems for recovery."

Julie started tearing up as she hesitantly asked the doctor, "Are you saying he may not come out of this?"

Doctor Martello reached out to Julie's arm and tried to comfort her "It is much too soon to speculate about that. We are doing all we can at this point."

Greg glanced over at Michael who was holding back his own tears. Then he held onto Julie's other arm to offer more comfort. Greg asked the doctor, "Can we go in to see him?"

"Yes, but only a few at a time. He is unconscious and may remain that way for several hours or even a day or two. A patient's reaction to this type of injury is very difficult to predict. He could regain consciousness at any time and could appear completely normal. This is called a lucid interval, but just as quickly he could descend rapidly back into unconsciousness. We will have MRI results back shortly, which will help with diagnosing the epidural hemorrhaging."

Julie turned to Michael and Lisa. "I know you want to see Doug, but why don't your father and I go in first?"

The two teens slowly shook their heads affirmatively. The doctor led Greg and Julie into the intensive care unit recovery area to Doug's bed. He was the only patient there. They expected that Doug's chest would be heavily bandaged, but were surprised to see his head was similarly covered in heavy white gauze. His face was partly visible, but his eyes were closed. He had an IV in his left forearm and several other monitors on his right hand and chest.

Julie petted his face and started sobbing. Greg stroked the bare portion of his son's arm and hugged his wife with his other hand. Julie tried to hold back her tears. She was shocked and angry, but knew she needed to be strong for herself, for Michael and especially for Doug. The two parents looked at and prayed for their son. They remained motionless for a while. Finally Julie kissed Doug's forehead and suggested they leave so that the others could visit him.

As they left the room, Greg told Julie he would stay with Jim and that she could bring Michael and Lisa back with her to see Doug. Julie held onto Michael's and Lisa's hands as they walked into Doug's area. Julie tried to remain strong as the two teens starting sobbing when they saw the usually invincible Doug lying so helpless and almost comatose.

Julie decided to leave the two teens with Doug and left the room. Lisa tenderly patted Doug's cheek as Michael watched the IV transferring fluids into Doug's left hand. Suddenly, something caught Michael's eye.

He stared more intently and saw it again. Doug's left index finger twitched. Seconds later he extended his curved finger straight out.

"Lisa," Michael cried out. "Doug moved his finger."

Lisa looked at Doug's hand and saw it bend and uncurl several of his fingers. Then his right hand started. Finally he moved his head gently from side to side.

"Oh my God," Michael said loudly

"Doug is coming to," Lisa whispered excitedly.

"I'm going to get Mom. She needs to see this."

Michael ran out of the room and within seconds Julie and Greg were alongside their son's bed as Lisa reluctantly stepped back. Doug slowly opened his eyes but could not recognize who was there. He tried to blink, but it was too tiring for him.

Julie gently held his hand and whispered, "Sweetie, this is Mom. Dad and Michael and Lisa are here also. Just try to rest. You're in good hands, so just take it easy."

Doug tried to speak but could not. He moved his head and focused his eyes on those around him. His eyes eventually locked on his mother's face and he smiled. Soon he was able to focus on the others as well. They all smiled back at him, though the tears were starting to well up in everyone.

Greg leaned over and hugged his son as best he could. Michael performed a gentle fist bump with his brother who seemed to smile back. Greg then took Lisa's hand and led her to Doug's side. Lisa looked at her boyfriend with warm, loving eyes that comforted Doug greatly.

"Why don't we let Michael and Lisa spend a few minutes alone with Doug," Greg suggested.

"Okay."

The two parents motioned they would wait outside and walked toward the doors. Greg offered to get Julie a cup of tea.

On his way he phoned Francine who insisted on joining them at the hospital.

As Doug focused on Lisa his eyes lit up. He raised hands and extended them to her. She leaned over and kissed him softly on his lips.

"I love you," she whispered to him. Doug tried to respond but could not. His eyes moistened with joy.

Lisa started tearing up as she held his face in her hands and stroked his forehead, bringing a peaceful look to Doug's face. Minutes later Doug raised his hands as if he needed to tell Lisa something. She noticed a small white board and marker sitting on a table off to the side.

As she picked up the board she asked Doug, "Is this what you want, sweetheart?"

Doug nodded as much as he could. Lisa handed him the pen and held up the board so he could write on it. His hand was shaking as he tried to scrawl a few letters on the board. The first three letters looked like *sav*, though the lines of the *v* looked more vertical and horizontal than diagonal.

The next letters were very difficult for Doug to print out. Lisa sensed his frustration and suggested he try later. Reluctantly, he handed the white board back. After some time had passed Francine arrived and entered the room. She gave her grandson a long, loving hug and offered tender words of encouragement. Then Doug slipped back into a coma.

Outside the room Greg offered to buy Jim a coffee which he readily accepted. On the way to the lobby Greg inquired about Jim's session with Lisa, "So Lisa wasn't able to identify the attacker?"

"Well, she wasn't one hundred percent sure. By protocol I had to show her pictures of others that were similar in appearance. She was pretty shaken up and just couldn't be certain. We may not have a current photo of this guy. But we may be able to put him in a lineup unless he can alibi out."

The two men each sipped a vending machine coffee. It tasted strong and stale, but was piping hot and satisfied their craving for some type of caffeine. They slowly walked back to the intensive care unit waiting room. As they arrived, Julie, Francine, Michael and Lisa came through the doors out of Doug's room. Julie looked drained. Greg hugged his wife and son, as all of them sighed. Greg stepped back and glanced over at Jim. Greg knew that Jim would like to pay a short visit to see Doug, so Greg led Jim into Doug's area.

A few minutes later the two men came out and joined the three others. Julie took Greg aside and said firmly to him. "I'm staying here overnight."

"What? Are you sure?" Greg asked.

"Yes. I want to be here when he wakes up."

"You know the doctor said that could be days."

"I don't care. I want to be here."

"Okay. I'll use Doug's truck to take the kids home. But call me as soon as he awakes, no matter the time."

Julie looked into her husband's eyes. She knew he was hurting as much as she and she loved him dearly for it. They kissed tenderly. Julie hugged Michael and Lisa and then they were gone. Julie found her way to the hospital's chapel and prayer room. She contemplated privately the future of her son and prayed for his recovery.

CHAPTER 18

THURSDAY AFTERNOON FRANCINE picked Michael up from school and drove to the hospital. Doug was still comatose. Michael grew quiet after seeing Doug still motionless. Francine tried to offer comforting words, but to no avail. Michael kept dwelling on how his relationship with Doug had started improving, and now this. Francine and Michael eventually hugged Julie good-bye and headed for home. An hour later Greg pulled into the hospital parking lot.

As he walked down the hallway toward the intensive care unit he detected the faint scent of antiseptics. He opened the door to Doug's area and took in the scene. Two other patients in less serious condition had joined Doug. Julie sat next to Doug and looked exhausted. She had not slept much in almost two days. The lack of sleep and the strain of urging her son to regain consciousness had clearly taken its toll. Her eyes drooped with bags and her face was etched with lines of maternal worry.

She welcomed the sight of her husband and the thought of him relieving her. Greg was concerned she might be too tired to drive but she convinced him otherwise. He agreed only after she promised to call when she arrived home.

Minutes after entering her kitchen, Julie called a relieved Greg and chatted briefly. Then she checked on Michael, who was finishing homework. They talked about Doug's condition with little new to report.

"Have you eaten?"

"I heated up the left over pork chops, vegetables and stuffing," Michael replied.

"Good. I'll think I'll do the same." Julie yawned. "But I'm really more tired than hungry."

"You look tired, Mom. You should go to bed."

"I will. But I need something to eat first. You know Grandma is taking you to school tomorrow, right?

"Yeah, I know."

Julie gave Michael a hug and kiss goodnight and then went downstairs to have a small meal. A short time later she entered her bedroom. She had just spent twenty hours at Doug's bedside, desperately wanting to be there when he regained consciousness, but the moment never arrived. She collapsed from exhaustion on top of her plush king-sized comforter and was instantly asleep.

Before long a buzzing sound stirred her awake. She blinked her eyes trying to focus on her alarm clock and saw it was nine-thirty at night. As the buzzing sound continued she realized her cell phone was ringing from inside her purse.

Frantically, Julie jumped up and flew over to her purse on the dresser. She was certain it was Greg calling about Doug. She braced herself in the event Doug had taken a turn for the worse, though she could not imagine his condition being more dire.

She fumbled with the fastener on her purse, struggling to open it before the phone stopped ringing. With shaking fingers she pressed the button for connection. As she was about to speak she noticed the ID indicated unknown caller. Sadly she asked, "Hello? Who is this?"

"This is Sam Philips. I run the county's anger management program. I am calling about Douglas MacDonald."

"Oh, I see." Julie could feel tears welling up at hearing her son's name. "This is Julie MacDonald. I'm Doug's mother."

"Mrs. MacDonald, I'm afraid I have some bad news for you. Douglas did not show up tonight. You probably know, one unexcused absence is grounds for expulsion. I will have to recommend he be removed from the program."

The events of the past twenty-four hours resulted in Julie and Greg completely forgetting to notify Doug's teachers and counselors, including Sam.

As she thought about what had happened to Doug, Julie was momentarily overcome with grief. She began sobbing into the phone, unable to speak a word.

"Mrs. MacDonald, I understand how disappointed you must be. Perhaps if you and your husband came in with Doug to discuss this, we could consider making an exception."

"No, it isn't that, Mr. Philips," Julie said.

"I'm not sure I understand."

Julie inhaled deeply. "Doug was stabbed last night."

"What? Oh, no. Where?"

"He was at Stephenson Park. It looks like it may have been gang related. But he also suffered a severe injury to the back of his head. He came to briefly but fell back into unconsciousness."

"Oh my Lord. I am so sorry to hear this. I had no idea."

"I'm sorry we didn't call you. My husband and I have been keeping vigil at his bedside so we'd be there when he awakens again."

"I understand. I was surprised when he didn't show up tonight and wondered what might have happened."

"He said he was starting to get something out of your classes. We were hopeful they would help him."

"I believe he was benefiting from our program. He seemed to be more self-aware."

"Yes."

"Mrs. MacDonald, is there anything I can do?"

"No. Not at this time. Nothing I can think of. But thank you. We will keep you posted."

Julie placed her phone on her nightstand with the ringer set loud. She did not want to miss Greg's call informing her Doug had awakened. The call never came.

Dawn broke with bright sunlight streaming through the narrow slits of Julie's venetian blinds. Normally the illumination would awaken her but not this morning. In her exhausted state she forgot to set the alarm and slept through the sunrise and three hours beyond. Minutes after nine o'clock Julie awoke, surprised at the time. She immediately grabbed her phone to call Greg.

"Hi, sweetheart. How is Doug? Has there been any change?"

Greg sounded somber. "No. He hasn't moved a muscle. They've changed his bandages a few times. That's all. The doctor said a brain specialist will be conferring with him later."

"That's good. I want to hear what the specialist says."

"I agree, sweetheart," Greg replied.

"I can't believe the time. I forgot the alarm and slept in."

"It's probably good you did. You needed rest."

"I guess."

"Francine called when she picked up Michael. They knew how tired you were and let you sleep. She had Michael finish breakfast and ensured he had lunch money. She left you a note in the kitchen."

"Wow. I'll have to call and thank her."

"Speaking of calls, have you contacted Eric?" Greg asked referring to Julie's boss.

"No. I'll call your mom next and then I'll phone him. He'd like an update on Doug's condition. He's really concerned and has been great about understanding my need for time off."

Greg welcomed Julie relieving him at Doug's bedside but assured her she need not rush. He suggested softly, "Sweetie, take your time getting ready. You need to prepare well in case it's another long night."

"Thanks, honey. I know. I'll try to arrive around noon. Francine will pick up Michael from school. Michael has a half day so they will join me at the hospital around one."

They expressed their love and then said goodbye.

/ / /

Just before noon Greg returned from the hospital cafeteria with a Cobb salad and iced tea. He noticed that the two new patients had been moved out.

"Good for them," he thought. "I hope they're doing well."

He stared at Doug. Nurses had changed the bandages on his head twice and two additional monitors had been affixed to his chest. Greg thought about the previous Friday evening Doug and he had shared, and how special it had been. His son had been so honest, so brutally candid, so adult. Greg had looked forward to repeating evenings like that, but now he was uncertain if another memorial night like that would ever occur again. Greg took another bite of salad and said a short but heartfelt prayer pleading for his son to get well.

As he finished his lunch the door opened. It was Julie. She was carrying a beige colored throw pillow and a small booklet. Pushing his table slightly to his side, Greg stood and extended his arms.

"Here, babe, let me have those."

"Okay. Thanks."

Greg placed the pillow on his chair and the booklet on the table next to his food tray. Freed of the two articles, Greg walked back and hugged and kissed his wife. Julie paused and slowly looked over at Doug.

She studied every part of his bandaged body as if trying to spot something out of place that she could remedy. Finding nothing to fix, she just silently watched him. Eventually she tenderly kissed his forehead and softly rubbed the back of his right palm. Her eyes followed the various plastic tubes that led from Doug's arms to their associated monitors. The faint blips emitting from the machines were the only sounds she heard.

Julie studied Doug's face. His head was bandaged but his face was exposed. His eyes were closed and his breathing was labored. His expression looked strained. She hoped he was not in much pain, but more than anything she wanted him to wake up again. She wanted to see his beautiful blue eyes that could convey so many emotions. She wanted to hear his voice that could communicate so many sentiments. She wanted to feel his hand that could touch hers in so many ways.

Greg saw how deep in thought his wife was and stood back quietly. Eventually Julie turned to face him.

"Just when he seemed to be doing better."

Greg remained silent so Julie repeated her comment.

"Don't you think he was starting to do better? I mean with the Tough Love Program and the anger management classes?"

"I can tell you, sweetheart, he was definitely doing better. When we went out for pizza last week he shared things with me that he never would have brought up before."

Julie added, "And his relationship with Michael is so much better."

Julie sat next to Doug's bed. Greg moved to the other side and sat on a folding chair. The two of them alternated looking at Doug and then at each other. Time passed until a nurse entered and spoke quietly.

"I just heard from Doctor Drake who specializes in brain injuries. He's been reviewing the results from your son's tests. The doctor would like to discuss these with you. Could you plan to meet with him here in about thirty minutes?"

The nurse checked on the various tubes and wires attached to Doug and studied their associated monitors. As she smiled a good-bye, Greg's iPhone buzzed. It was detective Jim Barnett.

"Hi, Jim."

"Hi, Greg. How's your son doing today?"

"The same. He's still unconscious. We're meeting with his brain specialist soon."

"Good. I met with the paramedics who treated Doug Wednesday. We inspected the scene of the attack as part of the investigation."

"Oh? Did you turn up anything?"

"The paramedics showed me where Doug fell. There was still a lot of dried blood on the grass.

"Then I started feeling underneath the grass where his head would have been laying."

Jim paused for a second and then continued, "Greg, there was a huge rock, almost a small boulder, embedded in the ground with a really jagged edge mostly hidden by the grass. It seems Doug struck his head on the rock when he fell. The paramedics said Doug's gash was consistent with such a fall. I'm sending you photos."

"Wow. So that's how his head got injured?" Greg mused.

"What is it?" Julie asked.

"It's Jim Barnett. They think Doug struck his head on a sharp rock when he fell."

"Oh no," Julie gasped.

Greg said, "Thanks Jim. This may help the doctors."

"That was my thinking. Listen, would it be okay if I brought

Sharon and Cheryl by later to visit with Doug. Cheryl and he used to play youth soccer, and she's been asking how's he's doing. They'd like to offer any help and support Julie needs."

"Yes. That'd be great. But you should all know he may still be unconscious."

"We understand. We'd like to be there for your family. Say around seven?" Jim asked.

"That's fine. One or both of us will be here."

"Okay, Greg, we'll see you then."

"Thanks. Be well."

Greg shared with Julie more of Jim's information concerning Doug's head injury. He showed his wife the photos of the bloody rock Jim had texted over. The graphic images were painful for Julie to view and she eventually turned away.

Twenty minutes later a distinguished looking man in his fifties entered the area. He had salt-and-pepper hair and wore a starched white shirt with a dark blue patterned tie. Julie and Greg immediately looked up.

He walked directly up to Julie and extended his hand saying in a deep voice, "Hello, I'm Doctor David Drake." As he spoke his gaze alternated between Julie and Greg. "I understand you are Julie and Greg MacDonald, the parents of Douglas? Is that correct?"

"Yes," Julie quickly responded.

Doctor Drake shook each of their hands.

"I am the director of the Department of Neurosurgery here. Why don't we go to my office? It's just down the hall on the left."

Doctor Drake had a spacious, well-appointed office with numerous degrees, plagues and awards of distinction which impressed the two parents. The doctor ushered them toward two stuffed armchairs, then sat behind his large mahogany desk.

"Let me start with the good news. We have been able to repair the damage from the two stab wounds. The one to the side of his abdomen did minor damage to his large intestine but they were able to suture that fairly easily. The center cut was deeper and penetrated part of his stomach and liver. Doctor Martello performed successful surgery Thursday to repair those organs."

Julie studied the doctor's face. He had a reassuring expression and sounded knowledgeable without being arrogant.

Julie liked his confident, take-charge demeanor and felt her son was in capable hands.

Greg followed up the doctor's statement with a question, "So those organs will be able to function normally?" Greg asked.

"Yes."

The doctor paused and then continued in a more serious tone. "Unfortunately, your son sustained a very severe head trauma. There are some things I need to tell you about his condition."

Julie looked very worried and glanced over at her husband who looked back. He held her hand in his.

"I specialize in traumatic brain injuries of the type your son sustained. I have treated hundreds of these types of injuries commonly referred to as extradural hematoma. After studying the results of your son's tests I must recommend additional surgery."

"Additional surgery?" Greg asked.

"Yes. The blow to your son's head was a severe traumatic event to his brain. It caused a tremendous buildup of blood between the outer membranes of his brain and the inner parts of his skull. When Doctor Martello operated on his skull early Thursday he surgically removed this buildup and reduced the pressure on his brain. As a result, your son woke up and seemed normal."

"But just as quickly he slipped back into unconsciousness," Doctor Drake explained. "The latest MRI shows the blood is continuing to build up. The pressure on his brain is increasing. The only way to relieve this pressure is to operate again. Because I am advising you of this I will need your permission to proceed. You need to understand the risks involved."

"What are the risks?" Julie asked.

"The risks involve damaging arteries, nerves and especially the delicate membranes of the brain that appear to have been pushed up against the inside of the cranium. I would have to drill what is called a tiny burr hole through each side of your son's skull. It would have to be deep enough to relieve the pressure and remove the blood clots, but not enough to contact brain cells."

"It sounds very precise," Greg remarked.

"It requires extreme precision. Fortunately this is one of the best-equipped hospitals in the country with advanced state-of-the-art machines and facilities. We use high-definition microscopic cameras to assist."

Julie inquired hesitantly, "Have you performed this type of operation before?"

Doctor Drake replied, "Yes. Many times. Successfully. I have been operating a long time. There isn't much I haven't experienced, but each person is unique in terms of cranial matter, brain tissue and membranes, and the formation of arteries and veins. Sometimes I find an arteriovenous malformation."

"What is that?" Julie asked.

"It is an abnormal connection between arteries and veins that bypasses the normally required capillaries. It could locate anywhere in the body but often occurs in the brain where it associates with the central nervous system. It's often congenital. It usually doesn't cause problems unless a head injury occurs. We won't know until we probe inside."

Julie frowned and asked, "What if we choose not to do it?"

Greg looked surprised. The doctor replied, "That is your right. I understand your concern. There are risks with any surgery, but if the swelling isn't stopped, matters will only get worse."

Julie asked Greg what he thought. He whispered back, "I think we have to approve. Don't you?"

Julie replied, "I guess so. It's the thought of drilling into Doug's head. Twice. What if something goes wrong?"

"We trust your judgment and agree to the operation," Greg said.

"Very good. I will have my assistant draw up the papers for you to sign. The sooner we operate the better because the swelling is slowly increasing."

Doctor Drake thanked them and escorted them back to Doug's bedside. His condition had not changed. Soon an assistant came and handed Greg the required papers and informed them Doctor Drake had scheduled Doug's surgery for noon the next day.

Half an hour later Michael and Francine entered. Francine embraced her daughter-in-law who thanked her for coming. Then Francine hugged her son, and looked lovingly and sadly at Doug. Michael also hugged each of his parents and then stared at his brother lying motionless.

Greg suggested to Julie, "Why don't we wait outside to give mom and Michael some time with Doug."

Eventually Greg and Julie joined the others to whisper their prayers and goodnights to Doug. Julie once again insisted on staying throughout the night to be there should her son awake.

///

At eleven o'clock Saturday morning, Doug's family and Lisa stood around his bedside. He was still unconscious. Lisa stroked his forehead. The others tenderly touched his arms, hands and fingers, and offered words of comfort and support.

Suddenly the two heavy metal doors swung open. Two attendants entered the intensive care unit wheeling a heavy-blanketed gurney. They would transport Doug to pre-op. Each person gave Doug a warm embrace in one manner or another, and whispered words of encouragement to him. The two attendants expertly lifted Doug onto the gurney.

As the attendants repositioned Doug, Doctor Drake walked in. He commanded a certain presence whenever he entered a room, and this was no different. Everyone turned to face him. He strode up to the side of Doug's gurney, glancing at the monitors still attached to Doug. Satisfied with the readings, he motioned to the attendants who then wheeled Doug out as Lisa and his family all waved goodbye.

Doctor Drake turned to Greg and Julie. "Your son is in the best possible care. But I suggest you try to get some rest. I know you've been spending much time here, and I understand that."

Julie agreed but said, "I know we should rest. But I just can't go home. Not with my son in surgery."

"I understand. But the operation won't start for an hour while we prep him. The surgery itself will likely take a few hours, and then there may be two or three hours when he will be in intensive care recovery."

Greg asked, "Is there any place here where we could grab some rest or shuteye?"

"Yes, there is a quiet room with couches that you could rest on for several hours. The receptionist in the lobby can show you where it is. I will get word to you as soon as I finish with the operation."

"Thank you, doctor," Julie said. Greg and Julie both shook his hand and said they would be praying for him. Then he turned and exited the room.

"I'd like to go to the chapel and say a prayer," Julie said to her husband and son. The two agreed to do the same, as did Lisa. Lisa had been carrying the white board with her that she had used with Doug the day before. As she walked past a nurse's station she asked one of them if she could make a photocopy of Doug's scribbling. She gladly agreed to do so.

As Julie made her way to the chapel she decided not to wait to begin her prayers. She was a woman of strong faith who started praying as they walked.

CHAPTER 19

AT 3:30 SATURDAY AFTERNOON Greg's cell phone buzzed. "Hello?"

"Hello, Mr. MacDonald. This is Doctor Drake. Your son is out of surgery."

Greg's heart rate and breathing increased. "How is he doing?"

"The pressure on his brain is eased, but I'd prefer to discuss his condition with you and your wife in person."

"Yes. Of course."

The doctor asked, "Are you in the quiet room?"

"Yes."

"Good. I'll be there in ten minutes."

"Okay. Thanks."

Greg slid his phone into his pocket and quietly walked over to awaken his wife.

"Sweetheart," he whispered.

She stirred slightly. "What?"

Greg knelt down and said in a soft voice. "You need to get up."

"Uh, okay," she responded and then started blinking her eyes. "Is Doug out of surgery?"

"Yes. Doctor Drake just called. He'll be here shortly to tell us how Doug is doing."

Julie experienced relief and dread. She wanted to hear about Doug's condition, hopeful the news would be encouraging. Yet she sensed all was not well. "Why would the doctor want to come in person?" she wondered.

Greg crouched over and helped Julie sit upright. He sensed her anxiety and silently stroked her hand. He felt just as concerned, but wanted to be strong for her and Michael.

Minutes later Dr. Drake walked in. His demeanor was somber as he pulled up a chair.

"Douglas is resting comfortably. I performed two craniotomies on your son's brain that significantly reduced the pressure."

Julie felt guardedly optimistic. "So that's a good thing, correct?"

"Yes. A very good thing, and the wounds to his abdomen are healing well."

The doctor paused, then continued.

"Unfortunately the injury to your son's brain is far more serious than it first appeared."

"What do you mean?" Julie asked.

"Your son sustained a major traumatic event to his head. He received appropriate treatment soon after the injury, and has been under constant observation. Pressure has been building up inside his skull ever since the accident. The operation Doctor Martello performed Thursday released some of that pressure. My surgery relieved more of it. Unfortunately, these procedures are only delaying the inevitable."

"The inevitable?" Greg questioned.

Doctor Drake briefly rubbed his hands as he looked at both parents. "Blood has been seeping into your son's brain for the past three days. We slowed it yesterday, but there's more damage to his membranes and brain tissue than tests first showed."

"How do you know this?" Greg asked.

"I drilled two tiny holes large enough to insert what is called an endoscope. This is a thin flexible tube with a light and camera on its end. I used the tube to insert tools which were used to clean out the massive blood clots, and that's when the extent of the damage became apparent."

"So just how extensive is it?" Julie asked.

"There are thousands of arteries and nerve endings in the human brain that control virtually every function of the body. While it is hard to calculate, I would estimate that up to ten percent of your son's brain was damaged beyond repair."

Julie started sobbing and Greg to hugged her. The doctor went on. "Despite our best efforts, the swelling in his brain is continuing to increase."

Doctor Drake had a pained look on his face. "I am so sorry." He paused and adjusted his sitting position. "For you and your family."

Julie cleared her throat and between sobs. "Doctor, he gestured to us yesterday. He looked directly at me. He looked like he was getting better."

"I understand. I know that on the outside he looked like he was improving. That he motioned. He grasped your hand."

"Yes. Exactly," Julie agreed firmly. "So couldn't that mean he's coming out of this?"

"Unfortunately no. We know now that the damage to your son's brain is irreversible. There is no longer any neuron activity in his brain and there is no longer any oxygen flowing to it. It is just a matter of time before his vital organs start to shut down."

"Shut down?" Greg asked.

"Which ones?" Julie added.

"His heart, lungs, kidneys and liver. The brain controls the nerves and signals to these organs. With his brain inactive and lacking sufficient oxygen, these organs cannot function without external support."

"Doctor, are you saying that our son is being kept alive because of an external life support system?" Greg asked.

"Well, what I am actually saying is—"

Julie abruptly interrupted him and started hyperventilating. Then she cried out, "Oh my God. You mean a machine is the only thing keeping our son alive?"

The doctor sighed and then resumed. "The fact remains that a machine is only ensuring your son's heart and lungs continue functioning. Your son is breathing but his brain is dead. I truly wish I could say Douglas is going to recover. That is what all of my years of training and experience have led me to do. To heal the afflicted. Not to keep their organs functioning through artificial means."

Julie closed her eyes and took a deep breath but the words kept echoing back like a satanic curse: your son is breathing but his brain is dead.

Greg swallowed hard as his throat dried and his voice cracked. "How long could the machines keep Doug breathing?"

"Indefinitely."

Julie was incensed. "If you really believe my son is brain dead, then why in hell are you keeping him on those damn machines?"

"I'm sorry. The last thing I want to do is upset you."

Greg reached out to his distraught wife. "Sweetheart, the doctor is doing everything he can. This is just as hard on me as it is on you." He tempered his voice and continued. "Let's let Doctor Drake explain the whole situation."

Julie stared at her husband, glanced over at the doctor, then stared back at Greg. She wiped a tear and struggled to breathe. Doctor Drake's eyes turned soft and compassionate. He shifted them between the two heartbroken parents.

"I understand how difficult this is, but I must advise you that the length of time your son is kept on the ventilator is completely your decision. His condition is worsening and his brain is not receiving enough oxygen and blood flow to sustain itself. This means that other organs will not be able to function on their own. They need external support to be able to function at all."

"Is that why the ventilator and other equipment are being used?" Greg inquired.

"Yes."

Julie sighed and resigned herself to the inevitable truth. "So essentially you are saying my son has already died?"

"I am saying that your son's brain has ceased all activity. From a medical standpoint, Douglas is characterized as brain dead. I am so sorry. We did everything we possibly could to save him." Julie started sobbing again. Doctor Drake reached behind him for a small box of tissues housed in a decorative container and handed it to her.

Greg tried to comfort his wife by stroking her shoulder. Then he asked, "Well, is there any way to know if he's in much pain?

Are the machines reducing his pain or adding to it?"

"It is unlikely your son is feeling any sensations. His brain controls the pain sensors throughout his body and his brain is barely functioning now. The machines would not have any effect on those sensations. Again, the decision is solely yours as to how long you would want to keep your son on the heart-lung machine."

Julie seemed overwhelmed and spoke barely above a whisper, "I don't know what to do."

Doctor Drake looked at Julie and reached out to her arm. She looked up in reaction to his grasp and composed herself. The power of this small, gentle gesture by Doug's physician was not lost on Greg. He knew the situation was just as difficult on the good doctor as it was on him and his wife.

The doctor slowly released his grip on Julie's arm and looked intently at each of them.

"I am very sorry. I think I should let you two think about this privately. If you have any other questions, or need me for anything, just let the nurse know. She will know how to get in touch with me."

The doctor stood up, nodded acknowledgment to each parent and then left the room. Greg came over and hugged his wife. His sobbing was drowned out by Julie's uncontrollable crying. Greg held on to his wife, as he had never done before. He knew how much she was hurting. He was hurting just as much but wanted to be strong for her. For well over an hour the heartbroken parents tried to comfort each other, saying little but sharing more feelings of compassion for each other then either had ever experienced before.

During one of these particularly quiet periods of reflection, the silence was broken by the creaky sound of the doorknob turning. The parents looked over as the door to the quiet room opened. A middle-aged man walked into the quiet room and introduced himself.

"Hello. I'm Phil Rodgers from the OneLegacy Foundation."

Greg looked up, "The OneLegacy Foundation? I'm afraid I don't know what that is."

The man's expression immediately became more compassionate. "Please forgive me. I thought you knew."

By now Julie's emotions had transformed from curiosity to anger. *Just what exactly did he know about my son? And why is he so sorry about him?* she thought.

Phil spoke in a gentle whisper, "First of all, I am so sorry to learn about your son."

Julie squinted her eyes. Her expression became only more cynical as he continued to speak.

"OneLegacy is an organization that administers organ donations. Were you aware that your son designated himself as an organ donor?"

Julie expressed surprise. "No. Are you sure?"

"Quite sure."

He reached into his pocket and handed them Doug's driver's license.

Julie stared at Doug's photo smiling back at her. He looked so alive, she thought, so vibrant and so hopeful of the future that he now would no longer enjoy. Julie dabbed at the tears in her eyes. Her son's photo brought back a flood of memories.

She had taken him to the Atlanta Department of Motor Vehicles a year earlier. He was so glad he had passed his written and driving tests with flying colors. Bursting with pride, he had run up to her at the DMV facility and given her the joyful news. Another degree of freedom for her son, she remembered thinking at the time. Finally, she looked down at the bottom of the license and saw where Doug had checked the box for organ donor.

"Did you know about this?" Julie asked Greg.

"He mentioned it briefly at the time, but I didn't think much about it," Greg replied. "He brought it up again last week when he and I went out for pizza."

"I don't think he ever mentioned it to me. If he did I don't remember," Julie said.

Greg turned his attention back to Phil. "So why are you showing this to us now?"

"Because you may want to consider this when deciding how long to keep him on life support."

"I don't see the connection," Julie said. "Shouldn't we keep Doug on the machines as long as possible?"

Phil understood Julie's position. "Normally I would say yes. But I asked your doctor about your son's condition, and he said that it is deteriorating rapidly. The longer we keep him on the machines, the worse it becomes. And the less useful his organs become."

As if a light came on, Greg saw the connection. "So you're saying if Doug's organs are going to be valuable to others, they need to be taken sooner rather than later?"

"Yes. For any of the organs to be viable in another human, they need to be removed as soon as possible." He watched Julie to gauge her reaction. She sat motionless and expressionless. Phil looked back to Greg and then spoke.

"I have two grown children. If, God forbid, one of them was in the situation your son is in, what would I do? How would I feel? How would I react? I know I would be torn by a decision like this. I understand how difficult this must be for you."

With pleading eyes Greg asked, "How long till we must decide?"

"A decision within the next few hours would be best. If you take much longer it could jeopardize the viability of the organs."

Julie drew another tissue and dabbed her eyes. "You're basically asking us to end the life of our son so that others can profit from his organs."

"I know this is an unfair request to make of any mother, but especially someone like you whose child is just entering the world of adulthood. You have not had a chance to see him reach his potential. You have only seen him prepare for what might have been."

Julie was jolted by the Phil's words. She said, almost defiantly, "It is completely unfair. He was just starting to turn the corner on so many things." She started sobbing almost uncontrollably.

"What are the next steps if we do decide to donate Doug's organs?" Greg asked.

"As your son's legal guardians, you will need to sign permission for us to remove his organs.

The parents sighed and then Julie asked, "May we see our son?"

"Yes, of course. He is in recovery. The nurse can lead you there."

Julie and Greg glanced at each other with a look of resignation and then thanked Phil who rose to leave. The two parents remained for a while, each weighing the implications of ending their son's life to prolong his organs for others. They talked slowly, hauntingly, fully understanding the enormity of their decision.

At one point Julie said, "I just don't know if I can sign papers to do this."

Greg gave his wife a tender hug and countered with, "I know, but we have to consider what Doug would have wanted. We have to think how this could save other people's lives."

The two of them were going back and forth on their decision when the door to the quiet room opened. They immediately stopped talking when they saw it was Michael and Francine. Greg stood to greet his mother. She could interpret every possible expression on her son's face, and she could see all was not well. Silently she hugged her son.

At the same time Julie rushed up to Michael with tears forming in her eyes.

"Mom, what's wrong?" Michael asked. Then his voice started to grow angry. "Did something happen to Doug? What's going on? Tell me."

Julie hugged her son tightly and spoke between tears, "The doctors did everything they could but Doug's head injuries caused permanent damage they couldn't repair."

"You mean that Doug is . . ."

Greg quickly interrupted. "Your brother is being kept alive by a ventilator right now."

"What?" Michael cried out. "No. That can't be. He's only seventeen. He's got to come back. He's got to come back."

Francine walked over to try to comfort her grandson. Michael and the two women sat on the couch with Greg pulling up a chair to face them.

"Michael, I understand you and Doug were starting to grow closer lately? True?" Greg asked.

"Well, yeah, like he was sharing stuff with me," Michael answered, slightly more calmed down. "Why? What's this about?"

"Did he ever say anything about donating his organs?"

Michael thought for a moment and said, "Uh, I dunno, maybe. Yeah, I think he did say something about that. It was like right after he got his driver's license. Why?" He paused for a second. "Are you saying Doug wants to donate his organs?"

"Yes, Michael. Your brother had designated himself as an organ donor."

Michael clearly was still wrestling with the thought that his brother might not pull through. "So like you're saying if he doesn't make it you will have his organs donated?"

Greg breathed deeply. "It's a bit more complicated than that?"

Francine seemed puzzled. "What do you mean?"

"Doug is being kept alive by a heart-lung machine. His brain is continuing to enlarge and is not receiving enough blood and oxygen to sustain it. Eventually everything will shut down, which will damage his organs beyond the point of use. The sooner the organs are removed, the more usable they will be."

Michael and Francine sat stunned. Francine finally asked Greg, "Are you saying they want you to take Douglas off of the machines?"

"Yes."

"No!" Michael shouted. "You can't just unplug my brother. That will kill him. He's got to stay alive." He pleaded with his mother, "Mom, you can't do this."

Michael was sitting between his mother and grandmother. They tenderly hugged him to calm him down.

Julie spoke softly to Michael. "I'm not sure I want to do this. I'm not sure I can do this."

Francine sounded perplexed. "That is such an unfair position for you two."

Michael looked at his grandmother. "You said the two of them. What about me? Like, he's my only brother. I should get a say in this." He looked over at his grandmother for support.

Before Francine could respond, Greg said to Michael. "I know you love your brother very much. I get that. We all love him, but we have to consider the reality of the situation."

Julie had remained silent but finally spoke up, "I want to go to the chapel for a while to pray for some guidance about this."

"Would you mind if I join you?" Francine asked.

"Why don't we all go," Greg said. "I think it would do us all some good."

Francine and Michael nodded in agreement. The four of them walked together, though each was alone with their individual thoughts.

Julie prayed for some kind of sign to help her with the decision about ending her child's life, but no divine inspiration had come by the time she reached the chapel. Just inside its entrance, flowers on each side welcomed visitors. Dozens of candles gave off a warm glow inside the dimly lit room. The four knelt and prayed in their own unique ways. After a few minutes Julie got up to leave.

Just outside the chapel, Julie noticed several plaques and small-framed posters inscribed with motivational sayings. They had been collected from noteworthy health and medical facilities from around the world. One plaque in particular caught her eye. It was a quote from Samuel Golter, the executive director of the famous California cancer facility, City of Hope. It read:

There is no profit in curing the body, if in the process, you destroy the soul.

Julie gasped at reading the words. She took a second to process their meaning, when suddenly it became clear to her. It did seem like a divine moment of clarity. She had been seeking guidance and meaning. The answer was apparent to her in those few words. Even if her son could be kept alive by machines for another few days, in a sense temporarily curing his body, at what cost would it be to him, to her and to her family? Most importantly, at what cost to those who could benefit?

Julie believed everyone has a soul that lives forever, but she also believed the soul is the essence of the person while alive. She felt those words spoke to her about including care and compassion in the treatment of a loved one. The whole picture of her son's condition needed to be considered, and that meant including the potential beneficiaries of her son's organs.

Julie was deep in thought when Greg came up to her. He carefully read the words she had dwelled on, and seemed to understand.

Quietly she said, "We need to let him go. Others will be able to live because of this."

"I agree," Greg whispered. For the first time in days, Julie looked relieved.

///

Francine and Michael joined Greg and Julie, who told them of their decision. Francine understood and agreed. Michael was another matter.

"What? You can't do this. You're going to let them unplug his machines so he can just die?"

Julie tried to explain that Doug's condition was beyond hope and that his transplanted organs could help others. Michael disagreed and flew into a rage.

Realizing he was standing just outside the chapel he whispered as loudly and forcibly, "So you and dad just want to end his life? You want to kill him? Is that it? You two don't always agree with his actions, but I love him. He is a good brother to me. How can you do this?"

Greg looked shocked and angry at his son's outburst. Julie was stunned and hurt beyond belief. Greg lost his temper. Then Julie joined in with an equally loud voice.

"Stop it. Right now. This minute," Francine demanded.

Everyone stared at her. Each of them became silent. She took a deep breath and then walked over to Michael. She put her arm around his shoulder. "Michael, I know you love your brother very much, right?" He nodded.

"Wouldn't you want to help him accomplish the final thing on earth that he would want to accomplish?"

Michael looked confused, "What do you mean?"

"Douglas indicated that if anything ever happened to him, he wanted to be an organ donor. He wants his organs to be used in a way that can help others. If your parents wait until he expires, his organs will be of little use to anyone. Do you think Douglas would approve of that?"

"Uh, I dunno. I guess not," Michael said as he started weeping. "I just don't want him to die. I just want him to come back."

Francine hugged her grandson tightly. "I know, sweetheart, I know. We all want him back, but Douglas will soon be at peace, and he's going to save the lives of others."

Michael composed himself and gave his grandmother a hug back. Then he gave his mother a hug, and before long everyone was embracing each other. They talked for a few minutes about Doug's life and how unselfish it was of him to be willing to help others. They finally all agreed that the sooner they make Doug's organs available the better. They went back inside the chapel to say a final prayer for Doug and the donation of his organs.

Then they headed back to the quiet room, each one silent in their own thoughts. As they walked Greg phoned Phil and told him of their decision. Phil informed Greg that he would be waiting for them in the quiet room. Along the way, Julie called Lisa and asked her to come over immediately. Julie wanted to tell Lisa in person of their decision about Doug's organs.

As they entered the quiet room, Phil stood up and approached them.

"Thank you for making such a courageous decision. Your generosity and selflessness will prolong and enrich the lives of so many others."

Julie sighed and Greg steadied himself as Phil continued.

"As I mentioned before, OneLegacy coordinates the donation of organs, bones, tissues and skin to qualified recipients. Now that you have decided to donate your son's organs, I am here to help you through the process and to answer any questions you may have. Why don't we talk in this small room where there is more privacy?"

Phil led the two parents into a small room while Francine and Michael headed back to the lobby for hot cocoa. During the next thirty minutes Phil described every aspect of the organ transplant program. He explained how a team of doctors would be put on standby once the final forms were signed. Each physician had a unique organ specialty including heart, liver, kidneys, lungs and even eyes.

For each of the various organs to be removed, Greg and Julie would have to sign multiple documents giving their permission to have the organs harvested, attesting that OneLegacy would work with accredited medical organizations to determine the most qualified recipient of an organ, and that OneLegacy would not divulge the identity of either the donor or the recipient to either party. Phil did clarify that if either the donor family or the recipient wanted to communicate with the other, the OneLegacy organization would act as an intermediary.

Julie and Greg decided to donate as many of Doug's organs as possible. Most all of his vital organs would be excellent candidates for transplant. Phil thanked them and told them that their son's unselfish act would result in many people's lives being saved, extended or improved.

Once all of the documents were signed, all of the procedures explained and all of their questions answered, Greg and Julie stood to leave. They shook hands with the representative, who quickly left. The parents entered the quiet room and joined Francine and Michael, who were sipping their hot cocoa.

Julie and Greg described the various organs that would be donated. Michael was especially pleased to learn that Doug's eyes would be donated, because Michael had always admired his brother's perfect vision. After much discussion about other aspects of the donor program, Doctor Drake entered.

He advised Greg and Julie that they could all go in and say their final good-byes to Doug. As they exited the quiet room and walked toward Doug's area, Lisa arrived and joined them. Julie informed Lisa about Doug's condition. Lisa became overwhelmed with grief and sadness, but understood and agreed with the decision to donate his organs.

When they entered Doug's area they saw his chest lift and lower in rhythm to the respirator. There were tubes, wires and lines that connected Doug to numerous pieces of life-support equipment. One by one each person leaned over Doug and said their final goodbye. Francine went first, followed by Michael, then Lisa and Greg and finally Julie. When they slowly exited the room, a team of doctors was waiting headed up by Doctor Drake.

He came up to Julie and Greg and offered them his heartfelt condolences on the loss of their son. As the parents prepared to leave they shook the doctor's hands. He surprised Julie by giving her a brief hug. After the family left, the team of physicians began their work of recovering Doug's organs.

As the family exited the recovery area Lisa started sobbing. Michael nearly broke down but his sorrow was tinged with anger. Julie suggested that they stop by the chapel to say a final private prayer for Doug's dearly departed soul. They all readily agreed, but each one prayed for a slightly different request. Lisa prayed that her boyfriend finally had found the peace and tranquility that had seemed to elude him his entire life.

Francine prayed that Doug would find contentment in his afterlife and that Michael would make some sense of all this. Greg prayed that this terrible tragedy would not tear his family apart but somehow bring it closer together. Julie prayed that the recipients of her son's organs could use them in good health for a long time.

Finally, Michael prayed that the person responsible for his brother's death would somehow be brought to justice. He did not know how, but in his heart he felt that would have to happen. He prayed for a plan to ensure that it would.

CHAPTER 20

AS THE FAMILY headed to their cars in the hospital parking lot, bright red and blue lights flashed from on top of two ambulances. Hospital workers, dressed in light green surgical scrubs, emerged carrying two silver, rectangular objects. As they approached, the group took pause. They could plainly see each attendant was carrying two metallic, refrigerated containers which they loaded into the ambulances.

Two police cars suddenly drove up to escort the ambulances out of the hospital driveways. Greg and Julie realized what was happening. The ambulances would carry Doug's organs to the airport where planes were standing-by to fly the organs to anxiously waiting recipients at various cities throughout the country.

All of them stopped for a moment as the emotional enormity of the event washed over them. Julie started sobbing quietly. She thought about all the memories her son had provided her during his seventeen years of life. She thought about how at one point he thought about becoming a forest ranger because of his love of nature, and how he wanted to help others appreciate it. Now he was being whisked away to others for a totally different, arguably more important, mission.

Lisa came up to Julie and gave her a small hug. Lisa cried as she thought about her decision to end her baby's life. Doug's life had also been ended, and she prayed they both were in a more peaceful place.

Greg and Francine held the other's hands as helpers carefully lifted the containers and loaded them into the rear of the ambulances. Then they watched the attendants delicately strap the precious cargo securely into place.

After a final check an attendant slammed the back door closed. The accompanying loud thump pierced the night air. Within a few minutes an attendant in the second ambulance performed a similar procedure. Then he banged on the side of the bus to indicate both vehicles were ready to roll.

Greg's family and Lisa watched as the police cars and ambulances turned onto the main thoroughfare leading away from the hospital. The flashing lights of the four vehicles momentarily stabbed their eyes. The occasional sound of their pulsating police sirens blared through the streets. The five onlookers all stood motionless, then squinted at the convoy that was transporting the life-saving organs of their beloved Doug.

As the vehicles raced away, Greg thought about just how upside down his world had become. A week ago his son had asked him to dinner, and that had meant the world to Greg. Now his son was gone. Along with him all the hopes and dreams any father wants for his child.

The flashing lights grew dimmer and dimmer and finally faded into the Atlanta night. Francine saw how distressed her son appeared and stood next to him. She had learned long ago that sometimes the best thing to say at a time like this was nothing at all. She simply looked up at him.

Greg knew that look well. It was the look of unconditional love. It was the type of undying love that he had always felt from his mother, a type of love that he felt now more than ever. It was exactly the tonic he needed. She reached up and patted his back. She could no longer reach his tall shoulders. He thought back to the times growing up when she had patted his back in a similar way whenever things were not going well. It always had the same soothing effect.

Greg thought about the now-departed ambulances, and the irony of the situation. Normally, ambulances would race in with attendants rushing to transport critically injured patients into the emergency room. But now just the opposite was happening. It was as if everything was reversed, and it occurred to Greg that maybe this was how it was intended. *Maybe Doug's mission in life was to save others. Maybe his passing had a greater meaning of saving others who could not otherwise be saved.* These thoughts brought considerable consolation to Greg.

Francine could tell from the look on his face that he had found some peace in Doug's passing. Nothing could have made her feel more like a mother at that moment. Greg leaned over and gave his mother a tender kiss on her forehead. She never felt closer to him, nor to her grandson, whose organs were on their way to save, improve or extend the lives of strangers she would never meet.

///

Greg and Julie had spent a restless Saturday night but finally managed a few hours of shuteye. They slept until mid-morning. Francine had agreed to help with some of the many decisions Greg and Julie would be faced with concerning the funeral and burial of their son.

Minutes before noon the MacDonald residence phone rang.

"Hello. This is Greg."

"Hello Mr. MacDonald. This is Phil Rodgers of the OneLegacy organ donation organization."

"Oh yes. Good morning."

"I know this is not an easy time. I hope you and your wife were able to get some rest last night."

"It took a while, but we both slept in and that helped."

"Well, good. On behalf of the OneLegacy organization I want to thank you again for agreeing to donate your son's organs. Your gesture will benefit many recipients, not to mention their family members."

"Thank you, but it was really my son's doing, and his wishes."

"I understand. One reason for me calling is to give you the status of your son's organs."

Greg listened as Phil described each of the organs that had been successfully recovered.

"The only organ that could not be donated was your son's left kidney. It had been too severely damaged by the stabbing from the knife. All of the other organs landed safely at their intended destinations and were healthy enough to be used by waiting recipients."

"We watched the eight metal containers being loaded into the two waiting ambulances," Greg said.

Phil explained how each of those initial canisters was specifically refrigerated according to the needs of the organ being transported. There was a container for each of the two lungs and other canisters for the healthy kidney, the liver, the eyes, bones and other tissue samples.

Greg then asked a question he knew interested Julie, "What about Doug's heart?"

Phil drew in a breath. "A heart transplant is risky and complex. It's even more difficult than a liver replacement. The procedure took more than four hours. Specialists were flown in to assist. So far, the organ recovery and transplant seem to be a success. But we will know more in a few days."

"That's good to hear," Greg replied.

Phil sounded more solemn as he said, "Your son's body has been prepared for release. Have you selected a funeral home service yet?"

"No. We're not even sure where to start with all this. It's all a little overwhelming," Greg lamented.

"I understand," Phil replied. He paused and then asked, "May I make a suggestion?"

"Sure."

"You may want to consider either Spangler Mortuaries or Jamison Funeral Services."

"I've heard of Jamison. They have been in business a long time, haven't they?" Greg asked.

"Over eighty-five years and still family-owned. They are very experienced with helping prepare decedents for viewing who have donated organs."

"I hadn't even thought about that," Greg said.

"We have worked with them often. They're great at helping

families get through an incredibly difficult situation like yours, with love, compassion and dignity."

"That sounds helpful. I'll talk to my wife about them. Thanks."

Greg joined Julie in the living room where she was selecting photos of Doug. Greg mentioned Phil's suggestion for a funeral home and Julie readily agreed. Minutes later she was talking with Richard Jamison from Jamison Funeral Services.

He discussed such items as the casket, clothing, flowers, obituary and the type of service desired. Richard sensed Julie was getting stressed and calmed her with comforting, supportive tones. His knowledge of the details made Julie feel comfortable and confident in her choice of funeral homes. That was important to a mother coping with so many conflicting emotions.

Richard suggested she and Greg come and meet with him. Julie checked with Greg who nodded yes. The three of them agreed to meet in two hours.

As Julie ended her call, the distinctive sounds of her personally customized doorbell chimes rang out. Normally, the soothing sounds would be a relaxing tonic at the end of a stressful day, but they brought little comfort to the grieving mother. What normally sounded like peaceful resonance of gradually fading reverberations on that day was like harsh sounds of clanging metal pipes.

Julie opened the door to Francine who immediately gave Julie a warm hug. Julie welcomed the affection. Francine knew that her gesture could do little to address Julie's pain, but also knew the healing effects of a heartfelt embrace.

Francine was a mother herself. She had been trying to deal with the death of her grandson. But she realized as much as she tried to imagine what her daughter-in-law was experiencing, she could not come close.

Francine thought about what she might have felt like if, God forbid, something had happened to Greg. No matter his accomplishments and his age, he was still her child. She would always be his mother. She would always feel his joy and his sadness. She would be heartbroken if he passed on before she did, and thought of the tremendous sense of loss she would have felt if he had died at a young age. That was what her son and daughter-in-law were feeling, and she tried to offer as much support and empathy as possible.

Julie invited Francine inside and they sat down in the living room. Greg had asked Michael to join them. They had much to discuss concerning the particulars for Doug's funeral and burial.

"Michael, your mother and I have several decisions we have to make about your brother's arrangements."

"What do you mean by arrangements?" Michael asked in a less-than-friendly tone. He was still very upset at the entire ordeal, and worried that the person who inflicted the injury on Doug would go unpunished.

Julie tried to console him. "We mean that we have to decide on all the various aspects of Doug's funeral. We are a family, and we would like you and Francine to be part of the decision-making for these things."

"Well, okay," Michael responded. "But, uh, like what kinds of things?"

Greg answered, "Well, the first decision was whether we wanted him cremated or not."

"Cremated! No freaking way!" Michael shouted.

"Calm down, right now," Greg said. "I didn't say we would, I only said it was a decision we needed to make, early on, because it drives so many other decisions."

Julie spoke up. "Your father and I prefer a traditional burial for Doug. Does everyone agree?"

Everyone nodded yes.

"The second decision is whether to have an open casket for viewing," Greg said.

Julie started tearing up at the image of her son laid out in a coffin. Michael felt his sadness quickly transform into a controlled rage as he kept dwelling on the violent death of his brother.

"And what did you decide?" Francine asked.

"We thought it best to have an open casket. It follows our traditions."

"I think that is a good way to go," Francine said. "Have you selected a funeral home yet?"

"Yes. We are going with Jamison."

"Good choice," Francine said.

Suddenly Michael looked up with a very disapproving expression as if he had just discovered a major flaw in their plans. "How can you do an open casket if like all his organs are, you know, like gone?"

"The funeral directors at Jamison's know how to do that," Greg said. "It's one of the reasons we went with them. Your mom and I believe they are the best at what they do. They will make your brother look good."

"Which brings us to what we dress him in," Julie said.

"He should be in his black jacket," Michael said.

"Absolutely not," his mother retorted.

"Why not? That jacket was the bomb. You know he loved that jacket. I think, like, he would want to be buried with it."

"I am not going to bury my son in some street hoodlum apparel."

Michael glared at his father. "You claimed you wanted my opinion on these things. So when I give them, Mom immediately shoots it down." Then he shot a glance over at Julie. "What you really meant was you want my opinion as long as it matches your own. Otherwise, you're just not interested." Michael walked out the room.

Julie and Greg were stunned and just stared at each other. Francine quickly got up and followed Michael into the kitchen. She sat down next to him and gave him one of the saddest yet most loving looks any grandmother could give a grandchild.

Michael looked back at her and just shrugged as if to say what could he do? It was as if the world was closing in on him and he had no way of knowing how to deal with it. Francine gave him a small hug and told him she understood how much he missed his brother. As gently as possible she reminded him of the talk they had several weeks earlier about trying to accept Doug as he was.

"I know you loved your brother very much. We all did, and he loved us all back. Maybe one way to show him that love is to show that love to your mom and dad. They are hurting as much as you are."

"I know but Doug was really rad on my suggestions about clothing. He and Lisa both."

"Well maybe that's something you could suggest to your mom and dad. Maybe Lisa should be asked about this."

Michael brightened a bit. "Yeah, that's a great idea, Grandma."

He stood and slowly strode back into the living room.

"Mom, why don't we, like, ask Lisa what she thinks about what Doug should be dressed in?"

Julie respected Lisa and believed her to be sensible. Within minutes Julie had Lisa on the phone.

They chatted for a few minutes about other aspects of the funeral before agreeing on a light blue high neck sweater with a striped collared shirt underneath. Julie asked what everyone thought and received thumbs up. Julie sighed in relief. One small skirmish was down, with the likelihood of others to occur.

The rest of the afternoon was consumed with a blur of decisions, activities and arrangements that the family had to make. These included the type of casket, time of viewings, content of the service, identifying the minister, whether a church would be included and the selection of the cemetery.

Another emotional task for the family was developing an obituary. The funeral director, Richard, had helped them recall many of the highlights, and some of the lowlights, of Doug's young life. Richard took down notes and a short time later provided the family with a rough draft that needed only a few minor changes. It was not lost on Michael that, at the end of a person's life, it is essentially summed up on a single piece of paper. There was so much more his brother could have accomplished and experienced.

///

Monday afternoon had turned overcast as the MacDonald's climbed into their Lexus for the drive over to the funeral home. Michael sat in back behind his mother with Francine next to him. Julie decided Michael would not attend school for two days. Normally the chance to miss two days of school would bring some joy to Michael, but there was no joy in the heart of the thirteen-year-old.

Just before two o'clock the MacDonald family walked into the funeral home and headed toward the viewing rooms. The mere sight of seeing their son's name on the entrance plaque to a funeral room sent shivers through Julie and Greg. They would soon experience more emotional sensations.

Greg entered the back of the room first with Julie and Michael at his side. Francine followed a few steps behind. There were flowers everywhere and they all sensed the pleasing fragrance of the numerous floral arrangements. Lisa, her mother Katherine and Katherine's friend Sylvia Jones had already arrived and were sitting halfway to the front. Lisa was sobbing non-stop.

Greg and his family started down the long central aisle. They glanced at all the flowers, but their focus was on the casket still far away ahead of them. They nodded to the three women who watched them as they approached. When Greg was about ten rows from the front he saw his son's face in the casket for the first time. It literally took his breath away. His knees buckled and had he not been holding so tightly onto Julie he surely would have fallen over. The sight of Doug resting motionless in a coffin was more than Greg could endure.

Michael had never before seen his father cry. Not so much as a single tear. Weeping was the only sound in the room.

After a few moments they resumed their walk to the front and approached the casket. Julie rubbed her son's hands which had been folded on his chest and lightly kissed his forehead. Greg and Michael did similar gestures. Julie commented on how peaceful he looked, wiping away more tears. She was glad she had decided on the blue sweater for him. All Michael could think about was why his brother had to die. Why couldn't he somehow come back?

By now Lisa and her mom and friend had joined the others around the casket. Each knelt for a minute on the small kneeling stand to say a prayer for Doug's eternal rest. A short time later other relatives and friends started arriving to extend their condolences. It was a very eclectic group of well-wishers. They included close and distant relatives from both Greg and Julie's side of the families. Even some of Francine's friends showed up.

There were co-workers of Greg's and a number of clients of Julie's that paid their respects. Additionally, dozens of Doug's and Michael's classmates, teachers, counselors, teammates, coaches and other friends attended. Friends from church and other organizations likewise stopped by to offer their sympathies. Other friends of Doug's also came including the rather large

Robert Henderson whom most knew as Tiny and who had grown closer to Michael.

Several of Greg's friends and colleagues joined him at the funeral home in the early evening after their workdays had finished. Jim and Sharon Barnett along with their daughter Cheryl extended their condolences and apologized for the absence of their son Kenny. Even Greg's boss Ted Riley came by to express his sorrow at Greg's loss.

Julie's boss and friend Eric Spencer was warm and sympathetic as he tried to console Julie. Several others came and went as the evening progressed. At one point Timothy Mallory, the Tough Love director, arrived with another man that neither Greg nor Julie recognized. Timothy introduced him as Sam Philips, the head of the anger management program with whom Julie had spoken a few days earlier. Both expressed their sincere sorrow for the family's loss.

The room slowly thinned out as the evening wound down. Eventually there remained just Doug's family. Richard came in and briefly went over the proceedings for the next day's funeral service beginning at the family's Christian church. Each family member knelt and said a short prayer for Doug before leaving.

CHAPTER 21

MICHAEL TOSSED AND turned all night. The vision of his brother lying motionless and lifeless in a white linen padded coffin prevented him from restful sleep. Just before sunrise Michael dozed off deeply, mostly from sheer exhaustion. The church service was scheduled to begin at one o'clock that afternoon.

Julie and Greg had not slept much better than their son, but by eight o'clock they were climbing out of bed. Julie immediately called the school saying that Michael would be out the next two days. Afterward, Greg came up and kissed her lightly on her forehead.

"Would you like to shower first?" he asked.

"No. You go. I have to shampoo my hair, and that always takes a while."

Normally Greg would have come back with a quick quip. It might have been something about the extra time she spends on her hair produces such an incredible result. Or that a queen requires whatever extra preparations she feels necessary. Or that a goddess is entitled to all the time she needs because it is so worth the wait. The normally frisky husband might have even suggested they take their showers together, knowing full well to where that would eventually lead.

Not that day.

Greg looked out of the window. The day was clear and crisp. It was the third Tuesday in December and slightly colder than normal. There was a light frost on the ground, which Greg knew would be melted by noon. Minutes later he climbed into the shower and adjusted the spray head. Soon he was pelted with the soothing warmth of the rushing water, but his thoughts wandered to the cold damp ground that his son's coffin would soon occupy.

The oversized bath towel Greg had set out felt refreshingly dry and warm. He realized Julie had snuck in and stuffed his towel in the clothes dryer briefly. It was a loving gesture Julie occasionally did to surprise her unsuspecting husband.

The simple act always impressed him and prompted affectionate words of gratitude. As he wiped his dripping limbs, he felt the usual pangs of appreciation and fondness toward his wife for her thoughtfulness. He would return the favor twenty minutes later when Julie stepped into her shower.

As grateful as Greg felt for his wife's small but meaningful expression of love, it brought him sadness toward his departed son. Doug would never experience such a tender moment as that of a loving wife expressing her love for him. Greg could not help but feel Doug had been cheated out of so many joys and wonders of living and loving. None of it made any sense to the bewildered father.

///

While Greg struggled to make sense of his older son's passing, Greg's younger son was focused solely on revenge. He had overheard his father's friend Jim from the police department they had no prime suspects for Doug's stabbing. Michael knew from talking to Lisa that the gang leader, Dominic Williams, was the person responsible.

Police could not arrest Dominic as the perpetrator because he had a defendable alibi that he had spent the night with his girlfriend, and because Lisa could not positively identify Dominic from the photos provided by the police. The mind of a thirteen-year-old was a wondrous thing. It was still part child and part adolescent. When faced with an emotionally overwhelming event such as the death of a brother with whom he was only beginning to bond with and understand, the reactions of a young teenager were unpredictable.

When Greg finished dressing it was just past ten o'clock. He heard a light rap on the front door and saw Francine standing outside carrying two bakery bags. Greg had suggested she join them for a light brunch before the four of them headed off to the church. Francine had stopped at a popular bakery on the way and had brought eight large, fresh cinnabuns, a family favorite, along with a half-gallon of orange juice.

"Here, let me take those," Greg said as opened the door.

"Thank you, Gregory," Francine replied, using the form of her son's name that sounded the most natural to her. "How is everyone doing this morning? It's a little chilly out," she remarked.

"Everyone is doing fine," he responded as he set the bags on the kitchen counter. Then Greg took in a whiff of the warm cinnabuns and said, "Wow. These sure smell good. Michael is really going to enjoy these. He loves cinnabuns."

"I know," Francine acknowledged. Then she smiled and said, "He isn't the only one in this family who enjoys these," referring to Greg's own preference for the tasty treats.

Greg replied, "Speaking of Michael, I better go see if he's up yet. Julie is just finishing up her shower. Make yourself at home."

"Oh, don't mind me. I'll be fine. How about I start setting out the dishes?" Francine asked.

"Sure," Greg replied. Then he headed upstairs to check on Michael. Greg could hear from the sounds of water that Michael was already in the shower.

Greg cracked open the door to Michael's bathroom and called out, "Come down as soon as you're dressed. Grandma is here with cinnabuns for us all."

"Okay."

Greg came back downstairs and stopped by his office to check on any urgent emails. He had broadcast an email to dozens of colleagues Sunday evening informing them of the family tragedy. Word had trickled out as to the passing of his son and that resulted in him receiving several dozen notes of sympathy and condolences.

By 10:45 Julie, Greg and Michael had joined Francine around the large wood kitchen table for breakfast. Greg suggested they all bow their heads and say a private prayer for their dearly departed family member.

Just after noon they all climbed into the Lexus for the fifteen-minute drive over to the church. Richard Jamison was already there and greeted them at the back of the vestibule. No one else was in the church. The casket was in front at the end of the long center aisle positioned perpendicular to it. Julie and Greg had decided to have it open for viewing until the service was to begin in case some friends had not been able to come by the funeral home the night before.

The four of them slowly walked down the center aisle. Julie held on to Greg on her left with Michael on her right. Francine was on the other side of Greg. One by one, each member of the family knelt on a kneeling pad beside the casket and said a final prayer for Doug. The family then sat in the seats that had been reserved for them in front and directly across from the casket. Lisa and her mother arrived shortly after and sat next to the MacDonald family.

It was half past noon and by now a number of friends and acquaintances had filed past the coffin. Each one paused to whisper a final good-bye to their dearly departed and to pay their respects to the family. Jim Barnett along with his wife Sharon and their daughter Cheryl were among the first to arrive. All three of them extended very warm and heart-felt expressions of sympathy.

Next came Eric Spencer. He tried to give Julie a hug, but she quickly extended her arm for a handshake.

"Julie, I'm so sorry."

"Thanks for coming."

Eric understood. Julie looked over to Greg and then back to Eric. Whatever fleeting thoughts she may have felt for her boss were washed away, permanently.

During the next thirty minutes dozens of friends and acquaintances had lined up for the final viewing. They moved slowly but reverently up to the casket and then back to the various family members. A number of Julie's clients had come out to offer their support. An even larger number of Greg's co-workers fought through downtown traffic to be there for their colleague in his time of need.

Many of Michael's classmates received permission to be excused for the afternoon to attend the service. Many of Doug's classmates, teachers and counselors were also in attendance. "Hello, I'm Carl Thomas from Doug's anger management group. I am so sorry for your loss."

Julie looked up and nodded her head in appreciation. When Greg heard Carl announce his name, Greg immediately recognized it.

After standing to shake Carl's hand, Greg said quietly and in a friendly manner, "Doug talked to me about you."

Somewhat taken aback Carl remarked, "Really? I'm surprised, because we hardly knew each other."

Greg took a small breath to compose himself. "He told me you gave him a different way to look at things."

"I really thought he had started down a new path."

"Oh, he had," Greg assured him. Both men's eyes became misty as Greg said, "He just got ambushed along the way."

Carl extended his sympathies to the other family members and then moved on. Not far behind him came the seven other males that had been in Doug's anger management class. They mostly kept to themselves. A few of them knelt to say a brief prayer.

A few minutes before one o'clock Richard Jamison approached the family and indicated it was time to close the casket. It would be the last time anyone would see Doug's peaceful-looking face. The four family members along with Lisa stood reverently around the head of the casket. Julie and Lisa both started sobbing as Richard closed and latched the coffin cover. Julie was standing between Greg and Michael, who helped her to remain upright as she slumped forward. At one point she reached forward as if to touch her son one last time. Then shortly they returned to their seats. Greg kissed his wife and stepped to a podium.

"This was not how I expected to be spending the week before Christmas."

Greg thanked everyone for attending and spoke about what a wonderful, intelligent son Doug had been. He described with a certain degree of satisfaction that while Doug had not excelled in academics, he had taught himself all there was to know about computers.

"Doug had become quite the video gamer. At eleven he wrote one of the gaming companies about an obscure programming error. When Doug received a typed response admitting that Doug was correct in pointing out the flaw in the software, he was so proud."

Greg paused.

"As was I."

Greg talked about several other aspects of Doug's life, including that he had designated himself as an organ donor and how several recipients would benefit from this. Greg then introduced Julie. She moved slowly as she ascended the two steps up and positioned herself behind the podium. Her hands were shaking slightly as she looked out at the large number of faces staring solemnly back at her. She cleared her voice and then began.

"Thank you all for coming. I agree with my husband when he said that Doug would be surprised to see so many of you here for him, especially in a church no less."

The comment brought some smiles and a few hushed snickers.

"Those of you who knew Doug well knew he was never big on pomp and circumstance. He had a few rough edges, but he also had some soft edges. That's what I'd like to talk to you about today. I'd like to tell you about some of Doug's softer sides. Many of you may be surprised to learn that for all his rough exteriors, he had a sensitive side as well."

Julie described some of her son's more gentle gestures. How polite he would be to her adult friends; how gentlemanly he would act around women; how well he treated his grandmother; his tenderness with pets. She mentioned that in recent weeks Doug had seemed to be growing closer to both his parents.

She looked out at Tim Mallory of Tough Love and Sam Phillips from anger management. Without citing them by name, she stated that Doug had seemed to be getting so much good from recent programs in which he was involved. This brought a tear to her eye that she quickly brushed away. Tim and Sam nodded back in appreciation.

Glancing over to Michael, Julie spoke tenderly about how Doug and his younger brother Michael had especially appeared to be growing closer to each other. She talked about how each of them had started sharing their particular strengths with each other. For Doug that meant giving Michael tips on computers, video games and basic truck maintenance. For Michael, that meant showing Doug some techniques on drawing and the use of colors and blends in artwork and clothing.

Julie concluded her remarks by saying one final public goodbye to her son, and then thanked everyone again for attending. The next person to speak would be Michael. He strode up to the podium and gazed out at the large number of faces looking back at him. He scanned the audience for a familiar face and spotted Tiny watching him intently. Michael was relieved to see such a friendly supportive person looking back at him.

Michael's hands trembled a bit and his voice was noticeably nervous at the start, but once he began speaking the sincere emotions of his heart calmed him down. Michael spoke briefly but lovingly about his brother. He reiterated and confirmed many of the things that his mother had described about Michael's relationship with Doug. He became teary when he elaborated on how Doug and he had grown closer in recent weeks. He ended with a simple, "I love you, bro."

Lisa was the next to speak and she had decided to read a poem that she and Doug had studied in school. It was entitled "Footprints in the Sand" by American poet Mary Stevenson. The poem described how the Lord was always there, and that in times of greatest need was when the Lord carried you. As Lisa walked down the steps to her seat she leaned over and placed a light kiss on the head of the casket.

The minister then arose. "Next to speak is Francine MacDonald, Doug's paternal grandmother."

Francine walked slowly but surely up to the front of the church. She began by saying how sorry she felt for her son and daughter-in-law, and for her dear grandson Michael on the loss of Douglas. She spoke of what a joy and a blessing that grandchildren could be to a grandparent, and that that was certainly true in the case of Douglas and Michael.

Then Francine gazed out at the congregation. "I have seen

much death and sadness in my seventy some years on this earth. It is never easy to lose someone you love. Especially someone so young." Francine stopped for a moment to take a breath and clear her throat.

"I have also seen how a tragic death such as this can shatter and harden your hearts. I ask you to please not let that happen. Please do not let Douglas's untimely passing replace the joy and love he brought to you with anger. I would like to share with you two brief stories that touch on this notion."

Francine described a famous painting of Christ by the English artist William Holman Hunt she had seen at St. Paul's Cathedral in London. Called *The Light of the World*, the painting portrayed Christ holding a lantern and standing outside a dark, closed door whose hinges and latches were only on the inside, meaning the door could only be opened from the inside. Francine clarified the symbolism by saying that the door represented your heart. "Christ is always on the outside knocking on your heart to come inside, but only you can let Him in." A number of heads in the audience nodded in agreement.

"My other story is about Mother Teresa," Francine said. Everyone seemed captivated by Francine's remarks and awaited her next words with interest. Francine explained how Mother Teresa had once said that there was one human ailment that was more prevalent and sadder than all others. The real tragedy, according to the saintly mother, was that it took so little effort to cure it. It would not require a medical breakthrough, or vast sums of money.

The ailment about which Mother Teresa referred was not violence, or torture, or murder, or rape, or famine or even poverty. She acknowledged that these were real problems in many parts of the world and that unfortunately she had seen far too many instances. She had met and seen millions of impoverished people from around the world.

The number one ailment that Mother Teresa believed was the most prevalent of all human conditions was that of loneliness. There were simply so many people who were so lonely. They had no one with whom to talk, to share, to love. Francine urged everyone to consider letting Christ into your heart so as to be less lonely, not more. She suggested they not close their hearts, but rather to open them.

"I understand that some people may feel that to avoid the pain of a broken heart it is best to harden their heart so that it will never be shattered again. If you would allow me to borrow an analogy from what doctors often say. You see, at my age I can afford to think of myself as a bit of an authority on doctors because I see them so regularly."

There were a number of chuckles and muffled laughs from the hundred or so of those seated in the church. It seemed to be the perfect tension reliever.

Francine continued. "Doctors say that when certain bones break they often heal stronger and better than before. Well, I would like to think the same is true of a broken heart. I know we are all saddened by what happened to Douglas. It was not fair. It was not right. He was far too young to die, especially in the manner he did."

Francine paused for a second to take a deep breath and then continued, "We are all saddened by this loss. Please don't let it close your hearts to love."

She briefly looked at Michael who stared back passively. Revenge was on his mind.

"Douglas's heart was starting to open up to the feeling of love he was starting to feel for so many others. I think one of the best ways to pay our respects to Douglas is to share his love, and your love, with others."

Looking toward the casket she said, "May you rest in eternal peace, my dearly beloved Douglas." She stepped down from behind the podium and returned to her seat. Julie and Lisa were both sobbing lightly but smiled at Francine as she sat down. The minister then approached the podium.

"The family would like to invite anyone else who would like to say a few words of remembrance for their son," the minister announced. A few others came up and spoke briefly.

///

A long procession of cars with headlights lit and funeral flyers in their windshields wound through the streets of suburban Atlanta with police escorts assisting. Once at the cemetery the pallbearers unloaded the casket and carried it the seventy-five feet to the burial plot. There were cushioned folding chairs adjacent to the elevated casket on which the four family members could sit.

Richard Jamison had carried the large floral display over to the gravesite and placed it on the center of the casket. Before Julie sat down she reached over to the spray of flowers and picked out three roses, one for Francine, one for Lisa and one for herself. The minister greeted and thanked everyone for coming. He quoted several appropriate passages from the bible and added some thoughtful interpretations to them. Then he asked everyone to join him in praying for the eternal resting in peace of Doug's soul.

The final act of the service was something arranged by Greg's boss. Two men stepped forward, each carrying a basket-weaved crate. They set the crates on the ground and at the same time released six doves from each basket. The twelve white birds flew together circling high above and then gradually off to the east out of sight.

Michael was mesmerized as he watched the doves soar overhead. He thought Doug would have been pleased. Michael also believed something needed to be done to avenge his brother's death, and at that moment Michael's plan of retaliation began to take shape.

CHAPTER 22

AFTER THE FUNERAL, dozens of friends and relatives arrived at Greg and Julie's home. People mingled back and forth among the kitchen, dining room and family room, munching on platters of food prepared by Francine. Michael sought out Tiny and took him aside.

"Hey, Tiny, let's go to my room," Michael suggested.

"Uh, okay," Tiny responded slowly, trying hard not to stutter.

Tiny had never been in Michael's room before and was fascinated by the objects on display. There were youth sports trophies, academic awards, graphic art posters, professional sports pennants and a host of souvenirs from the various national parks and historic sites he had visited with his parents.

"Listen, Tiny, like, I have a favor to ask, okay?"

"Alright," Tiny slightly stuttered in reply.

"I need a ride to Stephenson Park Thursday. Could you take me there?"

Tiny looked puzzled so Michael explained. "Mom's going to be with a client and dad has some after work meeting, so neither one will be available."

"Uh, I, uh, I guess so," Tiny replied.

"Great. Could you, like, swing by, like, around seven?"

"Sure."

"Would you like not say anything to anyone about this? I'm going to surprise some guys at the park and I, like, wouldn't want them finding out, okay?"

"Uh, okay," Tiny replied.

They left Michael's room and headed back to the family room. People were mingling, snacking and studying Julie's display of Doug's life. Many of them reminisced about their favorite memories of and experiences with Doug.

By eight o'clock Tuesday evening most of the guests had left the MacDonald home. Michael said goodbye to Tiny and confirmed he would pick him up on Thursday. Tiny just smiled his innocent, infectious grin and agreed. With this part of his plan in place, Michael fist bumped Tiny and said goodbye.

///

Thursday morning was a beehive of activity in the MacDonald household. Julie knew it would be a long day for her and Greg because of their evening appointments, and wanted to start everyone with a filling breakfast. So she prepared her popular flapjacks with all the fixings.

Greg also was up early. After showering he visited his office briefly to handle urgent emails. One was a reminder from Jim Barnett about getting together for lunch to compare notes about the progress they would present that evening at the monthly joint task force dinner meeting. As Greg finished on his computer, Michael bounded down the staircase and smelled the aroma of his mother's flapjacks.

"Hi, Mom," he said pleasantly. "These sure smell good."

"Thanks. Pour everyone some orange juice. What're your plans tonight?"

"I'm inviting Tiny over. We're gonna hang out for a while. There're some video games Doug showed me that Tiny wants to see. Is that okay?"

Julie gave reluctant approval. "I guess. Make sure you've finished your homework."

"Oh yeah. For sure," Michael replied.

Julie sat down to enjoy her breakfast with her family. The combined scents of pancakes, bacon, sausage and heated maple syrup added to the homey atmosphere. After finishing their meals, Greg and Michael kissed Julie good-bye and headed out. Minutes later Greg dropped Michael off at school and then drove to his office.

///

After a routine morning of reports, meetings and paperwork, Greg looked forward to walking to lunch at Dario's Deli. As he stepped inside the popular lunch spot, he smelled the fresh scents of homemade breads and spicy meatballs. It was a welcomed sensation. Greg loved many things about Atlanta. He relished the culture of the people, the history of the area and the excellence of the sports.

He especially enjoyed Downtown. He savored the small, specialty stores and eateries like Dario's Deli. Atlanta was always an interesting combination of opposites. In stark contrast to these tiny buildings were the towering skyscrapers that ringed the center of the city.

The only aspect of downtown that now saddened Greg was the fact that he would never be able to share it with his older son. Greg shrugged at the thought that he would never be able to show Doug why Greg had such a deep appreciation for all of the wondrous and unique traits of his beloved Atlanta. Greg was a man of faith who believed in an afterlife, and was certain he would be able to show and tell his son all about the magnificent metropolis.

Dario's was crowded as usual. Greg was glad Jim and he had made their usual arrangement of each one taking the other's order so that whoever showed up first would put in the order for both of them. Unsure whether Jim had arrived yet, Greg looked around for his friend. Finally he saw Jim at a small table along the sidewall on which Jim had placed Greg's sandwich, chips and drink order.

"You must have arrived early," Greg said cheerfully.

"I did. My meeting ended early and traffic was lighter than normal."

The two of them tore into their sandwiches. While eating they talked about the evening's meeting. All twenty-five of the key players on the joint IT/APD task force would be attending the downtown event hosted at an upscale restaurant.

After discussing minor details about their presentations, the two paused for a minute. Jim took a sip of his drink and said, "Greg, I am so sorry about what happened to your son."

Greg looked straight at Jim and replied, "I know. It is just so sad. I really believed he had turned a corner."

"I know," Jim replied. "I remember what you said about him during your eulogy, which, by the way, I thought was beautiful."

"Thanks," Greg said. Then he took a breath and asked, "Is there anything the detectives have on who did this?"

"Well, we think the Raptors motorcycle gang was involved. They've been known to entice high school kids to push drugs for them. Their leader has an alibi through his girlfriend, which I don't believe, and Lisa couldn't identify him."

"Well, couldn't you bring him in for a line-up?" Greg asked.

"Not without probable cause, but we're working on it. I'm confident we will get him one way or another," Jim said assuredly.

Then Jim said quietly, "Greg, I know you must miss your son very much."

"I do."

"Well, I know it's not the same thing, but in a strange way I feel like I know what you're going through."

Greg raised his eyes a bit and asked, "How so?"

"It's Kenny. Like we talked earlier, we haven't heard from him in months. His sister Cheryl tried to contact him about Doug's passing, but we haven't heard a peep."

"You haven't?"

"Nope, and it really pisses me off," Jim answered. "For all we know he could be out in California or down in Australia or God knows where else."

"Well, when's the last time you two talked?" Greg inquired.

"Hell, it's been over six months. Maybe longer. A part of me just wants to shake him like a kid and demand to know why he's treating us so badly."

"Yeah, I get that," Greg said.

"Another part of me feels like it's my fault."

"What do you mean?" Greg asked.

"I think I've mentioned I wanted Kenny to go into law."

"Yes. Because he was so interested in politics, right?"

Jim responded, "Not just interested. He was damn good at it. He won all of those student government elections in high school. He was president of the debate club and was singled out with distinction at the state high school debate competitions."

"Oh, yeah," Greg recalled. "Didn't he get written up in the newspaper?"

"Two newspapers. Plus his school's newspaper and the school district's newsletter." Jim shook his head and looked around the deli as if trying to find an answer. "I don't know, Greg. I know we're supposed to let our kids do their own thing, make their own ways, choose their own paths. It's just so frustrating that he wanted to go into police work and throw away the chance at a great career in law."

"Maybe he just wanted to follow in his dad's footsteps?" Greg offered.

"I don't think it's that. Not at all. We have been at loggerheads for the past few years on this. He threw away college, threw away law school and for what? He has seen the stress this job can put on a family, on a marriage. Why would he want that when he had so many better options? Sometimes I think he's doing it to spite me."

"I doubt that that's the reason," Greg protested.

"I don't know. It's just hard not to know where he is, and how he is." Jim paused for a minute and then changed his whole expression.

Greg noticed. "What?"

"Here I am going on and on about my own son when you just lost yours. I'm sorry Greg, I shouldn't have gotten so carried away."

"Hey, it's okay, buddy. If you can't vent to friends then who can you? I get how frustrating it must be to not know your son's whereabouts and how he is."

"Thanks Greg. You really are a true friend," Jim said with an appreciative smile as the two finished their lunch.

"So how much do I owe you?" Greg asked.

Jim waved him off. "This one's on me."

"Are you sure? I'm bumming a ride back to work with you."

"No way, my friend," Jim insisted. "I would have had to drive back anyway. Besides, consider it your fee for listening."

"Okay," Greg chuckled.

The two friends got up and headed for the door. Then they walked over to Jim's car for the ride back to work.

///

Michael arrived home from school and ensured he was alone. He dug right into his homework assignments in History and Algebra, which he wrapped up in an hour. The sun had already set as he came downstairs and strode into the kitchen. Michael wrote a note saying he and Tiny had decided to go see a movie. His intent was to buy time in case his plans for the evening grew longer than expected. He tacked the note on the bulletin board and then walked to his father's office.

One of the paybacks Doug had offered Michael for helping Doug shop for and select appropriate clothes for an important date was to tell Michael about the location, contents and combination of their father's gun safe. Inside it was a stash of ready cash.

The cash was not what Michael was interested in that Thursday evening in December. It was the Colt Model 1911A handgun that had been the focus of Michael's thinking for the past several days. He knew his father kept the loaded firearm in the locked gun safe.

Doug had told Michael their father kept the gun safe hidden in the lower left drawer of his desk. Michael opened the drawer and lifted the dark gray rectangular box out and set it on the top of the desk. It was heavier than Michael had imagined. On the front panel was a recessed square pad with ten numbered push buttons.

Michael pressed the pushbuttons marked seven, one and three and heard the faint sound of a latch releasing. He raised the sturdy thick lid and stared at the lethal weapon. It looked shiny, and new, and deadly. He knew it was loaded but he also saw that the safety was on so he gingerly picked it up. It was surprisingly lighter than he expected. After inspecting it from end-to-end and side-to-side, Michael carefully placed it in a zippered compartment on the inside of his backpack. Then he closed the gun safe and replaced it in the desk drawer.

At ten minutes after seven Michael started pacing in the kitchen. As he started formulating contingency plans he heard the doorbell and saw Tiny's truck outside.

"Come in," Michael called out.

"Okay," Tiny replied.

Tiny started apologizing for being late, blaming it on traffic and a gas stop.

"Hey, no problem dude. Are you hungry?" Michael asked.

"Ah, yeah," Tiny smiled in response. Michael realized that Tiny could have just finished a full dinner and would likely still be hungry. In fact, he had eaten only a light snack earlier and looked enthused about a meal.

"How about the Varsity for hamburgers before we go to the park?"

Tiny smiled broadly as they headed out the door. During the drive, Michael thought about the lengthy talk he had had with Lisa about what had happened at the park. There was no doubt in his mind that Dominic Williams was the person responsible for his brother's death. He had also learned from some of Doug's friends that on the third Thursday of each month there was an informal gathering of hoodlum motorcycle enthusiasts at Stephenson Park which Dominic always attended.

Michael expected to arrive at the park around eight thirty, late enough to ensure Dominic would have already arrived and early enough that he would not have already left. Michael planned to confront Dominic with Greg's gun and to force a confession out of Dominic. As to whether he would actually pull the trigger he believed he would put that in the hands of fate and take whatever action he felt necessary.

Tiny pulled into the Varsity parking lot at seven thirty. Tiny ordered double portions which did not surprise Michael. He paid for Tiny's meal with lunch money he had saved.

After both had finished eating Michael suggested, "I think we should go now."

"Okay."

At eight thirty-five the two boys climbed out of Tiny's truck at Stephenson Park. Tiny headed straight for the restrooms when Michael called. "Hey, can I have your keys for a minute? I need to get something out of my backpack."

"Okay," Tiny replied as he handed Michael his truck keys.

With Tiny in the restroom, Michael switched off Tiny's cell phone. Next Michael carefully but quickly removed the handgun from his backpack. Then he tucked it inside the rear waistband of his cargo pants, remembering to release the gun's safety mechanism. Partly as a tribute to his brother, and partly to conceal his weapon, Michael had worn Doug's black leather jacket.

///

As Michael inserted Tiny's key into the door of his vehicle, Julie inserted her house key into the door of her home. She read Michael's note about seeing a movie with Tiny. She thought it was a bit peculiar but not out of the ordinary.

Minutes later Julie's phone rang. It was Tiny's mother saying she was concerned about the safety of her son and that of Michael. Tiny's sister had just told her that she had overheard him say he would be taking Michael to Stephenson Park that night.

"Are you sure?" Julie asked. "Because I just walked in the house and Michael had left me a note saying that your son and he were going to a movie."

"Well, I suppose she may have misunderstood. Or maybe they were going to go there originally and then changed their minds to go to a movie."

"Teenagers do change their minds. But Michael never mentioned going to the park. Now I'm starting to get worried. Have you tried calling your son?"

"Several times. But it goes straight to voice mail as if he has it turned off."

Julie said she would try to call Michael and would call her right back. They ended the call and Julie tried contacting Michael three times but each call went right to voice mail. Then Julie's phone rang. She looked at the caller ID hoping it was Michael, but it was Tiny's mother. This time her voice was quivering.

"His phone is at the south end of Stephenson Park," she cried into the receiver.

"What? How do you know that?" Julie asked, now growing quite concerned.

"Because we have a GPS feature on his truck. I just keyed in an inquiry as to the truck's location and it shows it being at the south end of Stephenson Park."

"Oh my God," Julie gasped. "I need to call my husband. He's with a police detective and they'll know what to do."

Greg and Jim came out of the joint task force dinner meeting when Julie's call came through. She sounded frantic as she explained what Tiny's mother had just relayed to her. *Why would Michael want to go to the south part of Stephenson Park?* he thought.

"Michael had a friend take him to the south portion of Stephenson Park," Greg blurted.

"It's bike night there tonight," Jim said.

"What does that mean," Greg asked anxiously.

"Biker gangs get together to show off their customized motorcycles the third Thursday of every month. Michael's not interested in customized bikes, is he?"

"Hell no," Greg shouted back. Then a terrifying thought came to his mind.

"Jim, did you say Doug's suspected assailant headed up a motorcycle gang?"

"Yes. Dominic Williams. He heads up the Raptors but he alibied out."

Greg spoke to Julie. "Sweetheart, listen to me. I know you and Lisa talked for some time about what happened to Doug in the park that night. Do you know if she ever shared those details with Michael?"

"I don't know. Why? I'm getting a bad feeling about this," Julie replied shakily.

Greg tried his best to ease her mind, but his own mind was racing. Then, as if an avalanche had just fallen on him, a frightening thought rushed into his head. As much as he preferred not to, he knew he had to share it with his wife. He tried to remain calm, not wanting to upset Julie any more than she was. In a steady voice he asked her to go into his office and check his gun safe.

If he had hoped to calm Julie, his plan failed miserably. As soon as Greg spoke, Julie knew what he was thinking. Twenty years of marriage did not come without some degree of mental telepathy.

"What do you mean check the gun safe?"

Julie strode into Greg's office and stooped to open the lower desk drawer and pull out the heavy gun box. Her heart was pounding as she set the safe on the desktop.

With shaking fingers she pressed the numbers Greg told her and heard the latch of the sturdy lid release. She raised the cover and as she looked inside her heart skipped a beat. There was no gun inside. She slumped down and in a very despairing voice told her husband that the gun was gone.

Greg exhaled deeply and uttered a barely audible, "Damn it."

Jim quickly surmised what Greg had just learned and suggested that they take Jim's car to get to Stephenson Park immediately. Jim's car had flashing lights on the visors to enable his car to race through traffic. Greg quickly told Julie of their plans and that he would call her as soon as they arrived at the park. He then told her to call Tiny's mother to explain what was going on.

///

Michael began walking toward the restrooms at south Stephenson Park to meet up with Tiny who had just come out of the facility. Most of the hundreds of motorcycles that had been there earlier had already left. Michael surveyed the remaining bikes closely seeking out one particular design. Lisa had described for him what Dominic's motorcycle would look like because of its unique paint job.

Toward the end of the parking lot were two motorcycles off by themselves. As Michael and Tiny approached them, Michael's heart started racing. He had no doubt the motorcycle on the left belonged to Dominic. Lisa had described it as being deep purple in color with yellow and light blue accents including long narrow flames on either side of the fuel tank. Most distinctive were the words Raptor Warrior painted in highly stylized lettering.

The artistic side of Michael engulfed him for a brief moment as he admired the coloring and graphic patterns that were dyed and tinted on the various surfaces of the bike. Michael quickly came to his senses as he realized that the owner of this motorcycle had murdered his brother. The time for justice had arrived.

Michael did not want Tiny involved in this part of his plan, so he reach into his pocket and exclaimed, "Damn it."

"What?" Tiny asked.

"I think like I may have left my wallet at the Varsity. Damn. It has some notes in it I need for the friends showing up here. Would you mind driving back there to see if they have it?"

"Ah, okay," Tiny agreed.

The trusting Tiny walked to his truck and headed back to the Varsity. Michael figured he would be gone about forty minutes, more than enough time to confront Dominic. At gunpoint Michael figured to force him to confess to his brother's murder and to turn himself in.

Certain Dominic would show up soon, Michael hung back behind a picnic table not far from Dominic's bike. He was in dark shadows and not visible to anyone close by. Michael believed Dominic would soon come for his bike, giving Michael the opportunity to confront him.

Michael did not have to wait long. In the distance he saw two men walking toward the bikes. One of the men, with a slashed cheek and jet-black hair, strode off to the left to join a group who were exchanging packages in brown paper wrapping. The other man approached the distinctively painted bike. Michael suspected it was Dominic. The initials of DW on his belt buckle all but confirmed it.

Michael was nervous but realized it was now or never. He approached the man and called out, "Are you Dominic Williams?"

Dominic turned and squinted. He stared at Michael. "Who's asking?"

"You murdered my brother," Michael spewed.

Dominic seemed amused. "People say I've murdered a lot of people. Doesn't mean I've done it."

"His name was Doug MacDonald and he sold drugs for you at the high schools." Michael voice started rising as he continued, "And when he wanted out of the deal you stabbed and killed him with his own knife."

Dominic quickly grew annoyed. "Look, kid, why don't you go home to your momma before you get hurt."

Michael pulled the gun out and pointed it directly at Dominic. "You murdered my brother and you're going to pay for it. Go ahead. Admit it."

"You don't have proof of nothin'," Dominic mocked.

"This gun is going to provide the proof. You either confess to the crime or you die."

Dominic extended his hands. "Take it easy. This doesn't have to go down like this. Yeah, maybe your brother and I mixed it up, but he drew the knife."

"So you admit you killed him?" Michael demanded.

"Dude, he got what he deserved. He reneged on our deal. No one does that."

Michael aimed the gun at Dominic's head. "Bullshit. No one deserved that. No one deserved to die that way."

Dominic studied his young aggressor closely as well as the firearm Michael had trained at his head. That was when Dominic decided to bring the situation to a swift end. He pulled his own gun out from under his jacket and pointed it at Michael.

Michael summoned up all of his courage and pressed his finger against the smooth curved metal of the trigger. It moved about an eighth an inch and then stopped. Michael was unaware the secondary safety was still on. Dominic saw the puzzled look on Michael's face that quickly turned to panic.

Just then Raven approached from the side and began running toward Michael. In one rapid motion Raven pulled out his own gun.

"Drop the gun," Raven yelled at Michael.

Michael froze. He realized he was facing certain death and tried to comprehend the sheer senselessness of it all.

The sound of a firearm discharging pierced the night silence with a reverberating echo. Michael slumped to the ground, blood seeping out. The gunshot was heard at the Kozy Korner donut shop where the clerk called 911 and reported gunfire.

CHAPTER 23

THE FAMILIAR SQUAWK of the dispatcher keying her microphone grabbed Jim's attention as he and Greg headed to the park. There had been a report of a gunshot heard near the south section of Stephenson Park. Greg's heart skipped a beat as he listened to the dispatcher's dispassionate voice.

"All units in the area of Stephenson Park, additional gunshots reported in the same vicinity as those reported earlier on the south side of the park. Code two. Repeat, code two," the dispatcher reported.

"What is code two?" Greg asked.

"Lights approved for cars like mine," Jim answered as he pulled down the sun visors and activated a switch. Instantly red and blue flashing lights came on from behind the visors. Their bright reflections bounced off the sides of buildings as the car sped by them.

Greg's heart started racing almost as fast as Jim's car as he deftly maneuvered it around the randomly heavy and light traffic of Atlanta's streets. Jim's car was within a mile of south Stephenson Park. Greg looked around and was surprised there were not more patrol cars joining them on their race to the south portal entrance.

"Shouldn't there be other police cars joining us by now?" Greg asked.

"They'll be here quick enough. Most of the deployment tonight was on the opposite side of town," Jim explained. There had been a civil rights protest earlier in the evening there. Police officials believed there was a much stronger likelihood of violence at that event as compared to the motorcycle rally where gangs tended to police the area themselves.

Greg decided that now was the time he needed to call Julie back. She picked up immediately but just as Greg said there had been reports of multiple gunshots at Stephenson Park, his cell phone went dead. In his haste to call his wife he had not noticed the quiet beeping sound indicating his battery was low and about to go off. Greg swore at himself and asked Jim if he had an adapter that Greg could use to make his phone usable.

Jim reached into his pocket and pulled out his own smart phone and handed it to Greg. Not being familiar with this brand of phone, Greg took a second to study the various icons on the face of Jim's phone. Just as he was about to press the proper symbol, Jim pulled into Stephenson Park. Greg peered out of his window beyond the parking lot of the park.

///

Back at the MacDonald residence, Julie slowly closed the door to the gun safe. She tried to piece together all of the tragic events that happened over the previous two weeks, and especially now during the past two hours. She wished she had someone with whom to talk.

In all of the chaos, Julie completely forgot that there was someone there with her to share all that was going on, Francine. Julie had driven to a client's home earlier that evening to discuss potential redecorating of the homeowner's living and dining rooms. The house was located close to Francine's home. Julie had agreed to pick Francine up and bring her over to Julie's house to spend the night. Francine had been taking a nap in the guest room.

Julie quickly tip-toed into Francine's room and gently awakened her.

"Francine, it's Julie. Sorry to have to wake you, but we need to talk."

"Oh, okay," Francine said a bit groggily. She blinked her eyes a few times and asked, "Is everything all right?"

"It's Michael. A friend of his took him to Stephenson Park," Julie answered.

Francine sat up on the bed. "Why on earth would he go there? Particularly at night?"

Julie started sobbing. "We think he took Greg's gun with him."

"Oh no," Francine uttered.

"Greg thinks Michael may be trying to avenge Doug's death. I can't believe this is happening," Julie said in between sobs. She tried breathing heavily to compose herself. "Greg and his detective friend are on their way to the park right now. I am hoping to hear from him any minute."

Julie paced around the room. Francine could see this was not helping the situation at all and felt it would be better if they moved out into a more open space. "Why don't we go out into the kitchen? I'll make you a cup of your favorite tea."

Julie looked at her loving mother-in-law and smiled briefly. "Okay. Thanks. That sounds good." Unfortunately, the respite was short-lived as Julie soon started sobbing again while asking, "Why would he take a gun? What if he ends up being shot?"

The two of them walked to the kitchen. Francine began preparing the tea while Julie sat down at the side of the table. Eventually, the thoughts of tragic outcomes that could befall her son became overwhelming for Julie. She started breaking down, saying she could not bear the thought of losing her only other surviving child. "Both of my children brutally killed within a week of each other? How can this be happening? Where did I go so wrong?"

Francine tried to console her by saying that she was not to blame for Doug's death. She reminded Julie that she and Greg had done everything humanly possible to help Doug. Their efforts, directly or indirectly, Francine insisted, had put Doug on a more straight and narrow path.

"But don't you see?" Julie countered. "Doug's attempts to turn things around are precisely what got him killed."

"No, no, no," Francine softly replied. "Doug's attempts to turn things around are not what got him killed. A criminal person's greed, and pride and violent nature are what got Doug killed. Doug's attempts to turn his life around are what redeemed him in the end."

The vibrating sound of her smart phone startled Julie and got her heart racing. She saw caller ID showed that it was Greg.

"Sweetheart, what is going on? Where are you right now?" Julie asked in a voice that sounded urgent and almost panicky.

"We are within a mile of south Stephenson Park. Honey I need to tell you that gunshots have been reported being heard at that area. But we don't have any additional information about that right now. As soon as I find out more I'll—"

All of a sudden Julie's phone went silent. She first thought something was wrong with her phone. Surely Greg would not end the call so abruptly. It had to be her phone, she was certain. It never dawned on her that Greg's phone might be the source of the problem.

Francine immediately saw the panicked and depressed look on Julie's face and came over to console her. Francine had just poured a hot cup of tea for Julie but left it on the counter. Instead she came right over and gave Julie a warm, comforting hug without saying a word.

Francine knew she did not have to utter a sound. Julie would share her feelings soon enough. Julie tried to speak but could not. She was sobbing uncontrollably and struggling to catch her breath. Francine kept patting her on her back.

Finally Julie calmed down enough to cry out, "I can't lose Michael, too!" She took a deep breath. "Greg just said there were gunshots heard at the park. What if it was Michael? What if it was my baby?" The sobbing started all over again. Francine kept patting her.

"How I can lose both of my children in less than a week! Michael doesn't deserve this! Doug did not deserve this! None of this makes any sense! How can this be happening?"

"Julie, take a drink of this."

Julie took a sip of the hot brimming tea. Her hands were

still shaking, her eyes were still misty and breathing was still irregular.

"Julie," Francine began. "I can't pretend to know the depth of the pain you must be feeling right now. Whatever condition your son is in right now, both he and your husband are going to need you to be strong."

The thought hit Julie light a thunderbolt. In her preoccupation with the welfare of her son, it had not occurred to her the devastating effect this whole situation could have on her husband. She realized that both of the men in her life needed her to be there for them, in whatever capacity that required. Julie took another sip of tea and tentatively nodded her head in acknowledgement.

"Until you learn otherwise," Francine went on, "you must believe that Michael is still okay."

Julie nodded.

"Julie, I know you are a woman of faith, are you not?"

"Yes, I am," Julie said assuredly.

"Well, then, I suggest you put your faith in the Lord. I know you have been given a tremendous cross to bear. But I also believe the Lord will never give us more to endure than what we can bear. Would you agree?"

"I suppose so," Julie said hesitantly.

"Why don't we say a silent prayer for Michael and for Greg right now," Francine suggested.

"Okay. That sounds good," Julie responded.

CHAPTER 24

THE LAST FEW bikes from the motorcycle rally were departing the south section of Stephenson Park as Jim Barnett's car raced under the south portal. The flashing lights from his visors blinked red and blue on the sides of the giant archway as Jim's vehicle passed through the huge structure. Greg started squinting into the dimly lit parking lot looking for any sign of his son. Jim widened his viewing area to scan the entire horizon in front of him.

"There," Jim shouted, pointing his arm. "Over on the far right."

"I see them," Greg exclaimed back.

A tall muscular man appeared to be pointing a gun at one of two people lying on the ground. Jim parked the car but left the flashing lights activated.

"Stay back, Greg. He's got a gun," Jim instructed as he drew his own weapon and trained it on the gunman. Greg stayed behind Jim as the detective cautiously stepped forward.

"Drop the gun," Jim ordered to the man holding the firearm.

He planted his feet wide apart and anchored himself with a

perfectly centered balance. Then he raised his gun to eye level, cocked the trigger and pointed it directly at the man.

"I said drop the gun. Now," Jim said in the sternest voice Greg had ever heard his friend use. The eyes of the two men were riveted on each other like lasers. Neither was about to blink.

Finally the gunman spoke. "Okay. Setting it on the ground." The man turned his gun sideways and pointed it away from Jim toward the ground. Then he slowly bent his knees and squatted down to gently place the gun on the weed-infested dirt. With the gun out of his hand he stood up very slowly with his hands outstretched.

Jim walked quickly in his direction. "Back away and get on your knees. Hands behind your head," Jim barked out at the would-be assailant. The man known as Raven took several steps backwards. Jim reached the gun and picked it up while keeping his own gun trained directly on the disarmed gangbanger.

Behind Raven and to his left lay Dominic Williams, his gun still clutched in his motionless hand. Dominic's chest was covered in fresh blood that was still oozing out underneath his black motorcycle jacket. The red liquid puddled on the left side of his body.

Jim angled his way over to Dominic without diverting his gaze away from Raven. The detective bent down and felt for the carotid artery. No pulse. Dominic had been shot twice in the chest.

As soon as Raven started kneeling, Michael's prone body came into view to Greg who ran quickly to reach his fallen son. Even in the sparse lighting he could see what looked to be blood oozing out from underneath his son's chest area.

"Oh no! No!" Greg cried out as he came upon his son. Half a dozen fleeting thoughts started rifling through his brain. *What was his condition? Is he still alive? How did this happen? Who is responsible? How will I tell Julie?* Jim backed up to assist his anguished friend while maintaining eye contact with Raven.

The right side of Michael's head was lying flat against the ground and his eyes were closed. Greg leaned over and whispered, "Oh, Michael, my dear sweet Michael."

Then Greg noticed Michael still breathing. "He's alive! He's still alive!" Greg exclaimed. Jim rushed over after he issued an order to Raven, "Don't move a muscle."

"Let's roll him over," Greg suggested. Very slowly and carefully Jim and Greg rolled Michael over on to his back. Blood seeped from his son's chest. Jim immediately recognized it as a bullet wound and pulled out his handkerchief.

"Here, press this on the wound." Greg applied as much pressure as he could without inflicting any more injury to his son. A few minutes later Michael moved his head, slightly. He grunted and then gradually opened his eyes.

"Sorry, Dad, I just had to do this for Doug." His voice trailed off.

"Don't talk right now son, just be still." Then he turned his head away from Michael and yelled to Jim, "Ambulance! Right away!"

In less than a minute, sirens blared and police cars rolled up, followed by an emergency services truck and two ambulances. Attendants rushed up to tend both Michael and the other victim lying on his back.

As two emergency medical technicians took over the treatment of Michael, and for the first time Greg noticed that Michael was holding Greg's gun. Michael saw that his father was looking down at the gun.

"Sorry I took it, Dad. I forgot to turn the other safety off."

Greg hugged his son as much as the paramedics allowed. Then Greg moved to allow them to attend to Michael. They quickly saw that Michael had been shot in the upper left torso. While the bleeding was perfuse, it did not appear any vital organs were damaged, one of the medics said.

Greg had been so focused on Michael that he did not notice the other victim lying on the ground. Michael saw his father looking over at Dominic and told him that he was the person who had killed Doug. Greg just stared at the body of the person who had taken his son's life. Then he thought of Julie and knew he had to call her. As he figured out how to use Jim's phone, additional medical responders went over to the man who was lying on the ground. They checked his vital signs and declared him dead at the scene.

Jim heard Michael tell his father that he had left the safety on, so Jim verified that the secondary safety was still engaged. Jim inspected the gun and determined it had not been fired.

Someone else must have shot Dominic. Jim looked over at Raven with suspicious eyes and started walking toward him. Raven moved his right hand from behind his head.

"Freeze," Jim ordered.

"Please," Raven asked. "I need to show you something. Let me reach in and show you something. Please. It's not a gun."

"All right. But slowly. Very slowly."

Raven carefully extended his right hand into the left inside of his jacket. After opening a sealed pocket he slowly pulled out an object and revealed it to the detective.

"Oh my God," Jim gasped. He could not believe what he was looking at.

///

Julie was still firmly grasping her pink encased smartphone when her husband's voice abruptly stopped ten minutes earlier. She had tried calling him back several times only to hear voicemail.

Julie was so preoccupied thinking about what might have happened that initially she did not realize the phone in her hand was buzzing. Finally the vibrating sensation registered and she quickly looked at the caller ID. It was not a number she recognized.

"Hello," she said very cautiously.

"Sweetheart, it's me. I'm with Michael but he's been shot," Greg said rapidly.

"Oh no," Julie started crying into the phone.

"He's okay, honey, he's okay."

"What did you say? He's alive?" Julie gushed into the phone.

"Yes. Yes, he's alive. He's going to be okay," Greg confirmed. "The paramedics are tending to him right now. They're about to load him onto the gurney."

"Oh, thank God," Julie blurted out. She looked at Francine with an expression of total relief. Then Julie's expression changed from one of bewilderment to one of shame. She realized she had just thanked the Lord just minutes after all but despairing of His help. She silently said a prayer of repentance and appreciation.

"Michael was shot on his left side but it missed his heart," Greg explained to his wife. "The paramedics think he'll be okay," Greg repeated.

Julie exhaled another sigh of relief and asked, "Could I talk to him for a second?"

"He's not really conscious and they've got an oxygen mask on him."

"I see. Are you going to stay with him?"

"Yes. I'm going to ride with him in the ambulance to Atlanta General."

"Well, then I'll be right over to join you. I'll see over there."

"Okay. And sweetheart?" Greg paused.

"Yes?"

"You drive safely, okay?"

"Will do. Honey. I love you," Julie said sweetly.

"I love you, too."

Julie ended the call with her mind in a blur. She quickly explained to Francine what had occurred.

"I'm going to drive over to the hospital right now. Would you like to join me?"

"Definitely."

Within minutes the two women were on their way to the hospital.

///

Back at the park Greg watched as the paramedics gently loaded his son into the ambulance and secured the gurney. He yelled a "thank you" over to Jim who was still staring at Raven. Then Greg climbed into the back of the ambulance. Soon it was racing out of the park on route to the hospital with its lights flashing and its siren blaring.

Jim was still staring at the kneeling gunman. He was holding in his right hand what looked to be a laminated card. On one side was a police identification card and on the other an image of a police badge.

Jim asked in disbelief, "You're a cop?"

"Not just a cop. Not just undercover. Dad, it's me."

"What?" Jim uttered. As he neared the kneeling man, Jim was stunned as he realized the shooter indeed was his son Kenny. Jim lowered his gun and said "Damn. I hardly recognized you. What's it been? Six, seven months?"

"Nine. Good to see you, too," Kenny said with a smile.

Jim still seemed shocked. "You must have put on some twenty pounds."

"Twenty-five actually," Kenny responded. "Most of it muscle."

"I still can't believe it's you," Jim marveled. He was surprised, shocked and puzzled. Then he studied his son. The undercover makeup unit had given his son a scar on his left cheek, tattoos on both arms and his neck, and long jet-black hair.

"How did this happen? When did this happen? Did you shoot the gang leader?" Jim asked as his mind flooded with questions.

"Dad, I'll tell you all about it. Are you sure our perp is dead?"

"Positive. No pulse. No breathing," Jim replied.

"Well, does that mean I can stand up now?" the still-kneeling son asked his father.

"Of course. He's your collar, isn't he? Best you get your ass up and finish the job."

"Listen, Dad, I know you have tons of questions. Before I get buried with all the paperwork, why don't you let me buy you a cup of coffee over at the Kozy Korner and I'll tell you all about it."

Jim agreed. As he walked over to his car, he watched as the second ambulance transported Dominic's body to the morgue. He backed out of his parking spot while he watched his son mount his Harley and take off for the donut shop. *When did he learn to ride a motorcycle so well?* he thought.

The two men parked in front and walked into the coffee shop together. They made for a peculiar sight. One was a middle-aged man in a sport jacket with short hair wearing wing-tipped shoes and a business-casual dress shirt. He could have passed for a Wall Street broker except for the firearm he had tucked away in his rear waistband.

The other man was taller and much younger. His long jet-black hair was slicked back behind pierced ears that framed a tattoo on the rear of his neck. He wore a black leather motorcycle jacket with gang affiliation badges. The bottoms of his dark Levis covered expensive Harley-Davidson motorcycle boots. His left cheek contained a three-inch ugly-looking slash.

Jim could not take his eyes off of his son. Despite the drastic changes in appearance, some things with Kenny were the same. Jim smiled in relief when he heard his son order a Danish-filled bear claw and cup of black coffee with just a hint of honey added, a combination Kenny had loved since his mid-teens.

"I'm glad to see some things haven't changed," Jim smiled.

"Yeah, well, you know what they say, Dad," Kenny replied.

"No, I don't know, son," Jim answered. "In fact, at this point, I'm not sure I know what to believe."

Kenny just smiled. "Old habits die hard. I'm glad I'm back with you, Dad. It's been a really tough nine months."

"I can only imagine," Jim responded. As they talked Jim slipped off his sport jacket and draped it over the back of his chair. Kenny did the same with his jacket. As his bare arms came into view, Jim marveled at how muscular his son had become. He also was struck by the authenticity of the tattoos that adorned his forearms and biceps.

"That ink isn't real, is it?"

"Nah," Kenny replied. "But they look real, don't they?"

"Yes, they do. I always heard our makeup department for undercover was second maybe only to the LAPD who's usually in bed with Hollywood anyway."

They both laughed.

Kenny explained how he had so impressed his superiors with his undercover work in the junior high schools the previous year that they proposed another assignment. It would be more elaborate and dangerous than his previous assignment. It would involve infiltrating a notorious, murderous motorcycle gang with ambitions to significantly expand its network of drug use among early and pre-teens.

In order to transform him into a convincing motorcycle gangbanger, Kenny underwent a total makeover. He partook in a highly supervised and rigorous program of bodybuilding, weight-training and motorcycle instruction. The undercover unit had worked in concert with the FBI to provide a believable backstory for the character known as Raven.

They also helped to stage Raven's shooting of the homeless man in Stephenson Park to convince Dominic that Raven was a killer. As Kenny continued with details of the ruse, Jim was amazed and impressed at what his son had accomplished.

"So you mean it was you who shot that homeless slug?" Jim asked his son almost incredulously.

"Sure was," Kenny replied proudly. "That poor homeless guy was actually Keith Dedricks, another Sweeney," Kenny said using police slang for an undercover cop. "He's a part-time wannabe actor who's done some stage work. He played it a bit over the top, but he got Dominic's attention all right."

"So that's why there was so little said about his supposed murder right after it happened. I wondered about that," Jim mused.

"Exactly. The department and the DA worked together to keep it under wraps."

Kenny then explained how he had used new state-of-the-art contact lenses to 'wire' himself for evidence. One lens had a tiny camera in it while the other was equipped with a microphone.

"Our objective was to take down Dominic and stop the spread of his influence. He and his gang will be going away for a long time."

Kenny took another bite of his bear claw and washed it down with a swig of his coffee. He smiled with the satisfied look of having done an important job well. Then he turned more serious.

"Dad, I felt so bad about what happened to Doug. If I had been there just a few minutes sooner I might have been able to prevent it."

"Son, listen to me. You can't beat yourself up for something that someone else caused. What happened to Doug was tragic, and I feel so bad for his folks. You know his dad is one of my best friends, but you weren't responsible. Dominic, and only him, was responsible."

Kenny shrugged and took a breath. "I know. I just wish it hadn't gone down like that."

"You did all you could do. Doug's girlfriend told me you actually came back and showed her how to put the compress on him."

"Yeah. I also took his phone and dialed 911."

"So that the call could not be traced back to you. That was smart."

Kenny continued. "The package I handed Doug had fake drugs in it to keep him out of trouble, but to no avail. I feel terrible about it. Then not being able to attend the funeral. That just tore me up. Doug's folks must think I don't care. I plan to let them know, now that I can."

"I think they'll understand completely why you could not be there. Look at it this way, you being undercover is what eventually took Doug's murderer down. Plus, you ended up saving Michael's life."

"Yeah, I suppose you're right," Kenny finally agreed.

"So tell me. How exactly did things tonight go down with Michael?"

"Well, I saw Michael and Dominic each pointing a gun at each other. I yelled at Michael to drop the gun, but he just froze after realizing he had left the secondary safety on. Just as Dominic was about to shoot Michael I fired at Dominic, but he was still able to get a shot off. I fired at Dominic one more time to make sure he went down."

"In so doing you saved Michael's life," Jim repeated to his son.

"As far as I'm concerned, Michael acted in self-defense."

Jim suspected that Kenny was giving Michael the benefit of doubt, but Jim saw no need to challenge Kenny's version of the story.

"I agree. The MacDonald family has been through enough. So what's going to happen to you?"

"I'll be on desk duty for a few weeks while they investigate the shooting, and then probably be re-assigned to the Northwest Division."

Jim sat back and marveled at his son's appearance.

"You are one bad-ass looking dude. You must have had the biker babes climbing all over you."

"Not really," Kenny fibbed.

"Speaking of babes, we would have nabbed Williams ourselves if his old lady hadn't alibied him out. Not big on the truth, but she's smoking hot. She probably could have gone for you."

"You have no idea, Dad."

CHAPTER 25

IT WAS JUST past eleven o'clock on Christmas morning when the four MacDonald family members arrived home from church. At one point the pastor had explained what had happened to Doug and Michael recently, and asked the congregation to keep the two boys in their prayers. Julie prayed that God grant eternal rest on the soul of her departed son. She also said a fervent prayer of thanks that Michael had been spared.

It had been a week since Michael had experienced the deadly encounter with Dominic Williams. Michael had spent two days in the hospital and escaped with a deep flesh wound to his upper left torso. Fortunately the bullet struck no vital organs, and no ligaments connecting to his shoulder had been harmed. His chest and shoulder were heavily bandaged but doctors assured his parents he would enjoy a full recovery within six weeks.

Julie had experienced the typical religious reaction of many parents who had lost a child. *Why does a loving God allow bad things to happen to good people?* The often-repeated notion that God works in mysterious ways initially left Julie feeling cheated, confused, angry and disappointed. This normally very faith-filled person even started harboring doubts about the existence of God.

It was Francine who had steered Julie back to restoring her faith in the Lord. Francine recounted for Julie the many blessings she had been granted over the years, including the meeting and falling in love with Greg. Giving successful births to two healthy boys added to the list.

The most surprising hidden benefit of that whole process was how close it brought Julie and Francine together. They had not always enjoyed a warm and pleasant connection, but the support that Francine had provided to Julie during her trying times of grieving and coping had brought their relationship to a much stronger level of trust and confidence.

Francine had insisted she help Julie with their traditional Christmas dinner of honey-baked ham and smoked turkey. Greg had started preparing the smoker for the turkey by six in the morning. Julie and Francine were in charge of the ham and all the other fixings, with Francine specializing in her tasty deviled eggs, scalloped potatoes and stuffing.

As in previous years, Greg and Julie had invited Jim, his wife Sharon and their daughter Cheryl. Everyone was excited that for the first time in several years Jim's son Kenny would also be joining them. Kenny had stopped by a few nights earlier to give Greg, Julie and Michael a full accounting of his role in taking down Dominic Williams and Ramon Tartikof.

Julie had also invited Lisa. Both of them agreed that the most appropriate place for Lisa to be during her first Christmas without Doug would be at his family's home. Lisa arrived shortly before noon with mixed emotions. She was glad to see all of Doug's family and to spend time getting to know the Barnett's better, especially Kenny.

Still, Lisa felt sad that Doug would not be there to share in all of the warm and special feelings of the season. She asked Michael if she could visit Doug's room. Michael was only too glad to oblige. He had special feelings of his own in being in the room that had been the sole sanctuary of his brother for so many years.

Doug's posters and mementos brought back a flood of memories for Lisa. She walked over to the leather office chair by Doug's desk and sat down. Michael could see there was something else on her mind as she opened her purse.

"What's shaking with you?" Michael asked her.

She reached into her purse and pulled out a piece of white paper. As she unfolded it she asked Michael, "So, did you see the message Doug wrote me from the hospital?"

Michael was surprised. "What? Uh, no. I didn't even know if he could write. Like, what did it say?"

"Well, that's the thing," Lisa responded. "I don't know exactly. He could barely scribble, so it's hard to make out. He had written it on a small white board in his room. Later I had a nurse make a copy of it so I could take it with me." Lisa started tearing up as she said, "It was the last communication I had with him."

"Really?"

"Well, yeah, sort of," Lisa said.

"What do you mean sort of?"

"Well, I mean the last time he was conscious with me," Lisa explained. "I feel his presence from time to time. Like I feel his spirit is here still with us."

"Yeah, I know what you mean. Like, I've gotten that feeling he's still here. Like when I'm playing the video game he taught me, or doing some other stuff we used to do together."

"Well then you know," Lisa said. "I just wish I could figure out what his writing meant."

"He wasn't able to explain it to you?"

"Oh, no way," Lisa declared. "He wasn't able to talk at all. He was barely able to write. That's why his handwriting is so scribbly."

"Let me see it."

Lisa handed Michael the sheet of paper. He studied the two scrawled words. After his initial glance, he thought the first word looked like *sav* and the second similar to *my*.

"It looks like he was saying 'Save my.' What would that mean?"

"I have no idea," Lisa replied. "It's like I've been racking my brains trying to figure it out."

Michael tried to apply his artist skills to interpreting the letters. He studied the words closely. "Lisa, maybe the letters are not like what they appear to be."

"I don't get it. What do you mean?"

"Well, what if the *v* isn't really a *v*?"

Lisa looked intently at the letter. "If it's not a *v* what could it be?"

"Well, see how the slanted line on the right starts out a little above the bottom of the line on the left?"

"Yeah, so, like, what about it? I don't see, except, wait!" Lisa exclaimed. She finally realized what Michael was thinking.

"It could be an *f*," she proclaimed. "Do you see it, too?"

"Yes. I think it's an *f*, which means," Michael announced.

"Which means the word was probably s*a*fe," Lisa finished his thought for him. "So he was trying to write *my safe*," Lisa suggested.

"That's what it sounds like to me. I think there is something in his safe that he, like, wanted you, or someone, to find," Michael said.

Lisa asked, "So do you know the combination?"

"Me? No way. I thought you might have it."

"I have no idea," Lisa replied. "I know he told me he customized the combination to something he'd be able to remember. So maybe we can figure it out."

"Why don't we start with his birthday," Michael suggested.

"Okay," Lisa agreed. Then she looked at the circular dial of numbers and said, "That won't work. The highest number is sixty, and Doug's year of birth is way higher than that."

"Um," Michael thought. "Good point. Maybe he used his month and day and age. So it would be five, twenty-six and seventeen. Let's try that."

"Sounds good. Why don't you do the honors?"

Michael thought out loud, "I wonder if it starts to the left or the right? No matter. I'll just try it both ways."

He spun the lock twice just as his dad had taught him to make sure the tumblers all cleared before starting the sequence of numbers. He carefully turned the dial left, right and back left to the assigned numbers. Michael took a deep breath and looked at Lisa.

"Well, here goes," he said as he pulled the heavy, steel level downward. But it only moved a quarter inch and then stopped.

"Damn," Lisa said. "Maybe try it the opposite direction?"

"My thoughts exactly," Michael concurred. He spun the

dial a few times to clear the tumblers and repeated the same sequence of numbers except this time he started turning to the right. Again, the lever would not move downward.

"I'm going to try his age first followed by the month and day, and see if that works," Michael explained. Lisa was starting to grow anxious. She felt there was something important that Doug had locked away, and that he had wanted it to be discovered.

Michael tried the new sequence of numbers, first starting it left and then right, but neither combination worked.

"Try my birthday," Lisa insisted. She told him the numbers of her birthday and age. He tried the sequence of her age, month and year of birth, starting first to the left and then to the right. Neither attempt worked. The he changed the order with her age last. Again, both attempts failed.

"I don't know what else to try," Michael mumbled. "Let me see that paper again," he said to Lisa. She handed him the photocopy which they both studied intently. Suddenly, Michael's eyes widened.

"Lisa," Michael said excitedly. "Look closely at the *y*."

Lisa studied the letter. "Well, I admit, it's not a perfectly shaped *y*. It's like too straight."

"Exactly. It's too straight," Michael agreed.

"So like what are you saying?"

"I think it's an *i*," Michael said.

"Yeah, I guess it could be that. You're thinking it really says *mi*? What does that mean?"

"Well, it could mean my first name. Maybe he was trying to write *safe Michael*. Maybe the combination to the safe is my age and birthday."

Once more Michael knelt down in front of the safe and spun the dial a few times to clear the tumblers. He pressed his fingers onto the silver ribbed knob of the dials and slowly turned it to the right, stopping precisely at thirteen, then left to the four and right to twenty-four. This time he heard a familiar latching sound.

His sense of anticipation grew as he realized the locking mechanisms had all aligned. He pulled the heavy, steel level downward. The movement stopped briefly when the lever seemed to catch on something. Michael applied more pressure that caused the lever to continue downward a full sixty degrees. As it did so, he heard the clanging of internal gears and tumblers. Finally the lever stopped. At the same time the four locking rods all retracted. The heavy door swung open.

Michael and Lisa peered inside the dark enclosure. On the floor of the safe they noticed the stack of emails from Lisa that Doug has saved. There were also several photos of Lisa and Doug, and a few of Doug and Michael. This brought a warm smile to Michael's face. Then they noticed the main article in the safe. Just as they did, Julie called from the bottom of the stairs.

"Michael, Lisa, it's almost time for dinner. Can you come down in a little bit?"

"Yeah, Mom," Michael yelled back. "We'll be right down."

The two teenagers returned their attention to the safe. Michael quickly suspected what the peculiar looking object was. As soon as he was sure, he yelled back to Julie.

"Mom! Mom!" he practically screamed.

"Stop yelling, Michael. What is it?"

"Meet me in the living room. Right away. And bring Dad and Grandma and everyone else," Michael instructed. Within minutes Francine and Julie had joined Greg and the Barnett family in the family room.

"What's going on?" Greg asked his wife.

"I'm not sure," Julie answered.

At the top of the stairs Lisa turned around for an instant to check that Michael was right behind her. As they descended the stairs their senses were greeted with the pleasing aroma of a freshly prepared holiday dinner. Michael especially enjoyed the whiffs of ham, smoked turkey and other steaming fixings that were escaping out of the kitchen.

They did not come into view until they were at the bottom of the stairs. Lisa walked into the family room first and quickly sat down. Michael had followed her close behind. He carried what Doug had been securing in his safe. Everyone looked at the object and was stunned.

It was the crystal replica of the Eiffel Tower that Greg had purchased for Julie's twentieth wedding anniversary. Lisa informed everyone that Doug had told her he had been trying to restore it, but it had sounded like he was not having much success. Doug's sessions at anger management had prompted him to keep trying.

Julie began sobbing and Greg came over and gave her a consoling hug. Greg's own eyes were starting to tear up.

"It's just beautiful," Julie uttered between sobs.

"Wow. That took some time and effort," Greg marveled.

"It's amazing how intricate all the glued together pieces are," Jim commented.

"Well, he always was good at jigsaw puzzles," Julie said in a deep breath.

Doug's family thought he had thrown the shattered memento out the night he destroyed it. Instead, he had stored it in a box and kept it locked away in his safe. For ten days straight he had locked himself in his room and carefully laid out all of the fragments of broken crystal. Then he meticulously glued the pieces back together as best he could. There were a few tiny gaps here and there, but for the most part the crystal structure was intact. All except for one part.

When Michael had assembled the top and bottom portions of the tower he noticed a small part of the rear right corner was missing. It was only a minor piece but it included Doug's engraved name, and it caused the tower to tilt ever so slightly back and to the right.

"The only piece Doug could not include was the corner with his name on it," Michael said sadly. "I, like, accidently stepped on it and crushed it when I was helping him clean up the mess." Then he said wistfully, "I eliminated his name from our tower."

Julie walked over to Michael and comforted him. "You didn't eliminate his name. The piece of crystal may be gone, but Doug will never be gone from this family."

Lisa came over and gave Julie and Michael each a warm hug. Then Michael turned to Francine and asked her what she thought it all meant, and why she thought Doug spent so much time restoring it.

Francine smiled at her grandson. "I think it was Douglas' way of trying to make things right with his parents. I think it shows that no matter how much something seems to be shattered, with enough love, patience and commitment, it can always be put back together."

Greg came over and gave his mother a hug. "Amen to that."

Then he suggested they all go in the dining room to enjoy their Christmas dinner. As they walked out of the room Julie turned back once more and stared at the repaired piece of crystal. She voiced a quiet prayer of thanks, and then joined the others for their holiday feast.

EPILOGUE

A YEAR HAS passed since Doug's tragic death. Julie and Greg have invited Jim and his family over to join them for Christmas dinner along with Francine and Lisa. Julie had indicated that before they all sat down to enjoy their bountiful feast, there were three topics of memorabilia about Doug that she wanted to share.

The first concerned Atlanta's Centennial Olympic Park. Though Doug had not yet been born when the one-hundredth version of the modern Olympics was held in 1996, Greg had taken Doug to the site several times. While Doug was not very interested in participating in sports—computers and video games were his specialty—he had shown a keen interest in selected areas of sports history. One of those areas had been the Olympics.

Doug had enjoyed studying about the ancient Olympics in particular because of their sense of gladiators not unlike some of his modern video games. Any reference to modern Olympics held interest for Doug. So Greg had taken Doug to the Centennial Olympic Park on more than one occasion. They always had a good time.

The aging Centennial Olympic Park was in dire need of refurbishing. A fundraising campaign began in which donors could purchase a memorial brick to be placed in a renovated pavilion. The brick would be inscribed with a tribute to a loved one. Greg purchased two bricks, one for Julie and him to dedicate to Doug and one for Michael to do the same. Greg also purchased replicas of each brick that came with a glass display case.

The actual bricks would not be installed until after the first of the year. The replica bricks and their display cases had arrived a few days earlier and Greg and Julie were eager to share them with family and friends. Everyone was seated in the family room when Greg carried in two cardboard containers. Greg explained the story behind the bricks and then split opened the tape on the first box.

"This first brick is from Julie and me," he announced as he pulled out the paper stuffing. Then he smiled warmly at his mother. "And by extension this is also from Francine."

He removed the ceramic display case that had a sturdy rich wood base. Then he grasped the heavy brick that was surrounded in brown paper. Everyone watched closely as he discarded the wrapping.

He held the brick up for all to see and declared, "This is for Doug from his mom and Dad and his grandmother."

On the brick were inscribed the words:

In loving memory of our beloved son, Douglas

There was a collective *awwhh* from every member of the family.

"What a loving tribute," Jim's wife Sharon said.

"I am like so glad it will be there for all time," Lisa commented.

Greg inserted the brick into the specially designed display case.

"Can you set it on the mantel?" Julie requested. "I made some space for it."

Greg placed the brick and display case on the fireplace mantel just to the right center where Julie had cleared an area. Then he handed the second box to Michael.

"Here, I think you should do the honors," Greg suggested.

Michael stood up very seriously and accepted the cardboard container from his father. He split open the tape just as Greg had done. Slowly he pulled out the brick and unwrapped its paper covering. He stared at it for a moment and gradually became misty eyed.

"Michael, would you mind sharing it with us?" Francine asked gently.

"Oh, yeah," Michael quickly responded.

"It's okay, sweetie," Julie said, trying to comfort him. "Just take your time." She knew this was emotional for her son, and it would soon become more so.

Michael gripped each side of the brick and lifted it above his head. He turned slowly for everyone to read its engraving

The experience of a lifetime, a brother

This time there was no audible reaction. There were only the knowing nods of heads as they all smiled at Michael in knowing fashion.

After a few minutes Julie stood up and announced, "Michael has written a poem to his brother that he would like to read for all of us."

Michael set the brick and its display case on the coffee table and reached inside his stylish pocketed vest. He pulled out what seemed to be a few pieces of typed papers and slowly unfolded them. He looked out at each person sitting in the now hushed family room. Then he began reading.

"It's me again Lord, and I'm asking once more,
To grant me another request,
I know I ask often, but I hope this time You'll soften,
For this is one thing I truly do quest.

My petition involves, an issue only You can resolve,
A dilemma that I face all alone,
It concerns my brother Doug, whom I'd dearly love to hug,
But he's been called back to his eternal home.

Today Doug is gone, and it seems so sadly wrong,
For he left all of us far too soon.
Now he's with angels above, and experiencing Your love,
Amongst the heavens and the stars and the moon.

*I know I'm not the best, and that I'm making a request,
That I may not be worthy to afford,
But could You please think it through, and consider what to do,
When I ask, 'Just five more minutes, Lord?'*

*With Your power so divine, You could surely grant the time,
Just five more minutes with my brother?
I would use the time well, as to him I would tell,
How special he was to me more than any other.*

*It's just a few hundred seconds, but the need for me beckons,
To share with him all that I've stored.
So once again I must ask, if You would please do this task,
'Just five more minutes, Lord?'*

*I would tell him out loud, how of him we're so proud,
That includes me, mom and dad, and his grandmother.
And from my time as a pup, and all the years growing up,
How I so treasured having him as my brother.*

*With sentiments unscrambled, I'd try not to ramble,
And hope he wouldn't become too bored.
But to make this come true, I have to ask of You:
'Just five more minutes, Lord?'*

*I promise not to question, and will not even mention,
What were the factors that may have led,
To his sudden untimely passing, from which I still am grasping,
For I want inside his heart, not his head.*

I know You have the power, to give a fraction of an hour,
When once more I could just move toward
Experiencing again the fun, of playing our games til they're done,
'Just five more minutes, Lord?'

I really miss his unique style, and his warm, engaging smile,
And the funny goatee on his chin,
And the way he'd try not to laugh, if ever I said something rash,
Then eventually breaking out in a grin.

I'd ask about his rings, his music and other things,
And if asked give him pointers on his art.
But mostly I would say, on this and every day,
That I love him deeply with all of my heart.

It's hard to let him go, though I must—that I know,
But before I do, of You I implore,
Let me hear him at peace, before he turns back deceased,
'For just five more minutes, Lord.'"

Michael folded his papers back up and looked over at his mother. She beamed with more pride than she had ever felt before. Then she started sobbing. Lisa walked over to comfort her, but soon Lisa was weeping as well. After a short silent pause, it was Francine who finally brought things back to an even keel.

"That was a beautiful poem, Michael," Francine said through a warm smile. "I am sure your brother is looking down on you and commenting favorably on your sentiments right now."

"Thanks, Grandma," Michael replied sheepishly.

Eventually the others joined in with their various accolades. When the praiseful remarks subsided, Julie stood and addressed everyone in the room.

"I mentioned earlier there were three topics of memorabilia about Doug that we wanted to share with all of you. The first was the two centennial bricks and the second was Michael's beautiful poem to his brother."

Julie paused for a second and took a breath. Then she opened several pieces of folded paper she had been holding in her hands.

"As you all know, we donated Doug's organs per his wishes and ours. Much as we would have wanted to meet with the recipients, the organ transplant organization is very strict about preventing any communication between a member of a donor's family and the recipient unless both parties are in agreement."

Julie's voice started to crack as she continued. "We wrote to the organ transplant organization OneLegacy per their instructions and documented the fact that we would be willing to communicate with each of Doug's organ recipients. The organization in turn contacted each recipient and offered them the option of writing a letter to which we could then elect to respond to or not."

"I think that's wonderful, Julie. I mean that you would be willing to do that," Sharon said.

"Well not everyone responded. Administrators at OneLegacy told us that recipients and their families often feel survivor's guilt in that their family is benefitting from the tragedy of another's. We did hear from three of those who received Doug's organs. I'd like to share them with all of you."

Julie read the letter from a fifty-five-year-old woman in Ohio who received one of Doug's kidneys. The woman no longer had to go through the daily ordeal of dialysis and looked forward to twenty or thirty more years of a fulfilling life. She wrote that words seemed inadequate to express her sorrow at their loss. She was grateful for Doug's unselfish gesture, and was sure that such a generous man had to be at peace in heaven.

Another letter Julie read thanked them for the gift of sight that their eleven-year-old daughter received as a result of Doug's optic organs. The parents of the girl wrote that their daughter said she experienced a totally new world of light and color. The visual impact was much more dramatic than the girl had imagined. Julie explained the recipient hopes one day to be an artist, a fact that was not lost on Michael.

Julie placed all but two of the pages on the end-table and cleared her throat. "This is the letter that I treasure the most." She then read it out loud.

"Dear Donor Family,

Thank you for writing to OneLegacy and requesting to hear from me. I am the twenty-year-old male who received the gift of life from your loved one.

There is no way I can convey how much I appreciate the selfless act of your son who is responsible for me being alive today. It takes a very special person to do what he did. It also takes a very special family to agree to donate organs during your time of grieving and loss.

I do not know much about your loved one except that he was your teenaged son. I understand how you may be reluctant to share details of your son's passing, and I respect that. I do want you to know that he and your family are in my thoughts and prayers each day. It sounded like you would like to know a bit about myself, so let me tell you some things about me.

I was born with a weak heart that was complicated last year with a rare form of leukemia. Despite the best efforts of doctors with numerous treatments and operations, they eventually concluded my only recourse would be a heart transplant. I was cautiously hopeful when I was told they had found a match, but saddened to learn the donor was so young.

The operation took eleven hours. There were a few complications but doctors quickly resolved them. Eight months later I feel like a new man. I can run and hike and play sports for the first time in years. I am a senior at the University of Montana in Missoula. I am enjoying the big sky country and all that the beauties of nature have to offer.

I know I will never be able to thank you enough for giving me a second chance at life. But I can promise you I will try to live up to the example set by your son and *try to help others. I truly hope that life provides your entire family much happiness and prosperity. If there is anything more you would like to know about me, please don't hesitate to ask. Thank you again.*

God bless you all.

Your extremely grateful recipient"

    Julie neatly folded the papers and placed them with the others. She looked up at faces that were spellbound.
    "That was amazing," Jim said.
    "How courageous of that young man to write such an emotional letter," Sharon added. Francine, Greg, Michael, Cheryl and Kenny all had words of praise as well.
    The only person who remained silent was Lisa. She was deep in thought about the man who now possessed the heart of her former lover, the father of her ill-fated child. She kept thinking about this man's offer to ask him anything anyone would want to know. There was plenty more Lisa wanted to know about this man. Those revelations would come later.
    Julie stood up and led everyone into the dining room where they were soon immersed in the delicious holiday feast. It turned into a very satisfying day for them all.

ACKNOWLEDGMENTS

THERE ARE A number of people I have to thank for making this dream of writing a novel a reality. My agent, Leticia Gomez, helped to get me started on this path along with our good friend Harris Kern. Katie Sebastyan provided numerous suggestions that improved the story and its readability. Kari Kozuki, from OneLegacy, supplied pertinent information about the organ donation and transplant process.

Networking guru Betsy Ashton honed my ability to interact effectively with other authors. My use and knowledge of social media was significantly enhanced through the persistent efforts of Shari Stauch. None of this would be possible without the professional and thorough approach of my publisher, John Koehler.

Joe Coccaro was especially instrumental in ensuring the proper timing of storylines, the development of key characters and the overall editing of the work. Another person whose efforts I appreciate is Courtney Davison, our copy editor. Her ability to provide polish to the manuscript is amazing.

Most of all I want to thank my loving wife, Ann. Her patience, support and encouragement throughout this long journey kept me going and saw me through to the finish. She will forever have my gratitude, and my love.

QUESTIONS FOR READERS

1. To what degree do you feel the sibling rivalry depicted in this story was realistic?

2. Have you ever experienced a situation in which you thought revenge would bring you satisfaction, and did it?

3. How realistic was the family tragedy described in this story?

4. Can you describe personal tragedies in your own family or those of friends that are similar to the ones described in this story?

5. How informative to you were the descriptions of organ donations, transplants and recipients?

6. To what extent do you feel the discussions about adoption and abortions were thought-provoking?

7. How do you think the younger brother's development will be impacted by the influence that his older brother's life and death?

8. With which character did you identify the most and why?

CPSIA information can be obtained at www.ICGtesting.com
Printed in the USA
BVOW04s1908010916

460889BV00001B/58/P